A Richer Dust

A Richer Dust

Amy Boaz

·

THE PERMANENT PRESS
Sag Harbor, NY 11963

Copyright © 2008 Amy Boaz.

For information, address:
  The Permanent Press
  4170 Noyac Road
  Sag Harbor, NY 11963
  www.thepermanentpress.com

Library of Congress Cataloging-in-Publication Data

  Boaz, Amy
    A richer dust / Amy Boaz.
       p. cm.
    ISBN-13: 978-1-57962-159-9 (hardcover : alk. paper)
    ISBN-10: 1-57962-159-7 (hardcover : alk. paper)
       1. Women painters—Fiction. 2. Philosophers—Fiction.
    3. Artists—NewMexico—Fiction. 4. British—New Mexico—
    Fiction. 5. Taos (N.M.)—Fiction. I. Title.

PS3602.O25R53 2008
813'.6—dc22   2007048235

Printed in the United States of America.

For

Jane E. Carr and James David Boaz

There shall be
In that rich earth a richer dust concealed;
A dust whom England bore, shaped, made aware,
Gave, once, her flowers to love, her ways to roam,
A body of England's, breathing English air,
Washed by the rivers, blest by suns of home.

—Rupert Brooke, from "The Soldier"

"I only remember hints—and I proceed by intuition."

—D.H. LAWRENCE, *Fantasia of the Unconscious*

→ Part I ←

I set foot in New Mexico and I saw—crows. Sleek, oily black-birds perched in cottonwood trees around the desolate station. They scolded us as we stumbled out of the train at Lamy. They sounded nothing like the old squawkers I had known back in London, scurfy and starved that winter of 1924. These ravens were as big as my new black sombrero, bartered from the Chinamen as we came through New York. They ringed the station like the neighborhood bullies, eager to confront the newcomers. We looked up in astonishment. I held onto my hat—the birds were eyeing it—and Abe laughed. He laughed and the peril was broken. He turned to us, and said something I couldn't hear, and Vera pursed her lips angrily. She smacked her pockets for a cigarette.

We were stunned by the light. Above us, at last, was the open sky, unharnessed from the windows of the train. We could make out nothing but the mud-brick shed that stood alone, and served as a station somewhere on the way to Santa Fe. Inside, a few wooden benches and a ticket window—*Cerrado*. Abe stood on the station porch and squinted under his too-large hat; his beard caught the afternoon light and burnt a coppery red. He was watching the mountains: the swell of ancient hills, low-rolling, dull grey, and strewn about the horizon like kicked-off workers' boots. Over his shoulder rose the superior Sacred Mountain. He knew it, he indicated it to me. Then he stretched with satisfaction and squatted against the largest valise—Vera's.

She smoked and scowled at the ravens, though I imagined the scowl on her handsome face was meant for me. It was just the three of us now—our leader, his wife, and me, *making history*, Abe had said. But three was a crowd. Why hadn't the others come? Vera wouldn't sit down. She puffed on her cigarette and snorted in her faintly comical German accent. Where was Junior's cab that was supposed to be waiting for us? Hadn't Janie assured us that we would have a motorcar? And what did Janie think, leaving us stranded at the mercy of the elements, with Abe nearly spitting blood? Vera sputtered and fumed; I couldn't hear her words. I knew them without pulling out my ear trumpet. Her nostrils flared, she stamped her foot and made the porch shake. But then Abe shifted and she halted.

Something will happen now, he said, in his serene way, and Vera and I both stepped back, calmer, more certain.

A figure detached itself from the corner of the shed––tall with brilliant eyes, dark pigtails, smooth brown skin, and wearing a blanket over his shoulders. A young Indian man, who motioned shyly. We followed him, dragging our luggage. There was a wagon we hadn't seen, a flatbed drawn by two patient brown mares, and we clambered in. Vera was livid, tripping over her overstuffed parcels, and Abe and I tried not to meet each other's eye and start to giggle. Thus comfortably arranged, we left the station, and set off toward the violet hills.

We weren't inclined to speak. The desert appeared to me then as a *lack*—blank, flat, empty—defined by what is absent rather than by what is there. A landscape particularly suited to the deaf person, it seemed to me. But this was the beginning; I was terrified and knew nothing. We took turns sitting up next to the driver, who didn't speak much English, or English I could comprehend, and I wasn't about to thrust my trumpet under his nose while he held the reins, lest he drive off the shoulder in alarm. By reading his lips I managed to learn that our driver's name was Domingo, as in Santo Domingo, after one of the Pueblo tribes inhabiting these lands. I thought Domingo marvelously handsome and couldn't stop stealing looks at him. I didn't know anything about Indians when I first arrived in New Mexico; I didn't know about their dainty, symmetrical features and sand-colored skin and modest manners. The only Indians I had ever seen were in Buffalo Bill's Wild West

Show at the Crystal Palace when I was a child—festooned cannibals shipped from the wilds of the American West, we were told, arrayed in fiery paint and war bonnets, riding out on their painted ponies shrieking and shooting off guns. We were thrilled, the sons and daughters of the Queen's favorites, gathered in our sashes and sailor outfits with our nanny for a Sunday afternoon to watch these exotics. I recall the Indian on display was enormously tall and very red (had they *reddened* him?), pockmarked from up close where we four siblings sat staring in our select box belonging to our father the Viscount, and chewing on taffy purchased by Nanny— not any specific nanny, but one in a succession of aggrieved caretakers. We hopped in our seats to see the Indian beat his drum and wave his tomahawk. I remember him because of his ferocious lack of *shame*—the ruined rage he cast on our box stuffed with beribboned children of Victoria's gilded reign—clearly he hated us—and we clapped and clapped, delighted and not disappointed by his response, for how could a redskin behave otherwise when faced with the Englishman's instinct to be superior?

We bumped along in the punishing wagon, humbled by the darkening of the massive hills—the Sangre de Cristo, they are called, *blood of Christ*—mountains that undulate masterfully north to south, along the Rio Grande. Then sunset split open the horizon and spilled out a startling palette of orange and scarlet, igniting our ascent into deeper shifting ranges. We had gained height so that I could no longer gauge where we were, save that trees had appeared along our river route, glorious fruit trees in early bloom, for it was just April and we could smell them. The Rio Grande accompanied us to our left, deeply scored into the dry earth, giving way as we ascended to a comforting rushing noise like scampering footsteps heralding our arrival. The river was the lifeblood of the region. The air was cold and growing colder, and we had far to go—not as the crow flies (those gigantic bullies!), but rather as Domingo prodded the steady dual team, work horses patiently plying the pebbly ascent, and in no hurry to get home with the setting of the sun.

Occasionally we rounded a pass that was so narrow, a wagon approaching from the opposite direction would surely have collided with us. I ducked and trembled under a blanket in the cab.

Vera, at her turn seated next to Domingo, laughed at my nerves: she had none of her own. We watched the smoldering of her cigarettes, inhaled the sour tobacco odor as she smoked, and Abe described his last sojourn to Italy fleeing publishers who had censored his book because it propounded the equality of the sexes. I ferreted inside my sailor's bag for my trumpet and thrust it toward him, not wanting to miss a word. *War*, he was saying, *corruption of souls*, he hectored, *dying of a civilization.* He was pulling on his red beard, spouting his slogans in fine form, and I smiled happily. *The end of the end.* Vera rumbled in assent, patting her thick, spread thighs. The sainted air was going to benefit Abe, we knew it, and we would work at making *pure* art, and maybe (I thought secretly, deliciously) I would get a bath at Janie's, when we got there. But another thought swiftly dampened my joy: the recollection of Janie herself. I had observed her at a party once in London, holding forth on the uses of psychotherapy, a small person hungry for company and attention—for Abe's arrival in Taos was Janie's coup, and she would have to display him, and fête him, and I dreaded these gatherings because I heard nothing.

Taos, 1963

Akbar moves near me, a younger man, he doesn't know how much younger and I don't plan to tell him. He lights fires in my adobe grate, and attends to the mound of dishes in my sink. No dishes in the sink, he says sternly, mimicking his mother. He starts from his task by my laughter, then turns to move his arms clumsily around my bosom, struggling with the brassiere strap he has no talent disassembling—it's an unwieldy, old-fashioned thing. His square granny glasses magnify his grey blood-shot eyes, and lend his pale, freckled face a funny, determined expression, framed by a lion's mane of hempen coils. He doesn't believe in cutting his hair, or combing it for that matter, and it grows in tightly matted, wonderfully soft springlets that reach to the middle of his back.

He and the young people out here have a strangely old-world way about them—the ladies wear long skirts and cover their heads in white fabric caps while the men smoke cigarettes made from crushed aromatic herbs. I think Akbar fantasizes about seeing me in long skirts, and discarding the men's trousers I've always worn. He struggles with the ungainly brassiere strap. He's ready instantly, this fragrant lover in my house—his beard emits an odor of sandalwood incense, and the sweet herbs he smokes—startlingly ready to thrust himself inside of me and bring me to the quick. Really, at my age, I haven't had a proper lover. I'm an old lady—my hats have helped preserve my skin all these years in the desert. But Akbar doesn't see, in any case, doesn't mind, likes my smell of turpentine and fishing tackle, likes the *structure* of me, he indicates awkwardly, because he's a tree climber—he's still wearing his glasses as we tumble over the worn-out mattress. He feels for the latches on my pants and glides his hand down my thigh; then I hear him softly cursing, sweet, incomprehensible words, when he has to fool with my knife.

1924

We pushed the heavy furniture against the thick plaster walls and danced to Junior's drum. He brought out the thunderbolt for Abe, who asked to sample it, and we all drank except for Janie and Vera. There was a fire roaring in the blackened gouge of the wall. It was a deep, cavelike dwelling, constructed of mud as all the houses were, with interior walls painted white, though it had two storeys—everyone called Janie's adobe the Great House because of that. And because of Junior, no doubt, who was as tall as a silver fir, broad and commanding in his silence. The furnishings were fanciful: Pueblo pottery, New York photography, Chinese paintings. The heavy, carved doors to the dining room patio were thrown open and we could glimpse the crescent moon in a velvet sky. Had I ever seen such a marvelous expanse of sky? Domingo told me that the stars were the footprints of his ancestors. And where were they directed, I asked him? Home, he indicated, pointing south. I didn't know how high we had ascended, how rarefied the air became, how quickly drunk I grew. I didn't know the other guests at Janie's house: a sly-faced, tanned man I would meet another time, and a few roughed-up women who watched Abe with interest, and the Indians who were Junior's relatives. They stood around like pillars holding up the walls. Junior sat cross-legged on the floor and pounded his drum, the sweat glistening on his deeply tanned, impassive face, dripping to the ends of the black braids. He closed his eyes as he pounded rhythmically. Janie wore a prim dress and a blue ribbon tied in her short hair, like Alice in Wonderland. She was an heiress from Buffalo, New York. She was annoyed because she wanted to catch Abe's pronouncements and we behaved like unruly children. Over dinner of *sopa de lima* and chops and beans she asked me a few questions, then grew bored by my answers, or rather by my accent. She noted how frightfully *English* I was, and I felt the first of several reversals. Later, while dancing, tipsy from the liquor, I lifted Abe in my arms daringly—he was so slender and light. We turned around and around. Vera was disgusted by these public exertions, and went up to bed, and Janie soon followed her through the warren of halls and secret staircases in her curious two-storey adobe house built by the Indians. But Abe and I danced until I fell down, and the men laughed and laughed.

Junior saw us off on his black stallion at the gates of the ranch. The morning light staggered us, and we had to shield our eyes. The Sacred Mountain rose massively from the vaporous cloud rings behind Junior's blanketed shoulders, his pigtails wrapped to the tips in white ribbon. He lifted his hand in grave salute, and the pigeons rose from their houses in the cobblestone courtyard, circled once like a cyclone, then settled high in the cottonwoods. Junior turned his horse away from the rust-colored Great House to the Pueblo lands of his people. As Janie's husband he possessed a great deal of land and many animals to be tended to. We climbed into the back of Domingo's cab, fell over our luggage and provisions Janie had thought to pack for us, such as potatoes, onions, and bread, also furniture and mattresses, and we set out through the still sleeping town of Taos. Janie took her breakfast in bed and hadn't come out to say goodbye.

The town was made up of a paltry cluster of adobe houses, huddled at the great mountain's base and brilliant in the morning sun like Jerusalem marble. Soon the flat-roofed mud houses thinned, and the road north out of town unfurled before us. The land went on and on without interruption—the valley cascaded over unevenly eroded ranges. Presently we turned off through the pine forest onto a trail that was rough, rutted, and nearly unnavigable in parts. We ascended unsteadily in Domingo's cab, and sometimes he had to get out, grab the horses' bridles, and coax them over an unspeakable gully. We sat silent and pale, wearing our hats. Abe and I had terrible throbbing heads from the homemade whiskey, and at one point, when the sour smoke downwind from Vera's cigarettes assaulted us, he leaned over the side of the wagon and vomited. Vera looked the other way, satisfied, I thought, with a hint of a smile on her face.

So, she said, and smacked her lips. Strong medicine will kill you.

He didn't reply, but fell back against a mattress like a dead man. I fanned his face with my wooden palette and he opened one eye and winked at me. He hated his sickness, denied it whenever Vera referred to it—but he possessed the blue-lipped ethereality of the sick man. Vera had told me he nearly died from pneumonia in Italy the previous winter. And he couldn't drink, not like we could.

Dolly is the strong one, Doll can take anything, Abe said gustily, so I could hear. Vera scoffed.

And fall down on her face, Vera cried. What do you English know about drinking? You don't know how to drink. You're thin-skinned. The Germans know how to drink, we're famous for it!— She always touted the superior ways of her people. The Germans felt music intuitively, wrote the loftiest books, invented modern science, art, literature. The Germans knew how to conduct warfare.

Her pronouncements had gotten Abe surveilled during the war, and the couple was eyed with official suspicion. But what did it matter now? We had landed on the moon. Vera was quite sure of herself. She puffed away at her smokes. I don't remember her ever without a cigarette shoved into the corner of her mouth. Slowly we trod up the pocked trail.

Janie had offered Abe the homesteader's cabin outside of town on the main highway. It was a low, steady grade up Lobo Mountain. The pine forest opened at last to a welcome clearing on the slope. Two cabins became distinct from the pines, with patched tin roofs, sagging in disrepair. Domingo knew where to find them. The tribesmen, he said, used to use the place when hunting, and he indicated a large fire pit down the slope from the cabins. The larger of the two structures, the homesteader's cabin, so-called, contained several dusty rooms and an iron stove, and looked out onto a cleft in the hills, revealing the sweep of valley beneath them. The other cabin, several paces below, was more like a shed, big enough for a bed, a chair, a stove, and room to turn around in. This had to be my cabin, because there wasn't anywhere else for me. Moreover, it had two windows, one facing southeast, toward the larger cabin, the pine forest, and the valley well beyond; and one window facing north—offering a painter's light. I was turning around and around in the shed, admiring myself in the shaving mirror the last squatter had left hanging there, when I sensed Vera storming around outside. She spoke loudly, and didn't care that I heard.

It won't do, she can't stay here, right under foot!

Abe didn't reply. He was already sweeping out the rat shit in the cabin, making order. He and Domingo brought down the feather mattresses from the cab, struggling under the dead weight, and I could see they were too heavy for Abe to manage. Abe snapped, Vera, come here and stop fussing. And before I could leap up to help, Vera was enlisted to pull down the cumbersome things and drag them inside the cabin. She was a big lady, and had herculean strength, as we would learn, though she was sulky and offered her arm power grudgingly. She had better things to do! She tossed off her cigarette, set up her cuckoo clock, and took over the kitchen, such as it was, banging at the battered copper pots we'd brought from Janie's.

I can't live so close to that woman! she cried. I matter around here, too, I matter as much as you do!

Vera, be quiet. There's work to do.

Did I ask for her to come, too? Vera hollered. Do I have to share my peace with this—your—

Vera, that will do!

I imagined they were arguing out of a familiar necessity, shouting out their private brutalities that had little to do with me. I had enough to do cleaning out my own space, and I kept quiet. I liked the little shed—I wanted dearly to keep it. It was all I had to myself now and I felt like a child again, possessing few true belongings of my own. Everything I ever had belonged to my father, the Keeper of Her Majesty's Grounds, and I had given up my fancy flat in Bloomsbury with its pretty mantelpiece and French doors. I had returned the borrowed furniture to my parents' staff, and I had said goodbye and left all that. And here I swept and knocked out the cobwebs, pounded smooth the dirt floor, and Domingo and I mixed up some mud to repair the walls in both cabins. In time I would hang our artwork. Domingo would bring some materials from Janie's to fix up the roofs, but it didn't rain much in New Mexico and we didn't have to hurry. Abe got the stove working, and we explored the pine forest, gathering wood; Vera set to cooking with some of the provisions. By nightfall we were eating potato soup seasoned with wild sage and tearing at hunks of bread. We ate on the ground, leaning against the pine trees. We heeded the sloughing of the wind through the forest. The water hauled from the creek tasted like minerals, and Abe remarked that we'd have to clean out the stream. He wiped his beard, looking haggard, spent. The air was cold and sharp, freshly scented of pine and potato soup, and we ate hungrily. Domingo had fallen asleep against a tree trunk, snoring softly. We rested from our labors, content and hopeful. Then Abe sang softly—lyrics in an old English dialect I didn't understand, but rhythmic and sad and full of longing.

Evenings we made a big fire in the hunters' pit. Abe instructed, and we listened. I lay my trumpet at his feet.

I grew up in the slums of the miners, he said. I saw the devastation of grinding poverty on families with nothing to motivate them but the sweat of the father. The sweat of the increasingly weakened father was the lubricant of the industrial machinery. Bound every day to descending into holes of the earth to eke out a worm's living, and every day he was weakened, sickened by fumes, darkness, and pestilence oozing from the walls of the mines. What could he then offer his family? The wages were never enough, spread thin, and he grew ineffectual, impotent. His wife had little to feed the children, his children, spawned under hot sheets of fever and desperation—for what else does the poor working man have but the passion he brings to his woman, chosen for his desperate life's journey? His manhood, and the children, are the sum of this disabled man. They witness him daily weakening by the slave's work he must perform.

Abe possessed a quiet authority, a kind of medieval phrasing to his Midlands accent. *Spawned under hot sheets of fever and desperation* embarrassed me terribly. He went on and on in his comforting drone. He did not have to speak loudly. Vera was seated on a chair Abe had constructed for her, hands clasped over her belly, her cigarette dangling from one side of her mouth. The last of her fine breeding, Abe quipped, discarded overnight. She listened in a kind of hungry stupor, for she relied on Abe's words to correct the reigning imbalance in their relationship. She did not feel appreciated by her husband. Her handsome face betrayed a tension—did his words evoke memories of her own children? Was she wondering where they were, and whether they were better off without her? I never knew how it was with Vera, because she did not share with me, and she could strike me suddenly with the brunt of her anger. I was wary of her moods. I sat next to Abe, watching the fire, facing the brooding monolith that was most sacred to the Tewa Indians, the mountain that held their secrets. Domingo sat with us. He had brought his young wife, Rufina, who also worked at Janie's Great House, as the cook. She was Zuni, small and dark with brilliant eyes that watched Abe intently. Domingo and his wife listened, and sometimes Abe translated his thoughts into Spanish words, *la guerra* or *la machina*, and they nodded and murmured in assent. The others would come. The Indians used this place while hunting and the news would spread of this strange new visitor, and others would come to listen around the fire pit that they lent to us, the Indians who worked for Junior. They called Abe the Red Fox, because of his beard and his slender build, and also because of something that was wily about his nature. They were a little afraid of him, of his terrible pallor, his directness of manner, and the way he paused to consider before speaking about the plight of the working man and the dangers of encroaching society, industry, civilization. The Indians feared the evils of civilization beyond the borders of their pueblos.

After a while Abe ceased and I grew drowsy watching the fire die down. Then it became very cold and I felt the tiredness in my muscles from the day's heavy labor and the weight of my separation from life in England. Domingo and his wife had taken themselves away; I hadn't heard them go. Abe stayed, his look stony. I pulled myself to my feet to return to my shed.

Will you stay out long? I asked him.

He didn't answer, and I could see he was still wrestling with his thoughts. I blew at the embers, warming my hands.

He uttered, softly, The white man is finished. I waited, and he declared, The white man by his usurious finances, war machinery, and perverse systems of slaughter has ruined himself.

Vera, from the shadows, said: We left everything. Abe slowly turned to her. Had she spoken accusingly? I didn't think so, but Abe's face was dark and his tone held a dangerous edge.

You left your bankrupt life, he replied. You left your criminal bourgeois marriage.

Criminal! Vera cried.

You were an unfaithful wife before you met me.

You're judging me like a bourgeois, Vera fumed.

You had other lovers. You did not respect your husband. What kind of righteous union was that?

Ah, but he respected me, Vera retorted, and her eyes were glittering slits over the smoldering of her cigarette.

But not enough to keep you, evidently.

She got up. She was strong and could kill him with one blow. I backed into the shadows, toward my shed. Abe caught my arm.

She's blameless, he said.

Ha! scoffed Vera. She comes from the same world as I do. The aristocracy—my name, have you forgotten? *Von*—Lady Doll—we were gentry, landowners—we owned a whole county. Dolly and I would have gone to the same parties! Vera let out an operatic laugh.

I stumbled up the path to my shed and closed the door. Soon they would go up, away from me. I extinguished the candle and lay on the bed, breathing heavily. I imagined I heard the reverberation of Vera's laughter. I stopped up my ears. I thought of Abe and Vera's murderous, senseless arguments, and the sharp words they had thrown at each other rattled in my restless head—*criminal, righteous*. I hated them for spoiling what we had, what we had come to achieve. But these words soon blended into the night sounds: the hills were never silent for the sighing of the pines, the spooky calls of nocturnal beasts. The nights were alive in the pine forest, the time when the badgers and skunks and other industrious mammals performed the bulk of their work. Relieved of the paralyzing rays of the sun, the dark animals cavorted under the pull of the moon. Their ghostly chorus I found comforting.

When Akbar comes up behind me, I let out a little yelp. He finds me bending over in the garden—mostly I push around rocks and dust, occasionally tug at a weed in the wildly overgrown lavender patch—or he creeps up behind me when I'm standing at my easel.

He enters the house on silent bare feet, moves like an Indian, and I can't hear him, only sense the static crinkling of his locks when he's very near. Then I know him instantly by his smell—the sandalwood odor of his beard, his smoky skin. He buys his soap at the farmer's market from a woman he used to see, I think, but she's got a new man and barely acknowledges him when he loiters at her stall, deciding which soap to buy. She has a hardened face from standing over her vats of boiling botanicals, her hair coiled in the high crocheted cap the young people all wear. With her strong nose and long neck she looks in profile like Queen Nefertiti. She has a Semitic first name, Davida, Akbar tells me. He compares me to her. Davida talk talk talk, Akbar says, not like you. Davida no love Akbar for himself, says Akbar, speaking of himself in the third person, and nestles his fragrant face in my neck. Akbar give give and get no love, he says, thrusting his ready erection into my hand where we stand at my easel facing the north window. And I laugh, because he's like a kid. Akbar, you never grew up, I tell him, because he loves children, I've seen him gambol with them in the village when he goes to buy soap and sweet treats for our table, and if he doesn't have to climb trees Saturday mornings he watches *Popeye* on my television set. You're like a big kid, I tease him—but then his face grows thoughtful and sad, and for a terrifying minute I think that he's going to cry.

He has curious, solitary habits, my boy. I never know what he does when he's not with me. He likes music best of all—I find scattered 45s like oily cow pies all over the house, labeled with names of birds and girls he fancies: the Penguins, the Shirelles. He puts them on my old phonograph player, which was a gift from a visitor years ago and lies unused because I can't hear the music. Akbar laughs at me, blows off the dust from the machine, tinkers endlessly on hands and knees. He rolls the discs, and then he stands, with head cocked and mouth ajar, his expression enrapt. Crazy, he murmurs. He begins to rock back and forth, swaying sinuously from his shoulders and upper torso, scattering his locks—and this way he spends hours and hours, swinging his head to music I don't hear. I watch him seated on the floor or crouched over the record player, and I resist going to him, touching him; he is content, contained, perfect in his absorption. Although there are times I wonder if it's contentment that keeps him rooted to my floor, when the disc has long stopped playing and he remains still and immovable. He grows cold, like stone, and then I am afraid to touch him for fear of his crumbling into dust in my hands. Later when I look for him he's vanished, and doesn't appear again for days and days at my house on Avenida Mañana.

Victorian London, 1890s

I was the middle child, and not pretty. Or, I *was* beautiful early on when it didn't count, as all children with few exceptions are comely, possessing large inquiring eyes, softly rounded mandibles, and springy hair like fright wigs. As a result of my comeliness as a child, I gained the attention of my father, the Viscount, when he was free from pressing government errands, for he was a favorite of Victoria our Queen. My father wore a very high starched collar with necktie, a boater, and side whiskers that tickled our faces. But we rarely saw our father, occasionally in Hyde Park when we were escorted on an outing by Nanny—a succession of nannies, I don't remember which one—and we would wave sportingly to him, because our nanny told us to. My father thought us handsome children, strolling mid-afternoon in the park, though he didn't recognize us, seeing us so seldom in our youth, and he wondered aloud to his walking companion, Now why do you suppose those children are waving at me? At which his friend replied, Perhaps those children are yours, Viscount?

Nanny, too, thought I was pretty, and thus deserving of secret treat-giving from the pockets of her apron. I got rather chubby. These aging lady caretakers were propelled into exasperation after a few months running after the four of us: we would vanish mischievously in secret hiding places at Dunwoodie, our Scottish country house; throw our slippers in one concerted *bang!* at the nursery door after lights-out; engineer shoelace mistyings, whereby the elderly nannies, having fallen asleep after a couple of late-night nips of brandy and then springing up at a sudden noise, were left with a bruised skull. In short, we gave the old dames heart excitations. Sometimes, too, they softened toward us, ushering us into their lonely beds after the aforementioned toddies, and offering caresses, though we fought our way out. Nanny showered young me, née Dorothy, with special attention during the tender comely years of all girls, before the adolescent uglies set in. I sat for portraits on my pony, Tarts, chin on pancake wrist (not permitted for violin practice, however!), demonstrating my admirable early poise, or seated primly between my two sisters of more forceful personalities—the youngest, dark and pixieish, Sultana, and the older, graceful, strong-jawed beauty, Merveille, which means *marvel* in French, you know. Why wasn't *I* given a more volcanic name, like Artemis, which might have injected a more muscular element into my personality! I was dutiful, demure. My brother, in these portraits, the malevolent Abel, showed fire in his eyes—actually, he was poking me from behind with a silver forchette he had purloined from lunch. He knew I was the sister who wouldn't rat. Thus I was the most promisingly dutiful of the three girls, displayed on Tarts as well pleasing, if a bit startled by the attention, chubby from earning treats for my comeliness, and doted upon by Father, who entered the nursery late at night reeking of adult *going-out* smells and whispered words in my ear to sleep by—*sweet girl*. How could such a daughter not blossom stunningly?

Mother, however, was remote. Mumsy did not bother with her middle daughter's comeliness, having learned the overall uselessness of beauty when it came to the nuts and bolts of running a marriage. A Belgium countess, my mother was rather more impressed by her youngest daughter's canniness with the operation of mechanical devices such as apple corers and game instructions. Sultana was clever and learned how to take apart contraptions and put them back together, such as locks and timepieces, a skill that would serve her well during the war, when she and her young husband, a sheik, operated for British Intelligence. She had developed a passion for backgammon, having read about its popularity in the lands of the Rising Sun, and, wanting urgently to travel there herself (the Victorians believed that one's name formed one's destiny), she persuaded my mother to play it with her; dark, pixieish Sultana was the only one tenacious enough to learn the complicated arcane rules of the game, then teach Mumsy, who nonetheless caught on quickly. Mother was an intelligent person with precious little of cerebral content to occupy her in our lofty Mayfair house—the children given over to a succession of nannies left her a goodly bit of time during the days to make an elaborate toilette and call on friends in her smart brougham. With her keen, analytical mind she would perhaps have pursued mathematics, had she been a commoner and married for love. Instead, she attended the requisite ladies' luncheons of her set and attended book groups, where the members agreed on a fashionable new novel to read, perhaps chosen from *Blackwood's* magazine. Novels, my mother believed, contained life's true experiences, and Mrs. Oliphant's *Chronicles of Carlingford* series dictated her rarefied tastes. She scolded her daughters: Vanity will only win you a trifling husband! Then misery all of your evenings. My daughters will not be decorative creatures, in the fashion of the times. You must develop yourselves, my girls. You must develop your minds and your true gifts. You must arm yourselves against flattery and the temptations of venal indulgence. You will learn thriftiness and an astute judgment of character—and not make the mistakes most women make in taking a mate for life!

Yet Mother had married quite well. The young Geraldine of Belgium had been a beauty, darting-eyed and shapely in photographs, sheathed in gauzy layers of white fabric like bandaging, her wispy dark curls framing her well-molded face as she gazed off dreamily and rather near-sightedly into the distance. And into that near distance stepped the dashing Viscount Reginald (the second, alas), cutting a striking figure in his starched collar, straw boater, and muttonchops. Mumsy was small and amply figured, not unlike our battleaxe Queen, and tended in later years toward the same severe groundedness of physique, top and bottom heavy, from sedentary living as a daylong reader. Her eyesight suffered. My mother did not detect the unraveling of her middle daughter's comeliness until it was too late. I did not blossom, as expected. The problem lay in the chin: my cheeks filled out rosily, and the generous mouth sprouted many fine, lustrous, and useful teeth, but the chin did not firm up, leaving me with a rabbity expression—big eyed and toothy. My bosom, however, fulfilled the magnificent Victorian silhouette, and my jambs gained strength from riding and dancing lessons, at the Queen's own expense. I was going to be a strong girl, and I ate heartily, never suspecting, by the early teenage years, that I would be anything less in my father's eyes than his favorite. It had never occurred to me that I was not beautiful. And he, upon returning after a long trip on the Continent, having achieved the Queen's pressing exigencies, reencountered his slightly bewildered middle daughter, shyly pulling at her frock. He was aghast.

She's fat, he announced to Mother, and the current nanny, who indulged me with Bavarian sweets.

She certainly is *not*, retorted Mumsy, drawing up nobly her venerable girth. My daughters, without exception, are perfect.

She is *fat*, however, and must embark on a slimming regime immediately, persisted Father. No more sweets! And exercise for her—riding, dancing, every day.

Fat I was declared and a warning issued to Nanny to restrict the Charleston trifle I found infinitely comforting after knuckle punches by brother Abel. Nanny was helpless to stop my crying. Under the newly critical eye of my father, I fell from grace. My confidence faltered, chin withdrew, eyes watered in distress, and I ceded my reigning comeliness without a murmur to my two more cunning sisters, who already had husbands picked out. They knew it was the only way to get out of the house. But I was very attached to my glamorous, busy father and relied on his choice of me as his *sweet girl*—I did not want to leave his house.

One summer afternoon, on a rare excursion *en famille*, we all rode together in our elegant hansom, out for a drive to Richmond to enjoy the fine weather and observe the Queen's mounts. We watched the larks soar among the full, leafy linden trees as they tossed in the warm breeze. We four sat across from our exquisite parents and we admired them. My mother wore a preposterous bonnet on her small, dark head that lent her the appearance of an exotic bird. We listened with great pride to our father, because he had a marvelous deep voice, and he pronounced upon each of his children's gifts. Sultana was fearless on horseback and Abel took first in mathematics and Merveille had stolen the eyes of the young Grenadiers, hadn't she though? My mother bobbed her bonny head in assent. And when my father turned lastly to me, I didn't hear— panicked and dumb in the seat opposite, my ears smarting with shame. I didn't hear what my parents determined I would be. What else was left for me if bravery, genius, and beauty were already taken? I ceased to hear them at all.

It was the spring of Sylvie, the cow, which often ran away. She was a gift of a young couple who lived two hours by horse trail down Lobo Mountain, our closest neighbors. They invited us to their farm. They had heard about Abe through Janie, since there were very few of us then, the Eastern transplants. Kate, the wife, wanted to be the first to meet the controversial philosopher, or was he a Marxist? It didn't matter; he was famous, he was *new*. She was a potter, a tall, strapping American emerging from her farmhouse in a mud-splattered apron, pushing at her messy, pinned-up hair with an unabashed gesture. Behind her, Ralph, her husband, the poet from Chicago. He never really spoke, as I could hear. He seemed much younger than she, his hair already thinning, with nervous facial expressions and a particular gesture of rotating his wrist; he had a spindly neck and ankles. Ralph did not look strong like Kate, his wife, but rather dreamy and unstable, and I could never tell what he was looking at, gazing off just above one's head, into the middle distance. Their farm was small, modest, and unkempt, and contained a few imprudent chickens and scruffy dogs. My father had always kept dogs about when we were children, and they liked me. They sniffed with interest at my trousers, at the knife I had begun to keep secured next to my thigh for skinning fish. I had learned to fish at Dunwoodie when I was a child, and I was a good fisherman. Janie laughed at me for carrying around a knife secured to my thigh, but I reminded her a little huffily that I now lived out in the wilderness (unlike some people who got served breakfast in bed by their servants!), and one never knew what savagery one would encounter. She laughed, scornful of my English accent.

Ralph is a poet, Kate announced to us, or rather to Abe, as the young husband gazed off queerly into the middle distance. She was beaming with this announcement, pushing back her flyaway hair. She was delighted to be in Abe's famous presence.—He's from Chicago, she pursued. Ralph edited the poetry review and knows all the best poets. He writes wonderful verse himself.

Abe nodded, Very good, yes, and we looked at Ralph as if expecting him to spout his verses. He did not, merely smiled as he gazed above our heads. Abe asked Kate about her pottery, and we followed her inside the unpromising farmhouse mostly taken over by her implements of clay work. She had strong, shapely arms bared in a thin dress, and she addressed Abe in a saucy, quick, flirtatious fashion I was beginning to learn was the way in which women often addressed him. She demonstrated her coil method, then showed us some of her artifacts from the pueblos, and the stove out back where she fired her pots. Everywhere was a layer of dust and untidiness. Abe examined closely Kate's pots, complimenting her on learning so well from the Indian method. Then Vera spoke sharply,

How do you live here? She was poking around the kitchen, running her hands over the grimy surfaces.

Vera, mind your rudeness, said Abe.

But Kate shrugged not quite apologetically and did not seem to notice the need for a kitchen table. We get by—we are free, Kate announced, and looked out the window at her young husband, who was crouched in the squalid yard, feeding chickens from the palm of his hand.

He fought in the war? Abe asked.

Gassed, replied Kate.

Ah, said Abe.

How do you cook? Vera demanded, snooping around for some tea.

Oh, I'm a terrible cook, said Kate, laughing. I come from Boston. My mother never taught me to cook. I went to college. My mother wanted me to be a doctor, and I ended up at the *Globe* as a copy editor. But Ralph likes to cook a few things, she added, and we considered him through the window doubtfully.

How did you meet Ralph? I asked, thrusting my trumpet under her chin.

She started.—In the train, she shouted at me. He was returning from New York, interviewing a poet, and I intercepted him. Is that scandalous? She laughed again, shortly, and she meant: is that scandalous *enough*? She was showing off in front of Abe. He smiled pleasantly, sure of his conquest. But we have a cow that needs milking, continued Kate, turning brightly to Abe, and Ralph forgets to milk her, and she's grown so ornery and mean and sometimes, out of spite, won't let Ralph near her. Abe smiled at Kate like a steadfast beam. He only needed to stand in front of a woman and smile at her with his full attention and he got what he wanted. He wanted the cow, I knew that. Vera pawed at the ground, and turned on her heels, going out to join Ralph in the yard. He wasn't quite right, I was sure of it.

We led Sylvie out on her rope harness. She was a lovely fawn color and soft to touch, her udders fit to bursting. She was stubborn and mute until Abe gave her a little sweet from his pocket that he carried for the horses and then she came along with us, up the mountain trail toward our cabins. She bellowed lowly. She wouldn't let me lead her, content with Abe next to her, which pleased him in his homey proprietary way. By midday it grew warm. We stopped at the place called Open Mouth of Bear by the Indians, in honor of the mythical Yellow Woman, patroness of the hunt and crops—she was the first to give names to places of importance, Domingo told me. It was a flat ledge that jutted out over the mountain's side, resembling a bear's mouth (if you happened to know what one looked like), allowing a precipitous view of the valley. We ate what provisions we'd brought, and warmed ourselves in the sun. Sylvie, tied to a pine, munched on some greasewood, while Abe squatted next to her with his empty canteen and coaxed the milk out of her. He pressed his hatted head into her bony flanks, working her sore udders with his slender, nimble fingers, and instructed Vera on the art of milking a cow:

Vera, you squeeze gently, low thrusts, like this, he said, turning up an udder and shooting milk at her, as she shouted at him. Sylvie groaned in relieved pleasure.—And then pull firmly down and squirt into your bucket, in this case, a canteen, Abe said, delighted with himself. He was a country boy at heart, a miner's son. He handed the canteen around and we enjoyed Sylvie's fresh offering. Even Vera was glad and made a little homesick for her superior Alpine childhood.

I wish we'd asked for a chicken, too, said Vera, patting at her pockets for her pouch of tobacco, for she had begun rolling her own smokes, in the manner of the Indians. The girl had plenty of chickens, she said gloomily.

Vera, be satisfied with what you have, said Abe, as he was always telling her: Be grateful, lass, why do you want more than this? He wiped his mouth, took off his hat, and saluted the Sacred Mountain.

If you don't ask, it won't be given to you, she muttered. She licked the cigarette she had rolled and stuffed it between her lips.

I lay on the safe ground and tipped my hat over my eyes.

Janie wanted to know what Abe had said.

What did he want of Kate? she demanded of me. She stopped me in Fink's feed store. She wore her Alice in Wonderland ribbon in her hair and handed her parcels to Rufina, waiting patiently at her side.

Nothing, I said, trying to remember the interview with Kate and Ralph. I had provisions to buy in town with Domingo—tar and tin for the leaky roof. Salt and spices: Abe wanted to teach Vera how to cook food that *tasted like something*, he grumbled. But Janie would not be mollified.

But what did they talk about? she persisted.

Pots, I said.

Pots! she cried. And what else?

I don't think we spoke of anything else, Janie, I said.

You're lying, she said.

No. Maybe I didn't hear. . .

I spied Junior, taller than the others, speaking to some traders of jewelry, their wares spread on the ground of the Plaza, under the veranda. He saw me, too, though he did not smile, rarely smiled. He wore a white sheet wrapped around his massive shoulders, his face deeply tanned, impassive, majestic. When Janie spun away in a rage, he appeared beside me as silently as my shadow.

Fishing, he signed to me. We go fishing.

I nodded to him. I wanted to know—when, where? These were questions you did not ask of Junior.

We go, was all he would indicate.

Janie turned back to me. I'll come with horses, she said suddenly, as if the idea of a bribe hadn't occurred to her. I'll get him some horses. Tell him.

Yes, I said, and added, slyly: And Janie, he'd like to have . . .

Yes? she asked.

He wants an horno.

An *horno*? She looked puzzled. But why?

To cook like the natives.

Ah! cried Janie, her face lighting up.

I went away happy because Abe would be pleased with my trip to town.

Akbar starts at the backs of my knees. He knows I'm ticklish there, only there, maybe behind my neck, but not much. Not like Akbar, who is ticklish everywhere over his pale, freckled body. After our bath Akbar has discovered my ticklish zones by clambering around me on his hands and knees, thrusting and wiggling with his long, dry fingers. He is snickering gleefully. He's an imp, a big overgrown fool. He finds how contented he makes me by caressing my head, scraping his fingernails gently across my scalp. The skin on his palms and fingers is leathery from climbing trees, and I take his hands like lizard paws and try to soften them and the back of his sunburned neck with some lotion. I flip the hempen coils off his neck and rub the oil in the thick creases of his skin. He has a farmer's tan, and elsewhere his skin is bloodless and speckled. What's that, he asks, grabbing the bottle of skin emollient. He examines the contents closely. He is terribly far-sighted and lifts his glasses up off his nose to see better in the northern light of my living room. Oh no, he scolds me, squinting up with his pale grey eyes. Bad chemicals, he declares, make Akbar sick. He distrusts anything made by an American company—thinks the Communists have secretly contaminated the air, water, and soil. He replaces the bottle and looks at me sternly as if I have been trying to poison him. I take his hand and replace it on my bare skin; then he remembers where he was, at my breasts, which are as buoyant as ten-pound sacks of rice, and encumber me when I'm on top of him. He nibbles, using his teeth, and I have to tell him to stop. No biting! I cry, truly it hurts, and a rippling laugh escapes him and he moves on, to my underarm pits, pulling at the mouse-grey hair that delights him, then along my arm, and fingers, which smell like turpentine—everywhere touching gently with his mouth except where I want him most to touch. I coax him, nearly to tears—my fortune cookie at the Chinese joint in town declared I was to guard against being critical—I am determined to be a greedy lover finally, as men are. At the last moment, he's there, between my legs, peeling me open. Akbar's mouth belongs *there*, he tells me, before his crown disappears. And I agree, oh yes, nestling into the sofa, thrilled with this turn of events. I open myself. I'm going to drown with pleasure this boy brings me—I've waited a lifetime!

The Queen would hold dancing lessons for her young relations, and she had many. My father the Viscount could recite the dizzying lineage of Battenbergs before they became Mountbattens, and so on. Naturally, we were invited. On Tuesday afternoons we entered the newly opened Red Drawing Room of the palace, which was appointed in thick, sumptuous upholsteries, though the place stank of centuries of mold. We wore our best frocks and sashes and were accompanied by Nanny—one in the aggrieved company of nannies. Victoria had enlisted the mastery of Luigi Tucci, the legendary dancer she had seen perform at the opera in Venice. He was a smallish man, with black glossy hair and mustache, a pancake face, and slim, speedy hips that he maneuvered in tight toreador pants across the mirrored salon. Signor Tucci exuded the fragrance of lily of the valley eau de cologne, the favorite scent of the Queen's own granddaughter, the ill-starred Alix of Hesse, who was indebted to Tucci for preparing her successfully for her coming-out ball. Our Majesty, elderly, stout, and ferocious of expression, clad in her complicated black widow's garments and white lace cap, was wheeled in by her army of attendants. She had herself parked next to the classical bust of her deceased beloved husband, Albert, Prince Consort, in Caesarian toga and curls, the mirrors reflecting unforgivingly behind her. We faced her and her entourage, and curtsied awkwardly. Players on harpsichord, violin, and viola struck up a lively Bach bourrée while our Queen thumped out the time with her ivory-headed cane. Signor Tucci minced expertly, demonstrating intricate patterns of gigues and minuets. He was showing off for the Queen and hardly regarded us. We chased him in an attempt to execute similar moves and perspired profusely, knocking into each other. The Queen thumped the floor with her cane, emoting fiercely. There was no telling whether she was pleased or displeased. Sometimes her head drooped to her chest and she nodded off. Once I tripped over her footstool. One of her Indian guards grabbed me and whispered that the Queen would chop off my head. I wailed in terror. The Queen banged the padded arms of her wheeled chair and we froze and could not go on. With a flourish from Signor, the players started up again and we realigned ourselves. In the end our Queen decreed, waking with a start, that we were perfectly lovely, though Signor glowered at us and we knew we hadn't made him look any better. Dancing for our Queen, I was beginning to suspect that I was not beautiful after all.

We were returned in our brougham to Tilney Street, Mayfair, to show our mother what we had learned. Mumsy descended the staircase patting at her high hair, her eyes tired from reading the current novel by Mrs. Humphrey Ward. Presently she would ring for tea, and we arranged ourselves around our pretty mother in the drawing room and prattled. Sir Jeremy might be there, a large-bellied, fur-faced friend of my father who had served under Disraeli and came in the afternoons although my father was not at home, being a purposeful man with his days occupied. My mother would already be at tea with Sir Jeremy when we got home. He had a thin, high voice, unlike my father, and was expansive in a way that embarrassed our mother, who, however, could not decline the attention of a lord who had also served under a famous novelist. Sir Jeremy made himself quite at home, and was altogether an irksome presence in the house, because he monopolized the attention of our mother and we could do nothing to move her. Mumsy said, with a lift of her arm that seemed to cause her great effort, Show Sir Jeremy what you have learned! And we would prance through the dance steps once again, and end up in a heap of giggles. Sultana, a great mimic, imitated the ferocious expression of the Queen, which made us laugh the more, while Merveille, thrusting her hips side to side like a toreador, executed comically the precise moves of our legendary dance master, and Abel tossed himself over the sofa and clowned. My mother grimaced politely behind her serviette, but Sir Jeremy bellowed and slapped his squeezing knees. Jolly! he cried. Jolly!

I was shy in front of Sir Jeremy and held back from participating in our play because he watched us girls closely and even found me alone and spoke to me.—I say, he said, coming upon me in the pantry where I was rooting out the cache of Cook's tea biscuits, You're a very good dancer! I jumped to find him so close to me. I had not heard his approach. And I knew then what I had suspected by my father's critical glances and growing coolness toward me but hadn't completely grasped until that moment when

Sir Jeremy thrust his great grinning red face close to my own: that I was neither a good dancer nor beautiful. Because if I had been, like my two sisters, Sir Jeremy would not be speaking to me in this familiar manner, crowding behind me in the pantry of our kitchen. The realization crept sadly over me, making me feel helpless and overcome. I did not resist, but stared as if frozen at this large furry obstacle stinking sourly of his lunch. Sir Jeremy must have felt encouraged by my inability to speak, because he found me often in the house, on certain afternoons, when I was alone. He would creep into the library where I was bent over my schoolwork, and suddenly he was there when I had not heard him. I would leap up from my books, too terrified to cry out. He would appear in the library, sinking into the sofa like a dancing bear in collapse, and speak to me very gently.

Dolly, tell me what you did in school today, he said, motioning for me to come closer.

I stood in front of Sir Jeremy, who was very red in the face, breathing with difficulty and blowing out his whiskers on each side of his face. He smelled foul and stale like beer and fried meat. I was frightened of Sir Jeremy, but I was dutiful toward all adults. I had been well taught, and got up and stood in front of him, where he parted his sausage legs to make room. I recounted my school day in detail, though I could not hear myself for the blood pounding in my ears. I hardly knew what I was saying, I could have been speaking in Swahili, but Sir Jeremy didn't mind, as he fumbled with his fat red hands, taking hold of me. He was blowing alarmingly, squeezing my flesh, my poor fledgling bosom and hips, and I was afraid he would bust something either in me or him, before he exploded finally and reared back with arms and legs spread wide like Humpty Dumpty fallen off the wall. He was gasping and blue in the face and I asked quickly, Sir Jeremy, whom should I fetch? But his eyes rolled back in his head and he coughed, No one, lass, tell no one, and made me bring him a glass of water. Now get thee back to your studies, lass, he told me finally, more gruffly this time, and got up with difficulty, very sweaty and slick, leaving a darkish stain on the sofa. He left the library, to my great relief because I did not want to have to explain to Mumsy how Sir Jeremy had expired in my presence.

But he would find me again, in the library at my work or in the drawing room painting, left alone for a moment or two while the others were diverted by some activity. Putting aside my work, I knew to stand quietly in front of Sir Jeremy and recount my day briskly, and let him pinch me here and there, on my breasts and poor buttocks under my school frock. Subsequently, he would rear back in explosive agony, blowing his whiskers out the sides of his cheeks, flailing against the couch or the wall, if he were standing. He was a rank, meaty presence and always left a greasy residue of the public house on my skin. I would fetch him a glass of water and he would mutter, Tell no one, lassie, and I would be dismissed. I was disgusted by Sir Jeremy, but I was dutiful first and foremost, and told no one.

The first time we painted together we rode down through the pine forest in the morning on horseback. We rode Janie's horses: Abe had Jefe, who was tall, black, and spirited, and I rode Vera's slow brown Betty, strong and big-bellied. I hadn't ridden since I was twelve—English saddle, of course. Abe hoisted me up and I managed to stay on. He seemed a little concerned about the wild bumping I took in the saddle but I never looked down. He always rode ahead, and looked back from time to time to see if I was still with him; there I doffed my hat and gave him a little regal salute. We found a clearing and set up working in the dappled sunlight. It was still cool in the mornings and we wore woolen ponchos over our rough shirts and trousers. Abe parked himself under a tree, notepad on knees, and began to write, fluidly, as he did, as if effortlessly taking up in his sermon where he had left off last. I stood out in the sunny field and adjusted my hat, easel, and paints. I began a painting of the Sacred Mountain. The clean early light revealed a startling array of blue and grey to the earth, the clouds injecting the barest of flaws in the sky, and I worked quickly, hoping to capture the sweet clarity of the New Mexico morning. While Abe, writing his essays and speeches, pouring forth evenly and without stop, seated under the tree on the other side of the field, lent me determination and reassurance. I wondered if my presence gave him such a feeling. We lost track of time. At midday we broke. He signaled to me, having tired after a few hours of his concentrated cerebral activity, and I joined him under his pine tree and we ate what we had brought—cheese, bread, and nuts. I brought to him my painting and said, Look, Abe, what do you think? He gazed at it a very long while, sighed, and said finally,

Doll, *look*. The mountains have toes, do you see there?

I must have looked puzzled, because he grabbed my paintbrush and raked at the base of my mountain, scraping up what looked like erosion indentations into the violet volcanic soil.

Now, do you see? he cried, and I did see, though I felt a little sorry for my painting. Now look harder, Doll, he insisted, and deeper, and what do you see elsewhere and everywhere else? I stared, wanting to see what he saw in his rapture—the phoenix, rising from the red dust.

But I don't want the world behind my mountain. I only want my mountain, I returned, sulkily.

But to ignore the nature behind, and the spirit above? So put it in scale, the way you see it, Abe said, and gave me back my painting. He took a nap under the tree. Later I woke him up and said, Abe, and showed him my painting of New Mexican hills budding like adolescent breasts behind the Sacred Mountain. Abe cried out,

Yes, Doll, that's it! I felt a flush of pleasure. But he wasn't finished with my painting yet. He wondered, What about the ranch? Where is it? He pointed to the dip in the valley, beneath the mountain. Though I grumbled, he went on, And what about us? Shouldn't we be there, too? And the horses, and all the rest? So I went back to it, enthusiastically now, because Abe said so and because his artistic sense was sharper, in most cases. I trusted his instincts; they were usually better than mine. I painted our ranch and the straight pine tree under which he loved to work, and I even put in ourselves, although Abe stopped me again.

I'll paint myself, he suggested, and took over where I had put him squarely in the center of the canvas. He took the canvas between his knees, and, hunched over, dabbed at the tall slender figure straddling Jefe. Behind him several paces there was the slightly smaller figure, more unassuming in her round-brimmed Chinese sombrero, astride big-bellied Betty. I was the figure holding back. We laughed at ourselves depicted there, stepping back from the easel to admire our work. Then Abe said, Ah, but something's missing. I looked at him and shrugged at the painting. What? What could be missing after we included all of nature and the sky and even ourselves?

Vera, he said.

We stared at the canvas and exchanged looks. Now we couldn't go back to the ranch with this painting the way it was. I was crestfallen. But she can't be on a horse! I whined, and made Abe promise that he wouldn't remove me from Betty and paint Vera instead. And it's my painting!

All right, Dolly, said Abe, and he went to work. We'll put her in the yard, what do you say? Like this. He took up a brush and dabbed at the white paint and created a liebfrau bending over the cabbages in the garden. I watched him tinker painstakingly with the apron the figure wore, embroidering it with flowers in the Tyrolean fashion. And I wondered at his love for her—for he *did* love her, despite all the fighting. He worked with his brow furrowed, turning his head from side to side to consider the effect, then peeked at me.

Do you like it? he said at last.

I suppose so.

Don't sulk, Doll. Now will *she* like it?

No, I don't think so.

Oh, why not?

She's not in the center, *you* are. And you've got her in an apron. . .

The apron is the most beautiful object in the painting, said Abe. He laughed and laughed, throwing his head back. I saw the soft pale skin of his neck below the red beard, and the rings of dirt. She'll like it, said Abe, you wait. And I laughed, too, flushed at the thought of the fuss she'd throw. We gathered our things and rode back, wordlessly.

At the sound of the horses Vera roused. She was lying down on the bed when we returned. I caught sight of her through the window, smoking and reading. She came out onto the front step looking cross.

I am waiting, she declared. Cooking.

All right, we're here, said Abe. She watched us dismount, already suspicious.

Why so long today? she asked.

The land is beautiful in this light. We have been painting, said Abe.

I held the horses and began to loosen the girths and unsaddle them. I sniffed the air for the smell of food, but I smelled nothing. Abe headed toward the back door, the canvas under his arm.

What have you got there? Vera asked.

Doll's painting, said Abe, and he showed her. I hid by the horses and watched. Vera pondered the canvas, murmuring darkly.

Ach so, she said, admiring the mountains. And this figure, here? She pointed to the matronly figure in the apron. Who's there? Your mother, Abe?

Abe grunted. Why, no, Vera, don't you recognize yourself?

Ach so. Well, hmm. She needs chickens, don't you think?

He handed Vera the paints and she sat heavily on the front step with the canvas in her lap. She painted her chickens, white fluffy blurs scurrying around the bottom of the canvas.

There, she announced, as we watched over her shoulder and tried not to smile at each other. That's better. Now, Doll, she declared, struggling to her feet. She handed back the canvas: This is your best painting yet.

We had arrived in early spring and the nights were cold. In my small shed, I had my wood-burning stove and much wood that Abe and I had chopped and piled neatly, and soon the place was toasty warm. In the evenings we sat side by side in two chairs and sewed. Or, Abe sewed, because he managed beautiful stitching he had learned from his mother growing up in the Midlands. Also he enjoyed it, and I did not. Abe ended up patching my clothes, while I read aloud from a book he was reading or from a newspaper Domingo had brought us from town. The news was full of the presidential election we knew less and less about—the news of a greater world penetrated from a very long distance. Through my window, the moon cut a brief dash above the feathery pines. We were content to sit quietly, sewing side by side, or reading and sketching in the warmth of my shed. I didn't wonder what Vera was doing, didn't even think of Vera, though I imagined she was lying on her bed, reading German novels and glad to be rid of us.

I felt the earth tremble with the approach of hard bodies and then there were noises of the tribesmen. Abe got up and donned his blanket. Stay here, he told me, and went out, but I snapped the knife to my thigh and shot out behind him. The air stung my face after the cozy warmth of the shed; I shivered and pulled my poncho tighter around my neck. The tribesmen had set up a fire in the side field, at our pit, after a hunting expedition. First they placed a grouping of feathers around the fire as a way of asking favors of the gods for our meetings—turkey feathers and tails from the rainbow crow. The fire was stoked into roaring flames, snapping at the night air, and the men and their wives stood quietly around it. They shared this land with us: they were the stewards and we the squatters. They gathered after their hunt and they stayed when we were present, and eventually they came to hear the Red Fox, too. Someone tossed a log into the flames—Junior, wrapped in a sheet, his face glowing a deep, hardwood red. He greeted Abe in the traditional gesture of the people, touching his forehead, heart, then bringing the flat of his palms together—a harmonious integration of a body's I's, as Abe described it. Junior beckoned Abe to sit at the hearth. The others watched. I knew Janie wouldn't come. She had guests from the east, and there were meals to attend to, prepared by Rufina, and bedrooms to fill. But Domingo was there, sharing the pipe that was passed around.

And Abe spoke, calling, We are refugees from the Old World! For this is how he began his instruction as we nodded and hummed.—We have been scattered with the rupture of war! cried Abe. We are exiled from the lands of our fathers and mothers. The old country has descended into barbarism. The grasping among nations has escalated into unprecedented and unsustainable military aggression; the warlords have marched against their own people. Millions have been murdered, swept to the grave under the thrust of machinery and guns. At a certain point, no one, not even the leaders of this collective destruction, is sure what the fighting is about, except that the machinery, once put into motion, can't cease its relentless onslaught, its murderous momentum. Able men and women, in the prime of their lives, have sacrificed themselves willingly to this mayhem, to the subjugation of their reason and higher faculties. Why? Because they saw no other way except despair and suicide. This is barbarism. We are refugees from this madness! cried Abe. We come to the new land to start over.

Yes, nodded the tribesmen. They were the Old People of the sacred desert lands and they would harbor us, the refugees.

Behind us is disintegration, Abe continued. The war has broken down all old forms of class, society, and family. The father has been expelled from the family to fight a shadowy foe he feels nothing against, and the mother is left to fend for herself. Poverty stricken, she may be left homeless by the violence around her, forced to leave her children, forced into slavery or drunkenness or prostitution. Brothers are pitted against each other in a senseless civil war, children pushed out prematurely into a malevolent world to beg or work in factories to support the machinery of war—children abandoned, maimed, starved, robbed of their safety, and scarred for life. The family unit is broken up and scattered.

Soft gasps of alarm hung in the night air. Someone wept. The flames snapped toward the spangled sky. The Indians were peaceable people. They did not know of civil war and the metal-thirst of machinery.

Who suffers most in this scenario of bloodshed? asked Abe softly. There was silence. The women and children, of course, he told them. The nations can reassemble themselves from the broken backs of the people, but shattered families cannot rise from the ashes. The treatment of its women and children is the standard of a nation's sense of itself, of its own humanity. And by this standard— measured in the forced disintegration of the family, the rupture of the home, and impoverishment of wives and children—the Old World demonstrates its utter barbarism. We have turned our back on this scene of devastation, Abe said, opening his hands. We have removed ourselves from harm, cobbled a new family together from the wreckage. We reject the barbarism behind us, and we have come here, to make a new covenant with you, the Old People. We came to learn from you.

He paused again, staring into the flames. He would speak for hours like this, without raising his voice, steadily gaining momentum, building point upon point from his vast reservoir of memory. We sat as one body, hypnotized.

The basic way, he resumed, is to raise the human conscious-ness. That is why we are here. The higher a man is spiritually, according to the nature of his interests, according to his natural abilities, the more he will demand from himself and his friends, male and female; the stronger the connection is within the com-munity, the more difficult it is to break. Man must demand more of himself. He must integrate the various parts of himself, the spiritual, emotional, physical—integrate his *I*'s into a harmo-nious whole. He will not be content to serve others, to subjugate his body, his intellect, and emotional life to inferior, warlike, bar-baric behavior. He knows he is made for a greater purpose than slaughter. He will work with his neighbor, never fight against his neighbor. It is not in his interest.

And the woman? There came a clear, unmistakable shout from the back. Startled, we turned around to look. It was Vera, standing slightly outside the circle of the fire, in the long shadows of the pines. The tribesmen stirred uncomfortably.

Ah, the woman, said Abe. She votes, she drives, she smokes— in this country she is enfranchised, emancipated. But is this the whole story? He turned back to the fire and I detected a change in his face. Was it a hint of a smile? They had rehearsed this then, I surmised, and relaxed a little.—The woman is, he continued, the living point where all the decisive strands of economy and culture intersect. It is impossible to speak of a new human consciousness without addressing the basic condition of the mother—the source of the nation. The ages of slavery, hunger, epidemics, and war have not passed without a trace: they have left behind in the living organism of the family deep scars and wounds. The woman is still in bondage within the family, still tied to the drudgery of house-work, cooking, and raising of children. Her toil is not respected, and she hungers for work to enlighten and ennoble her. How to release her? She must be awakened and shown the way. Freeing the mother means cutting the last umbilical cord linking the people with the dark and barbaric past. She must be the equal of man, his partner.

How? cried Vera. How to release her?

She must become fully man's partner. A new woman.

And if he won't allow it?

The new man will. The new man wants it, wants to be stronger, more humane, and thus to meld with the woman only strengthens him.

Ha! she cried, raising her voice. I think instead he believes that to join with the woman only weakens him. Is that not the case? She glanced around, appealing to the tribesmen.

No, said Abe.

There were rustling noises, sounds of impatient movement. Abe was losing them. Deep furrows darkened his face. He set his lips—his beard was burnished by the flames. At last the Red Fox stood up.

Enough, he announced. We are one here. Someone handed him up a pipe. He scowled at it, his train of thought broken. Why did she do it? Why did she interrupt his sermon, muddle him, needle him? He took the pipe and abruptly sat down again, and the murmuring of voices resumed. Vera went up, back inside the homesteader's cabin, and slammed the door. We did not heed her anger. Indians laugh at anger, Domingo told me once, when I ham-mered my finger and cursed and carried on. They believe that the gods laugh at you when you make yourself ridiculous. You had to invite the favor off the gods, not make them scorn you. So we did not heed Vera's anger. Maybe we were wrong. Soon the interruption was forgotten, the people began to sing, and there was dancing. Junior sounded his drums. And though we didn't get back to sewing that night, Abe and I, how could I mind? Happy to sit on the terra firma, the unmoving earth, among them, a part of the harmonious whole.

Akbar works in the trees. He is harnessed to ropes, then hoists himself higher by clinging to the tree trunk in a lover's embrace. He grapples until he reaches a troublesome branch that needs correcting. The branch hangs over a roof, inviting rodents, or grows in such a way as to throw off-balance the rest of the tree. A saw is pulleyed up to him by the crew watching below; he steadies himself with one arm and maneuvers the saw with the other. Patiently, steadily, he severs the branch of the tree, and the branch is lowered slowly by rope to the ground, then broken down and bundled by the men below. Akbar is not a strong man, and when I watch him, surreptitiously from my woodie station wagon, I wonder where he gets the strength for this dangerous work. He is slender and has no meat on him at all, unlike me. He's a vegetarian, in fact, hardly eats. A shrimp, is how he refers to himself, or how others have referred to him. He has never been an athlete. His naked legs are spindly, undeveloped, and I have only just learned that he sometimes has trouble breathing. I discovered inhaling medication in his bathroom, along with a contraption of tubes hanging from the back of the door that remind me of my nurse's old douche—in those days, used as a form of birth control. I ask Akbar, What is that contraption hanging from the back of the door? He looks abashed, and mumbles. An enema, he says. I must look stricken. He murmurs something about cleanliness and good hygiene. It's good to fast, too, he adds, knowing that I do not. However, I don't ask him about the inhaling medicine, which shocks me more.

After he leaves my little house on Avenida Mañana in the early morning to go climb his trees, I find it hard to stand and paint with the smell of him still on me. I already miss the dear boy—an old woman's folly. I stand in front of an empty canvas, or one half executed like a half-cooked cake, and shift restlessly from foot to foot; I hop up to readjust the light, tidy the living room, or seek out a bowl of cornflakes in the kitchen, though I'm not really hungry. I can't settle down—I hunt up the car keys and take off in my yellow woodie to cruise the town. Maybe he's mentioned where he'll be working that day, and anyway, the town isn't so big that I can't find the Lucky Tree Service truck idling along the streets, outside the nicer adobes in town. It's a '57 white truck marked by a picture of a leafy green canopy. I park down the block where he won't see me—I don't want him to get distracted up in the trees. Sometimes I spy him already hoisted in an old gnarled cottonwood. He's one of two climbers on the crew; he wears a wool cap to keep his locks out of the way, his green official shirt, climbing gloves full of holes, and cargo pants, and he's wrapped up in ropes and pulleys. If he spots my car he'll know it's me—nobody else has an aged yellow station wagon as long as a New Mexico block. I bought it when I finally started selling paintings. It's big enough to hold ceremonials, I tell him, when he asks why I don't get a proper truck. He thinks I have money, but I don't have any real money. I give him some, when he needs things, like provisions for his mother, but he gives it back when his mother subsidizes him, and says it's not right to take money from me, la señora. He's proud only when his mother scolds him. I want to buy him the hard hat he talks about, to keep him safe on the job, but it's no use handing him money. I have to be sneaky. I buy him dinner because he returns from an entire day climbing trees, scratched up and very hungry, and I know he doesn't feed himself properly. I take him to the Chinese joint in town he knows won't poison him and I order lots of spicy dishes. He chews cautiously, very slowly. I pile his plate but he won't eat with any greater gusto, despite his evident hunger, not like I tend to gobble if the food is lying around. He doesn't say much. Me, I'm dying for conversation. But his mastication is serious and dignified, and I sit back, wait, and let the boy catch his breath. Occasionally it occurs to me that he's embarrassed to be seen with me—a white-skinned old lady with clothes mismatched and splattered by paint, a turban I threw on to cover my crazy static hair. I forget to don my armored brassiere and my venerable Victorian bosom now grazes my navel. There's a buzzing in my hearing aid, and to make up for it I have to talk loudly in a public place.

I park down the block from where he's working on Kit Carson and pull out a sketchpad. Akbar seems most at home in the trees. He straddles the limbs to balance himself and shimmies his way higher. He works with great care, slowly, cautiously, and does not look down. Sometimes he disappears within the luxuriant spread of a laurel and I can't see him for a while. I watch the sway of the ropes, the jerk of pulleys—a saw is hauled up, the incessant grating of it vibrates the air, and I have to switch off my aid. Then I don't mind the occasional traffic, or the noise from the saw or the men's shouts, and I can remain insular—my own island. I'm used to retracting into my carapace. I sketch Akbar: sometimes I make nine sketches of him before I have to move, relieve myself, and get back home before he sees me. Then he's down, the crew takes a break, lounges on fenders, smoking pungent cigarettes. There are jokes Akbar will crack to me later. The men are companionable and at peace after work. I steal away with a notebook of precious sketches. One day I'll have a whole notebook of sketches of Akbar and I shall make them into a painting—several paintings—a whole series. He's never seen my sketches. I'm afraid I'd scare him away. The folly of an old woman.

My hearing loss was noted at an early age, and duly ignored. I took more years to finish school than is usually the case. Sir Jeremy, while odious, was astute enough to recognize that by my mid-twenties I had better figure out something to do with my life. Clearly, my father the Viscount was no longer interested in me, having been disburdened by what was most useful to him, my comeliness; my mother was too distracted by the nuptials of her other daughters to concern herself with me; my brother, Abel, was sent away to officer training in preparation for war against the aggressive Germans and he couldn't torment me. I was not turning into the lady they intended, and I had no interest in marriage. Indeed, who would marry me? There was no one to steer me. I had only ever been good at one subject—art. Sir Jeremy, growing too girthsome to do any more harm to young protégées, and feeling rather sorry for me because I had turned out chinless and dumb, declared that I would go to the Slade School.

Anyway, you'll have more fun at art school, said Sir Jeremy.

But. . . what about my family? I asked, timidly, knowing little about fun.

I'll handle your family, declared Sir Jeremy with a great blow of snuff from his roseolar nostrils.

He seized my portfolio of pretty drawings and sent them to the influential director of the Slade, Marcus Willoughby. In three months I had enrolled in the school for the fall and Sir Jeremy, the doomed brute, at last crossed the Stygian ferry.

At the Slade, I was given a term to prove myself. A personage of my class was rare, and took the place from a more deserving student. I cut my hair. Rather, Lorelei cut my hair, and she was my new friend. I had never had a friend who was not intrinsic to my social set, apart from kitchen staff and groundskeepers and stable mates and, of course, the succession of nondurable nannies. I had been kept occupied by dancing lessons before our Queen. But the Queen had died with the new century, and our randy Edward VII had ushered in new fashions, although he was recently deceased as well, leaving his ungainly brother George V at the helm. The Slade was an urban school, attracting gifted artists from the industrial towns of Manchester and Glasgow, for example, and in this terrifying new milieu I met Lorelei, who did not concern herself with peerage or matching hats but with ideas—modern ideas, an attitude. I entered the cafeteria after studio class one fall afternoon and knew no one; I felt the dread of the forsaken who has to eat dinner by herself. I felt a hundred disapproving eyes on me and the fashionable getup my mother had insisted I bring; my valises were filled with useless clothing. I fetched my tray of food and sought a table by the tall windows where a group of young students was chattering happily. I hoped they wouldn't move away when I sat down. One of the girls who seemed to be their leader eyed me suspiciously, from my high, knotted hair and striped mannish blouse to my oiled button boots. She was trim and terribly intimidating with her short, dark hair and the many shades of red she wore at once—her lips, too, were full and bruise-colored.

I say, said the girl, leaning over and addressing me in a formal manner I later learned was not her own. I say, she drawled, is that a man's *cravat?*

She pointed. I put down my spoon and tugged at the canary-yellow silk Edwardian knot I had painstakingly executed in my tiny dormitory mirror that morning. My sisters had instructed me how to tie it in the smartest way. This? I asked.

She nodded. Do you know the way old Tum Tum used to walk with his hands in his pockets, fingering coins? Yellow, she noted, is the color of *money.*

The blood bulged at my temples. Had I heard her right? The girls were staring at my increasingly scarlet neck. They snickered. The scarf was indeed beginning to chafe at my adam's apple as if weighted with gold. I pulled hard at the knot and loosened it. I don't know, I mumbled. I suppose it could be. Do you want it? I asked suddenly, ripping at the thing and wanting instantly to be rid of it.

Divine! cried the girl. I wouldn't mind.

I handed her my mother's silk cravat. She grabbed it with tobacco-stained fingers and held it up against the windows, shaking it out, to the amusement of her table companions. She considered where to wear it, trying it first coquettishly around her dark helmet of hair like a charwoman—the other girls wrinkled their noses—then with a shrug she stuffed it deep into the bodice of her dress. It flared at her deep cleavage like the crest of a feisty cockatiel. The girls laughed and clapped.

Ho, ho! Lorelei, they cried. Now won't old Marcus flip his wig!

Later she offered me cigarettes for my gift of the scarf, and I took them. Lorelei would teach me to smoke, though I never mastered the art of it. I ended up bent double, hacking up the smoke from my lungs. Not like Lorelei, who struck her attitude, bodice yanked low under a short, smart jacket, thin skirts revealing her undeniably curvaceous form, and ankle boots that were always in a muddy state. She lounged over the dorm's threadbare couch, gazing at scandalous prints and smoking languidly. Lorelei was very attractive. She bemoaned having to make her own living tending to the hair of the bourgeois ladies in her working-class town of Birmingham. She talked about the genius of homosexuals, whom I had scarcely known existed. She told me about her poor mother, who raised her and her younger sister, when their father died after an incapacitating injury in the mills. She wanted to be a real artist like the Viennese she had heard about who painted subjects that people cringed to see. She scoffed at pretty pictures. She didn't mind my thrusting my trumpet under her chin when she spoke; she thought it was an original gesture, and thereby endearing, I supposed. Lorelei went to cafés at night in Soho without an escort and dropped names. She knew where to get a good meal for one shilling six pence—with wine! Lorelei wrote poetry when she was too lazy or hungover to paint. And she spoke about men.

Is it true that aristocrats like it in the bum? she asked me, as if I'd know.

What's that?

Doll, what do you think of Marcus? she changed tacks. He likes his ladies no-nonsense, like you. Though she wouldn't tell me what that meant.

He doesn't like students *of my kind*, I told her. He resents the privileged classes. He's hoping to fail me.

Prove him wrong, said Lorelei.

All the girl students had crushes on Marcus Willoughby. I was late to come to know this. I was always late to catch on and the girls poked fun at me, but not maliciously. I only knew Marcus as the formidable director of the fine arts wing. He led the evening techniques class, and criticized my work for its clumsiness. I was an undisciplined painter, I was not organized, I needed to step back and ponder the possibilities, said Marcus. We worked in a lofty studio from models fully clothed, of course. We worked on perspective, composition, tone. Lorelei's technique was better than mine, but most of all, she was bold in her portraits, using black outlines suggesting a worldly grittiness I knew nothing of—gashes of vivid color that evoked wounds and orifices, like her own fuchsia lips. Her paintings were shocking and exciting to me. I was silently thrilled as I sat on my stool next to her, toiling at studio. But Marcus was not shocked. He was a man of blunted height and robust build, with tormented angles to his nose (probably broken and refigured, I suspected) and steely hair a bit longish and curled over the collar. He reminded Lorelei that a painting should be startling, but also memorable. Keep your wits about you, Lorelei, he muttered, as he strolled by with his brush held aloft like a conductor wielding his baton. She arched her back as he passed and leaned to inhale the wake of his man-sweat scent. He scowled and pretended not to see, and behind him we hooted soundlessly.

Marcus was my first real teacher. He would cure me of my ridiculous sentimentalism, as he called it. My style was not muscular enough for him; it was weak, flowery, sugary, feminine—*chinless*, he might have added. I used too much paint, I overdid the effect, spoiling it. My series of landscapes of Dunwoodie, the Scottish setting of my youthful summers, elicited from scornful Marcus a theatrical drawing of a bow across the violin strings. My portraits of my sisters with their large kittenish eyes sent him into a fit of feigned weeping. Derivative, he hollered in my ear. When will Dolly command her own style? What will she bring to her canvas that which is truly her own? I despaired of pleasing him, as all of us desired to do. And only Lorelei did. Lorelei was an original, and Marcus respected her talent. Was she sharing her teacher's bed? She didn't say, only smirked, and spoke of his poor bedridden wife who had once had an illustrious painting career of her own, before the passel of bairns arrived. You should see her paintings hanging in his flat, she cried. Marvelous! Such suffering! Scenes of child and madonna so achingly pure and melancholy—the work of a desolate heart, waxed Lorelei, who threw adjectives such as *aching* and *desolate* around, to bolster her attitude. How had she come to see Marcus's home, I wanted to know?

Doll, we've all been there, for this and that, replied Lorelei, in her blasé tone, and I felt small indeed. She had attended the school two years, though I was older. He holds contests, she explained, and the winner gets a party.

As part of our portrait assignment, I painted myself. This was new for me—exciting, rather forbidden territory, and I could hardly recognize myself at this important juncture. But Lorelei had cut off my hair one bleak, motionless winter's afternoon in our rooms, snapping off the heavy tresses with sheep shears and leaving my neck exposed pitiably. Ah Doll, cried Lorelei, you have a neck! She clapped at her handiwork, stepping back. She handed me a mirror and I gazed on this new person with wonder. I looked startled, but brave. My dark eyes seemed larger, huge actually, my cheeks emerged, in spite of my lack of a strong jaw, my lips full, my nose upturned. Really, I had a nice nose, a holdover from my comely infancy. And out of a perverse curiosity, I painted what I saw in that mirror, the girl with cropped hair gazing with startled, bold wonder at the viewer, her lips slightly parted to disguise her rabbity childish teeth, her neck elongated in a mannerist fashion. A portrait of a girl in transition, regarding herself as a woman for the first time, and with a bit of apprehension. My portrait arrested the attention of Marcus Willoughby. He let me stay at the Slade School four years.

I was acquainted with Akbar's mother before I knew the son because I used to see her husband the doctor for the rheumatism in my hands. I know her as the woman who takes care of his office, cooks the midday meal, and opens the door to his house on the Plaza for patients; I don't realize she is the wife. I think she is the maid, the silent Mexican servant. Dr. Feliz is large, gruff, and very old, older than the woman who cares for his house. He takes my hands, muttering under whitened brows, massages my knuckles with his thick thumbs, then applies an ancient rancid elixir. He sends me on my way stinking of camphor and menthol. Later he dies—I read the obits of the local paper to learn the fate of all the old ones because I am one, too—and I think nothing again about the woman who cares for his house on the Plaza until I see her with Akbar, who prunes my trees. She arrives in my backyard on Avenida Mañana bearing baskets of food.

I say, Akbar, how did that lady get here?

Bus, he replies.

But why is she here? She worked for the doctor.

Akbar's mother bring lunch, he tells me, as if this is the most natural thing in the world.

He sits with her under my trees, a small, tidy woman in a dark woolen shawl, her long hair gathered back in the old-world fashion, her eyes beady and constantly on the move. Mother and son speak softly together. Something about her black beady stare frightens me off and I don't dare approach her. I wonder whether she remembers me from the doctor's house. Akbar climbs my trees for two days. I stare up at him from my studio window. I can't work with him up there in the trees, shimmying higher and higher with his long thighs straddling my knotty limbs. His mother catches me squinting up at him, and later she sees Akbar reaching for me under the table where I sit for tea. She jumps up as if poked from behind and lets out a stream of incoherent invective. She slams the fence to my garden. She waits on the highway for the bus. Akbar ignores her. He doesn't have any more trees of mine to prune, but still he comes over.

What did she say? I ask, as he straddles me across the chair.

She say you're old. As old as she is.

She's right.

Nah, she ain't, he says. Dooby doom. He laughs lowly and pumps away, gazing into my eyes.

A doctor's son, I had no idea. Not from the way he eats, like a farmer, all elbows and hunched back, mashing up his egg and cheese omelet distrustfully before shoveling it on toast and cramming it in his mouth, his napkin bunched at the side of his plate.

Or by the way he writes, with loopy, illiterate scrawls. He rejects the letters I leave for him on the table as he sleeps, says he can't read my writing, and I suspect he can't read script. I print. I add pictures of him in the trees. He's happy. He writes back in capital letters and leaves me a photograph of himself, weaving on an old-fashioned loom. Who snapped the picture? I ask, considering.

Akbar's mother, he says.

Is it her picture? She'll be angry that I have it.

Nah, says Akbar vaguely.

Once I take him to a fancy restaurant in Santa Fe for his birthday and he balks at the entrance, draws back, won't enter. What's the matter? I ask. This is my treat. No, he says, they's no vegetables here. I assure him, Oh yes, they *is*, I checked for you. But No, Akbar won't enter. Too much money, he protests, and Akbar has sad clothes. He wears ruined cargo pants and a checked flannel shirt with a long, lugubrious jacket dotted with Buddy Holly buttons. He swiftly tucks his riot of hair into his "crown," the woven cap he wears for climbing and that I believe he looks more attractive without. The hat swells hugely because of the high volume of his locks. His little square glasses flash. He looks earnestly official in his cap and jacket, like a young postal servant. Why oh why have I chosen a child for a lover? Now I am angry. Akbar, you come with me, it's high time you learned how to sit in a nice restaurant! I shout. I pull him in and watch him squirm uncomfortably. The hostess tries to insert us in a brightly lit area next to other tables, two inches apart. Dining heads swivel and stare. Akbar is about to bolt. I whisper to the hostess that we'd prefer something more secluded and she obliges me cheerfully, ushering us to the back by the loo. Akbar, traumatized, can't look at the menu. I order a salad with goat cheese, even though he will not eat the goat cheese, he pronounces; and a large vegetable pie, since the restaurant is known for its regional specialties. Vegetables, he insists, as he is very strict about his diet, and I assure him, Yes, yes, lots of vegetables. He sucks down a glass of water, frowns, then takes out the jug of special water infused with electrolytes he carries in his rucksack. He tips it back and guzzles it.

The waiter arrives with our salad and Akbar looks panic stricken. He lowers the jug to the floor. Removes his postal jacket, rolls up his sleeves, and tucks into the plate of fine greens. I let him have it all, watching from behind my glass of gin on ice. The medallion of goat cheese, fried to a delicate golden color, puzzles him. He spears it with a fork, sniffs at it, then hurls the entire cake into his open mouth.

It is to be savored, I warn—too late.

I think his eyes are going to pop out of their sockets.

He knocks back another glass of water (my own). He coughs and hiccups. His skin reddens. Once his eyes have cleared, he gazes at me. He smacks his lips, leans in, declares solemnly, *Me encanta.*

We clink glasses.

I dream that I enter Akbar's mother's house without her knowing it. I do what I manage to do only in my dreams: I fly. I become my own airplane. I fly over her head while she is distracted, talking on the telephone. I fly out the open window and join the great expanse of sky. The light is blindingly white and the air unbearably soft as it rushes about my ears. I feel like I'm joining the angels. And as I fly I feel my body, my sleeping body, quake. I gasp for breath and my heart thumps wildly in my chest, all the while my other self, my sleeping mind, my soul perhaps, is fleeing to join the spiritual world. I feel distinctly these two realms. The physical exertion in my dream begins to waken my sleeping body, but I'm not sure my other self, this ethereal, fleeing soul, *will* rejoin it— whether my various selves will merge harmoniously. At last I settle back to earth, and wake up, breathing with difficulty. I decide that I have had an out-of-body experience. I decide that the dream means that I am feeling guilty for stealing into Akbar's mother's home, literally, and taking away her son. I fly over her head when she isn't looking, because she won't understand the way we love, and she can't see, and maybe it is better that she can't see. I fly off and into the skies, which are the same shade as Akbar's pale grey eyes. That's where Akbar will take me, I'm sure of it—up, up, and away.

I tell Akbar about my dream. I am very excited. He coughs and starts an unrelated conversation, or maybe I haven't made myself clear, as it happens sometimes.

The young wife came on foot, without a hat, swatting at her frothy, ill-pinned hair. She stepped out of the pine forest. Kate appeared in our yard one early morning with brambles stuck to her dress. I watched from my window. She held her shoulders at an awkward angle, making a curious circular dance, her head turned to the side. I came out from my shed and saw there was something at her shoulder, clinging perilously. It was a ball of fur, a small marmalade kitten, gripping her shoulder with thin lethal claws and looking terrified.

I brought you this, Kate said, and tried to disengage the kitty, which clung with raptor talons to the fabric of her shawl. She laughed, bringing it close to her chest with a coquettish toss of her head. I knew by that gesture she hadn't brought the cat for me.

So young, I said, not making a motion to pet the thing. Abe would take it. Abe would take in anything stray.

You don't like cats? asked Kate, and I scowled and nearly replied, What difference does it make whether I like cats or not? But she was looking around the yard, seeing no one.

Not here, I said. They're at the stream mixing up mud. For the horno.

She nodded. She held the kitten to her lips and stroked it under the ears. Why didn't you go? she asked me.

I didn't hear them go. I was sleeping.

Indeed I was annoyed at being left behind. Abe worked before the sun was up, though he had promised to wake me.

And where's your husband, Ralph? I asked, and remembered the vacant-eyed young poet feeding the chickens from his hands. I moved closer to where she stood so that I could hear her answer.

He's resting, she replied, growing more serious. Some days are difficult for Ralph.

Why? I asked. What's wrong with him?

He's touched, Kate replied, stroking the kitten. The war destroyed his confidence.

That's very hard, I said. For you.

He feels isolated out here, she said, but he won't think of going back. Some days he just sits and stares. He won't write. Other days he writes for hours and won't stop to eat. He took off walking last night and I didn't know where he went.

He came back?—She nodded.—And what did he say?

He said nothing. Just lay down and now he won't speak.

You came to see Abe? I asked, more gently.

Yes.

I showed her into my shed and gave her some coffee heating on my stove and a piece of hard molasses cake. She held the kitty close to her, feeding it crumbs. It began to explore, and she leaned over my bed and let it roll on the blanket. Suddenly at a noise it leaped off the bed. Kate scooped it up and dashed outside. I became aware of the clattering of the wheelbarrow up the hill, and voices.

Abe emerged from the forest, pushing the wheelbarrow. He saw us and anchored the wagon filled with mud on the level ground. He removed his hat, wiped the mud from his face with his forearm, and gave a gallant bow. Kate held up the kitten in her arms, beaming.

I brought you this, she said.

Ah Kate, he said.

Behind them, Vera, in her ratted straw hat and with her arms covered to the elbow in mud, snorted and moved heavily up the hill toward the cabin. A mice-catcher, I trust, she said, brushing past them.

Oh yes, a good one, Kate assured her, if he's anything like his mother.

Lookee here, said Abe to me proudly, and showed the contents of the wheelbarrow. Sacred mud for our sacred oven.

We'll have to let it set a bit, I said, a bit peevishly.

Yes, ma'am, a day or two, he said. Have a good beauty sleep? he asked me with a devilish wink as he led the way up the hill.

Vera went in to wash and didn't want to have anything more to do with us. Abe set out the tea implements and arranged chairs in the kitchen. Kate admired the details in the wood where Abe had been painting, around the shutters and headboard of the bed. He painted intricate details of flowers and animals he had observed in nature. Then she told him about Ralph—that he hadn't spoken in two days, he had disappeared the night before, and stared at nothing.

Abe listened. He's in psychic pain, he announced at last. He's like a man possessed.

Possessed, repeated Kate. But of what?

Impediments gnawing away at the human personality from the inside. We are deluged by demons daily. For some of us it's worse than for others, especially after experiencing the trauma of battle. Some of us aren't equipped to resist the onslaught. What does he write about? Abe asked. Do you read his words?

Maimed bodies and slaughter, Kate replied. Watching friends die after a mortar-shell avalanche. The fear of dying in the trenches, wounded and forgotten.

Ach so, hissed Vera from the bedroom.

Bring him here, said Abe.

When? asked the wife.

Tonight. Bring him round, said Abe.

I thought I detected another snort from the bedroom.

Kate put the kitten on the floor. We watched it bat at the dirty cuffs of Abe's pants and he laughed.

The hour to milk our recalcitrant cow, said Abe. He stood up and reached for his hat. He moved toward the door. If I can find her, he added, and went out.

Kate, hair swinging, lunged after him.

My self-portrait arrested the attention of Marcus Willoughby. He stood in front of my canvas at studio and considered. He squinted and shifted his weight. Normally I did not arrest his attention, only exasperation, and I often suspected that I had gotten into the Slade by virtue of my connections rather than by the virtuosity of my work. Everyone knew of my family, that my father sent a monthly allowance, and that I had an account with his seamstress in Windsor. People would mutter, Lorelei heard them, and she told me what they said.

They're jealous of you, she told me. They can't believe that a person of your . . . *privilege* . . . could be a serious artist.

Jealous of *me*? I cried. Who had ever been jealous of me in my life? Rather feeling sorry for me, I thought, the girl without hearing, beauty, or *chin*.

You're quite good, insisted Lorelei. Your technique is improving, Marcus says so. You need confidence.

And here Marcus was considering my self-portrait. I examined the worn brown stuff of his wool suit, the steel-grey hair grown long so that it curled over his collar. Who took care of him? Close up he smelled like tobacco and old sweat. His light eyes, while piercing, were almost deeply sad, his nose long and crooked in a thin face, and there was a tortuous crease between his brows. He did not seem a happy man, rather bowdlerized. The fault of his needy children, the depressed wife? His hands were smallish for a stocky man. An artist's hands. Whenever he wiped his brow he used the back of his fingers, as if to keep from contaminating his fine thin skin.

This one we can work with, he pronounced of my portrait, and I detected something like a smile at the creases of his twisted mouth. He turned from the canvas to me, and I suddenly felt terribly self-conscious in my new short hairdo. I touched my exposed neck.

You have caught the girl-woman, he pondered. There is movement here—life! Keep at it, Doll, he said, and moved on, rapping his brush-baton twice against the side of my easel.

I learned that my self-portrait would be considered for the spring show. Feeling elated and vindicated, I wrote to my father at Dunwoodie: *At last I have hit on a profession, and it is to be an artist!* My father the Viscount did not scoff. In fact, old Reggie had entertained fantasies of immortality himself, as he wrote to me, in an extraordinarily forthright reply, as if the news of my unimagined talent as an artist suddenly allowed him to confide in me his shared artistic passion. He always hoped to write the chronicles of the keeper of the Queen's Public Works. I had known that he wrote fastidiously in his diary each evening when returning from his official post, a regular Sam Pepys in recording the minute gradations of his life as it revolved around court. He had never considered taking a sinecure in the far reaches of the Empire because he could not bear to leave his beloved England. And Reggie embodied the glory of that Empire. He stepped out each morning in his high hat and stiff collar tied with an ascot, his whiskers waxed and unquivering in the raw English morning; he made the rounds of Windsor Gardens with dark coattails flapping and umbrella tap-tapping. He made copious notes. He wanted, he wrote to me, to be feel sure that his indentured life, as he called it, though the finest and highest, had meant something—summed up to *gravitas et memoria*—to be added to the annals of the Empire. He was keenly aware all his life that he would never hold the rank of First Viscount (that went to his older brother), and he had never known another life outside of the seasons of the court, e.g., morning appointment with the Royal Highness (first mother, then son), rounds of the gardens and public works, official functions, meetings with staff, club lunches, then dressing for state dinners. It was an endangered life, headed the way of the dodo, to be sure. He had rarely seen his children growing up, and he knew less and less of his wife. If there was another way of life to be lived, he hadn't done it, didn't know it, and he felt secretly rueful. Was I reading him correctly? The world is changing, he wrote to me, alluding to the cacophony of war in the distance already making itself heard, and you, Doll, are finding your own way in it.

For the first time, he hadn't complained about the bills that were sent to him on my behalf (art supplies, dinners for my impoverished friends, clothing), or wonder what kind of hoi polloi I must be fraternizing with. His tone was forgiving, even wistful, and if I had been more perceptive (and more emotionally mature, despite my years), I should have been alarmed rather than flattered by his change of heart. The Viscount was watching the skies, sniffing the air. The old order was crumbling, and he was bracing for the new.

I didn't win the prize that year, but in another two years I did. There was a party at Marcus's house for me. I had heard much about his soirées and was surprised to find ourselves in a dark little flat off Piccadilly with two front rooms to move around in and a warren of tiny bedrooms for his family in the back. Marcus had at least four small, furtive children, I counted; they appeared fleetingly around corners and in doorways, then vanished. I never learned their names—the oldest was a girl about ten and missing some teeth. The two front rooms were covered wall to ceiling with paintings, many on the top tier executed by his wife, who sat quietly unmoving on the brown beaten sofa with a plate of food balanced delicately and untouched in her lap. She was pale and pretty in a kind of sad, defeated way, her hair streaked with grey, and she nodded her head with a vague smile when spoken to. It was rumored she had once enjoyed an unparalleled talent. The other paintings were by Marcus's students, making a name for themselves in London and on the Continent; they had given him their work out of gratitude. Then amid the other entries to this year's Spring Show there hung my prize-winning painting: a ceremonial dance of women holding hands, moving seriously in a circle, wearing long dark dresses and hair tied at the nape. It was called *Danse Macabre* only because Lorelei said that's what it should be called, as it evoked a feeling of solemnity like a burial ritual, she insisted, though I didn't agree that the painting was intended to feel *macabre*. By *macabre* I always thought of Charles Dickens. Rather, I found the figures light on their feet as they moved in their circle, heads inclined to one side or the other, and if the dark dresses and hair in chignons didn't exactly appear gay, there was a reassuring solidity and regularity about the figures (some with swollen bellies) that I liked very much. They could have been Pilgrims celebrating the first harvest in the New World, for example. But this interpretation came later, I think, when I arrived in New Mexico. Still, when I think back to Lorelei's title, *Danse Macabre*, I find it chillingly prescient, for couldn't the painting be depicting a dance of widows on the eve of the First World War? But people were always projecting what they wanted in my work, and I didn't have any real idea of what my paintings were *about*. Where did the idea come from? they nosily asked, and I couldn't ever answer adequately. Lorelei tried to coach me on how to give smart, quotable answers, because a painter should know what she is doing, such as that *The painting is a metaphor for the sacred connectedness of life,* that was a good one, *Indeed it appeared to me as a vision while strolling along the Clontarf,* but then she gave up in exasperation. I could not sound convincing. In any case, it was my first ritual dance, and little did I know where the chain of this theme would take me.

We dressed in velvet trousers and wore silk scarves around our heads. We had cropped our hair. It was 1914 and this was the Slade girls' modern uniform. We dressed for Marcus, of course, and tried to outdo each other to curry his attention. But I don't think he could be bothered, absorbed in conversation with his former students who had become famous. Lorelei, adorable in her scarlet breeches and scarves and cigarette holder held aloft, would always win in a beauty pageant with me. Yet I had the winning painting hanging in the place of honor in Marcus's front rooms, and I was happy.

You see who he's talking to? Lorelei whispered to me. She pointed with the tip of her lipstick-stained cigarette holder across the stuffed little room. Marcus was engrossed in conversation with a slender, pale man with a fiery red beard.—It's Abe Bronstone, she whispered excitedly. The writer. The revolutionary. Come to your show!

The writer? I repeated, dumbly, having encountered few revolutionaries in my life.

A genius, a philosopher, a prophet, my stylish friend pronounced.

Really? He looks a bit scruffy, I said.

He's brilliant, Doll. He writes subversive literature in a journal called *The New Man* where he advocates sexual equality between men and women. He writes about socialism, economic slavery, and resistance to authority. He is very high-handed. His books are always being banned. I understand his next book will be called *The Emancipated Woman.*—Lorelei snickered behind her grubby hand.—But he's *most* famous for running off with the wife of his German professor.

Is she here?

She is. The Wagnerian figure, there.

She jabbed the air. We examined the curvaceous, blond figure standing next to him, nearly his height (as he was not tall), with high, flat cheekbones and clear white skin, and clad in a kind of matching ensemble meant to be fashionable. She carried an absurd little purse dangling from the crook of her bare arm. There was a certain classical solidity about her figure. She caught our scrutinizing gazes as we bore into her from across the room, and her smile came quick and rather deadly. We turned to each other, Lorelei and I, coughing and blinking so that we wouldn't laugh.

Later, Marcus said to me, You are your own painter now. He nodded toward my canvas.

What's that? I cried, not wanting to miss a word. I thrust my trumpet under his chin.

Your. Own. Painter.

Oh certainly!

What are your plans? Marcus asked me.

I'm going to Paris, I announced proudly.

There's a war on the way, my friend.

My friend! I thought happily, and here he was looking so meaningfully into my eyes.—Do you think so? I asked. You won't go to war, will you? I added, suddenly panicked. You're not leaving the school, are you?

I'm too old for this war, he murmured. But the men—your fellow students, Doll. The young men will desert us at the first alarm. Abe Bronstone says that all over Europe and Asia the workers have risen up against their masters. The Balkans have exploded. The Russians have opposed the despotism of the czar. The old order is bankrupt. The whole underbelly of society is fomenting for expression, liberty, modernity. And we artists are no longer chained to the ideas of the past.

It's a marvelous time! I cried enthusiastically.

He laughed at my naïveté, showing brown teeth. I was still quite young, it was early in that fateful year, and we had paid scant attention to Continental aggression. He tilted his head, looking at me. And I recognized, at this moment, with my first-prize work hanging in his flat, and wearing bobbed hair and velvet trousers, and being young, younger than he in any case, I knew he did like me.

Do you have a boyfriend? Marcus asked me.

Oh, no—no, no, no, I stuttered. What did I know of the power of a young woman? It was my moment to wave my wand and wield the magnetic force. But I was clueless where this conversation might be going. I must have stared at him, melting under his look, as young ladies do, eyes widening to swallow up their man, and reflect back at him his own ardent gaze. I was sweating under the lights, in the heat of the crammed room, and dying to itch my scalp under the baking turban. I merely stammered, and the moment passed.

A child appeared around the corner, holding back shyly, or Lorelei insinuated herself between us, or Marcus's attention was snagged by the departure of more important guests, and the moment of my triumph slipped away. I was left standing alone, more or less in the same position as I had begun the evening. And yet, No. Marcus had gazed into my eyes. I didn't know a thing about how to woo or make a man love me. But I didn't care, really—love was too hard won. I would never be desirable enough, not in the conventional way. Still, my painting hung in the place of honor, and I had gained something like confidence (Marcus said so), and if love could be won another way, maybe this was it.

They gathered at night, and more of them came. The fire was stoked in the great pit down the slope of the cabins. Feathers were arranged around the hearth, and prayers recited to mollify the ancestral spirits. Couples sat together, huddled under blankets, or men sat alone. Some were smoking, but they did not drink their strong liquor, their *pulque*, made from the maguey cactus; it was too early, and the mood was solemn, expectant. The night was cold and clear, and we watched the grey-wreathed Sacred Mountain a little anxiously. Kate and Ralph sat together, wrapped in a kind of imperturbable silence that set them apart, while Janie appeared just behind them, very small and nervous. Was she looking for Junior, or Abe? I sensed the presence of Junior in the shadows beyond the fire, his stealthy, masterful self, even if I couldn't see him, and the mass of quietly shifting shades around the pit were tribesmen he had brought with him. Horses whinnied in the distance; I caught the scent of their sweat-brown bodies. I watched from the other side of the fire, wondering what would unfold this night. I felt a sense of dread I couldn't account for.

I sat at Abe's side and held out my trumpet like an almsman's cup.

The New Man, he intoned, is neither Republican nor Democrat. The New Man has developed new allegiances, and no longer holds to the static old order. By being thrust out of his home to fight a war that is alien to his nature—to abet the murder and mutilation of his fellow man—the New Man has experienced a complete rupture with his old life. There is no going back, and this he recognizes with sorrow and some confusion. What is ahead of him, if there is nothing behind? How can a human being who paraded severed heads on pikes be the same gentle father nursing a helpless infant in his arms? He feels hollowed out and alone. He no longer has to serve the master he worked for all his life—the feudal ties have been snapped by revolution and war. He is no longer a slave, yet he isn't sure what he is—how to *be*. His family, who waited long for his return, and suffered innumerable hardships in his absence, look upon the wreck of him with shame and pity. He seems to them weak and ineffectual. If he no longer works for someone, what does he work at? How does he work for himself? How to support his family? However, his wife no longer recognizes him. His eyes are hollow and she sees no life there. She is

frightened, because once she relied on him as provider and support, and now she recognizes his inefficacy, his shattered state. She
will have to care for him until he mends, or she will leave him.

Kate clutched at her shawl. Ralph stared at the fire, without
expression. And Abe went on:

Ideally, our man will not gaze behind him, but look to the
future. He will not indulge in self-pity. He will not wallow in
dreaminess, or laziness, or drunkenness—states that yield nothing
fruitful or productive. He may feel disgust, aye, disgust for himself
and what he has formerly been—a lackey, a slave, a hired murderer
for national slaughter—yet disgust against the limitations and the
vulgarity of the old life produces a motivation for the artist's way of
escape—as the *only* way of escape. He is being propelled forward,
and thus the old disgust is liquidated, transformed positively. Our
new man must reinvent himself.

There were some subtle rearrangements of place, obscured
by the dancing flames and smoke. Junior materialized briefly
and tossed a massive log on the fire. When the sparks and smoke
cleared, I saw that Abe had moved next to Ralph and had taken his
hand. Ralph stared blankly at the hand offered him.

This man is suffering, Abe said.

Kate gathered herself silently.

He is possessed by memories of shame and destruction, said
Abe. He is haunted by the specter of the past. He has not made
contact with his New Man. Comrades, called Abe, over the general
murmuring of the assembly, who is unlike this man, really?

We agreed by general assent that we were all like this poor
haunted soul.

Who has not indulged in self-pity? Laziness? Dreaminess?
Drunkenness?

A swelling susurration of assent from the assembly and a nodding of heads. Yes, we had all degenerated into these shameful
states.

But how to show this man where it is possible to go? cried
Abe. How to move forward, and not back?

Learn him a trade! someone called from the crowd.

Yes, agreed Abe, and Ralph is a poet, a man who wields words with his hands as a sculptor manipulates wood or metal.

Tend to his garden, came another suggestion.

Good! said Abe. To begin measures of self-sufficiency for himself and for his family.

Where are his children? called another.

It wasn't shouted in malice. Still, we sat in a pained, embarrassed silence. Kate quietly wept into her hands.

It's not his time yet, friends, said Abe. He hasn't arrived yet, hasn't found his momentum to move forward. Behind him is the destruction of an entire civilization—and what makes him believe that there could possibly be hope for new life before him? To sire children is to look forward, to be optimistic, and what does this man, nay, any of us, myself included, have to look forward to but death?

He asked rhetorically, almost sadly. There reigned a heavy silence among us. We didn't know, could only ponder.

Abe beckoned toward the Sacred Mountain.—Harmony, comrades! Look around us at the harmonious setting we've arrived at. The mountains emerge from the desert victorious, the valley is peaceable, the cosmic balance of all points in nature is maintained. The heavens ensure our safety, balance, equilibrium. The constellations and planets know their gentle rotations, the seasons are unalterably established—nature is eternally poised here. Everything knows its place—there are no tanks ripping up our earth, firestorms from machine birds sweeping down to destroy our homes, invasions of armored aliens bent on slaughtering us. This is a civilization enjoying its day in the sun.

Have you forgotten the native myth of the Five Suns? cried Abe. The myth of the indigenous Old People? In successive past ages, the sun was thrown out of the sky by an upset in nature, and eventually raised again by gods and superhumans. Finally, by the era of the Fifth Sun, what Hesiod called the Fifth Age, civilization reached its most fully evolved, most advanced state. The last civilization before the coming of the white man—the Spaniards—was the Fifth Sun. Then war and disease erupted, and earthquakes occurred. Men learned to manipulate nature to the mass destruction of humanity—learned to do what only gods can accomplish. The balance of nature was upset, and the equilibrium destroyed. So what had to happen? What *has* to happen? One civilization annihilates itself, another has to take its place. Harmony is regained, chronology restored. Is that what has happened? Have we surpassed the era of the Fifth Sun, only to look back at our civilization in ruins behind us? Are we arrived at a precarious moment in our collective humanity?

We listened and waited for Abe to tell us the answer. I felt a rise of panic in my throat. Had we come all this way across the ocean fleeing war only to be turned back by hopelessness and futility in the new world? Was there no place for us, then? I couldn't think of returning—there was little left for me back in England. My chances at making a name as a painter were feeble, my father and brother were dead from exploded hearts (a hereditary condition), my sisters scattered in marriage, and I only had the monthly stipend of my inheritance. I had met Abe, and he offered me something—a mission. He wouldn't abandon me now?

A small voice ventured: Can't we stay here, on this mountain, and be safe?

It was Kate. Abe replied comfortingly, Yes, we can, Kate. We've reached our refuge. We *are* safe.

But not for good?

Nothing's forever.

And Ralph's sickness?

He needs to realign his misplaced *I*'s, said Abe. To bring into harmony his physical, intellectual, and spiritual selves. He needs to raise his human potential.

How do we help him?

We give him our breath, our life, our—

Blood, said Vera.

I hadn't seen her. I had imagined she had gone to bed, impatient with our *hocus-pocus*, as she called our nightly assemblies before the fire pit. She called us a bunch of witches. Yet I knew she would want to hear what was said.

Vera, said Abe, having anticipated her interruption, go on.

The Aztecs used blood sacrifice to appease the gods and reestablish the equilibrium you speak of.

Yes, said Abe.

Blood, said Vera. Blood was needed to maintain their Fifth Sun, their glorious civilization. Blood was needed to forestall the plagues, flood, earthquakes, wars, conquest—all was coming, wasn't it? The gods fed on human blood—hearts.

Hearts, said Abe. Yes, that's what we give to Ralph. Our hearts.

Bah, she replied, standing now so that she was fully illuminated before the fire. She wore a shawl over her white dress and thrust back her shoulders, appearing to my eyes as large and indomitable as a Teutonic princess.

You're speaking metaphorically, said Vera. What do these people know of literary distinctions? They weren't schooled in your corrupted civilization. I mean *blood*, Abe—are you afraid to shed some blood to save this man?

I don't understand you, Vera.

He needs help.

You suggest bleeding him? said Abe, smiling derisively.

Not with leeches, no, certainly, she replied. But let's see what his wife is willing to sacrifice to save him.

Vera, warned Abe. He wanted to silence her. But Kate, the tall young wife, stood up bravely. Her bright blue eyes shone with determination.

I will, she declared to the assembly.

There were quiet murmurings among us seated, and we looked to Abe.

You are interfering, Vera, said Abe.

Let her, said Vera. She wants to help her husband. Don't you want to help your husband? she asked Kate.

Yes, said Kate. She raised her bare arms forward from her sides.

She wants you to bleed her, said Vera.

I can't do that, said Abe.

Bleed her! came a voice from the assembly.

Yes, here, cried Kate, thrusting out her arms.

Why not? cried Vera. Open her up. Let out the life blood in her, let it flow to her husband—feed it to the mountain!

Cut her! came another shout.

I felt a spasm run through the assembly around the pit, and I was one with it. I felt a current of fear and also something like joy surge through us. We had become one body, a mass compressed and communicating soundlessly, by warmth or nerves or vibration, and together we thrilled with the sensation. We moved together, our voices joined.

Yes! we cried. Bleed her!

Kate turned the undersides of her vulnerable wrists upward, pressed together. Abe stared at her, and then at the radiant faces. Ralph gazed up at her with a kind of wonderful love in his eyes. The crowd was singing, Yes! Yes!

Vera called to me loudly, Doll, give me your knife.

I looked at Abe: I could see the terrible battle waging in his face. I wanted to run, back to the safety of my shed. The congregation was moaning, faces uplifted toward the flames. Vera barked orders at me. I fumbled at my thigh, pulled up my pants' leg, and brought out the fishing knife.

The assembly cheered. Someone grabbed the knife out of my grip. The black blade flashed, the knife passed from hand to hand until it reached Abe, and then he was holding it. Lifting my knife, showing it to the Sacred Mountain. The blade gleamed in the moonlight, held by Abe's trembling hand. Held aloft, clean, glancing over the exultant face of the young wife with the outstretched arms. And swiftly it dipped and danced and changed colors, then fell to the ground. The flames rose, and we roared in unison.

When hostilities erupted in Europe, Lorelei and I shared a cold-water flat on Logan Place, London. My father had found the studio for me, since he and Mumsy were fed up with my having to use their house on Tilney Street when they went up to Dunwoodie, as they did more often. They had heard (from the servants) that we had unschooled gatherings, and that the place was left in an appalling state. But our new flat had a bathroom, and promised thereby to be a popular haven for my bohemian friends. There were two small rooms my roommate and I each laid claim to, and they were bright and pretty rooms, separated by French windows, the walls painted a vanilla white (obscured soon enough by our artwork and those of our friends), and a fireplace that often blacked up, but looked elegant all the same. The hearth stood in the farther room, toward the windows overlooking the street; this was naturally the brighter room, and Lorelei possessed it, though I paid the lion's share of the rent. We understood tacitly that Lorrie needed the light and air in order to convalesce from the lung sickness that was beginning to debilitate her. Moreover, Lorelei attracted people, especially men, and sometimes they stayed over, and we agreed without having to discuss the matter that she needed the privacy. She fashioned curtains for the French doors—she was handy, and could even sew, though she didn't like to admit it—and always had flowers picked up from somewhere in a vase on the mantle. On a silver tray in her room she kept many delicate and costly bottles of perfume, also procured from mysterious sources, I wasn't sure where because Lorelei never had any money, and when she did she spent it instantly and frivolously. By common consent we entertained in her room—the flowers, the smell of perfume, and the light from the windows kept the place cheery and bolstered our spirits. It was a bleak winter and the world was at war.

Lorelei worked at cutting hair. She was going to make it as an artist, it was just a question of time. Her friends displayed her work in their flats and galleries, and she knew everyone, many significant names she dropped effortlessly, though with the bloody war on and people half out of their minds, she needed regular employment. Her mum was sick, dying of liver disease, and Lorelei had to send money back to Birmingham as well as help her friends keep going during the crisis. These were her homosexual friends who were always at our flat and sometimes stayed over so that at night it felt cozy, like a rooming house. In the morning I'd run into Todd or Gary coming out of the bathroom in Lorrie's pajamas and robe. Todd was very small and sleek, with dark glossy hair combed back like a bat. Doll, you precious, he'd murmur, and brush my cheek with his scented fingers, or ask to borrow something of mine he liked such as my velvet breeches. Gary was a big, affectionate stevedore from Gibraltar. He would bring cargo that had fallen off the hauler—boxes of Norwegian candles, Alabama salted pork, cashews from South America. I couldn't understand his accent, but nonetheless we got along fine. They approved of my trousers, and I rarely wore anything else, even then, and an embroidered bolero vest my sister Sultana had sent from her honeymoon in Casablanca. Divine, they declared. Lorelei smoked and grew increasingly sad.

We held Tuesday evenings. Lorelei reclined, struck an attitude, and looked genuinely spent, one arm listlessly unwrapping her turban. She ran her fingers through her dark helmet of hair. She smoked, while Gary with his noble profile stroked her feet and Todd passed her up a glass of champagne. I sat quietly and sketched them like attendants to Bathsheba at her bath, after a Rembrandt I remembered. Their conversation covered the currents of fashion or psychology, and went typically like this:

Lorrie: I've never had an orgasm.

Todd: I can't believe my ears.

Gary: Are you sure?

Todd: How do you know? How do you know you've never had an orgasm if you don't know what one is?

Lorrie: I would have known, don't you think. With all the fuss you men make about it!

Natasha (a red-headed girl from the Slade, the wayward wife of one of our friends who had left England as a conscientious objector): It's different with women.

Todd and Gary (together): Yes, it is.

Natasha: With women it's *internal*.

Todd: Spiritual.

Natasha (her sharp little eyes finding me mischievously, wanting deliberately to embarrass me): How is it with you, Doll?

Me (sketching, aiming to remain inconspicuous): How? It's. . . it's. . . a singular pleasure. . .

General laughter. All: Oh Doll! *Singular!*

Lorrie (to general sighs): Doll's smart. She takes her pleasure singularly, and she's never left with a heartache.

I was a kind of mascot at these occasions.

Our guests filtered out into a cold night. Lorelei and I pondered silently. Often we turned off all the lights and listened to the wounded city from Lorelei's bed—the dark days of London, the Blackout—the sounds of panic, when officers on the street paraded with placards announcing "Take Cover" and we were bombed from the air by the German zeppelins. Other times, there reigned a graveyard silence as if all the denizens were holding their breath. We read about the initial disasters of the British Expeditionary Force and felt hopelessly sad. We braced ourselves for the encroachment of the Germans on Paris. We heard about the atrocities of the Huns. We learned from soldiers returning about the horrors of trench warfare. We dreaded a forced conscription for the armed services, as would happen in two years and rake up the remaining glory of our generation. We followed the machinations of the Liberal Party and the imperial ascent of Lloyd George; we feared the country was growing increasingly conservative. Bolshevism, Irish Republicanism, the establishment of the Ministry of Munitions to generate the mighty war machine—all terrifying developments. My father, when not occupied with stirring up propaganda for king and country, wrote me letters, urging me to quit London and move up to Dunwoodie. I was surprised, suspecting that he was tired of supporting me and receiving irate letters from Windsor tradesmen demanding payment for petty collegiate purchases totaling £13 with 5% interest. I read these querulous letters to Lorelei, who hooted with laughter.

You *aristocrats*! she spat. You hightail it off to Scotland and hide for the duration of the country's war and let the rest of us tough it out! That's rich, Doll, and why hasn't the Viscount ever taught you something useful, like how to type?

Yes, I agreed sadly, though I was stung. Lorelei was right, I wouldn't argue with her.—My mother thinks I am neither dutiful enough as a daughter nor adept enough at attracting a mate.

Why don't you just tell them to go to hell? Lorelei shouted, then stopped at the look on my face. Oh poor Doll, she said, more kindly. It's not easy being severed from your class, is it. You are a painter. You'll always be an outsider.

She didn't entirely approve of my background, used it often as a butt of a joke, though I knew it came in handy when she needed an entrée to a function or party.—Who do you know at the Henslowes'? she might ask. Who can you introduce me to among the. . . ? Lorelei was deeply conflicted this way. I think at heart she believed me essentially without purpose in the new world order, and she felt a little sorry for me. She and her slave boys, as we called them, referred to me as the Virgin Aunt, for she didn't take anyone seriously who didn't have a certain animal magnetism. Lorrie stood in continual amazement that I couldn't cook, clean clothes, change sheets, blacken my boots, darn holes, and hike two miles across London in the rain after a party when we couldn't catch a taxi cab. She could whip up a palatable soup on our two-burner galley stove from wilted leeks and bully beef. She could take an old castaway coat and add smart, oriental touches. She rearranged furniture, added flowers. I suspected I was in Lorelei's way. But she was wrong about my uselessness in the war: I would have joined the effort, had I been able to hear. I was afraid, simply—afraid of being run down, afraid of being rendered dumb mute by the din.

Instead, I retreated into my artwork.

We had many visitors over the first winter of the war as people decided what to do. I sketched them in a red notebook I carried everywhere, tied with a string. I didn't aim to flatter, but to keep myself occupied ("idle hands are the devil's workshop"), and from dying of boredom when talk I couldn't follow billowed interminably with the smoke. The truth was my hearing had grown worse—though Lorelei claimed that I had tuned out the world. My trumpet was clunky and ineffectual in a crowd. I had visited a doctor in London and had been taking some injections in my rear end that did no good. My sister Sultana claimed that the tropical weather of Borneo would cure my affliction. But on account of the war I never made it there, so I resigned myself, and like the resident dumbbell I sketched in a corner in front of the marble fireplace, under a vase of fragrant flowers Lorelei had salvaged from a neighbor's rubbish bin. I sat wherever I could catch some light, and I captured my latest subject (victim, if you will) while he was swigging from a bottle of rationed spirits, or when Lorelei was raking her fingers through her hair or leaning in to have her cigarette tip ignited by Gary or Todd. I learned that people *said* more with their faces and body movements than they did with their speech. One refugee to our flat was Lorelei's mother, Mrs. Dearley, who smoked incessantly like her daughter, except that she had a horrible death-rattle cough and immediately upon hearing it we all hushed and leaned in to see if she would come out of it. She did, and talk resumed. She was a nut-skinned creature with bony, hunched shoulders who carried about her person a strange, sharp odor, probably from the decay of her health. Her hands were frankly swollen and work-worn, her face scored by years of drudgery— long, drawn cheeks and a thin line for a mouth. What I saw in her face was literally a life of having worked herself to near death after her husband died from a mill accident fifteen years before (actually, *drowned himself in gin*, said Lorelei), and this misery I'm afraid showed in the sketch that I made of Mrs. D. But Lorelei liked it because of that—my friend never cringed from the facts of real life and she hung the portrait in her room, though she did not have a chance to give it to her poor Mum.

And beside the friends from the Slade, artists and pacifists who had places in the country to repair to while the war raged on the Continent, and whose portraits I executed routinely in exchange for fresh farm vegetables or wine or cheeses we could no longer get in the London shops, my father came to see me. He was chairman of the Imperial Defense Committee, in charge of sanitary measures for the army hospitals, and soon to be moving to Paris with Mumsy. He came to say goodbye—rather, had heard reports from the servants at Tilney Street that we were entertaining *men*, or so I imagined the true cause for his visit. He wore his top hat and carried an umbrella, and with a squeeze to my heart I noticed his whiskers held fringes of grey. How had I not noticed that he had changed so? I reckoned by his own crestfallen look that he was probably wondering the same about me.

So this is how you do, he murmured, taking in the flat, and the bit of mess we lived in. He went to the lavabo to wash his hands and discovered the place didn't have hot water. He was very tall and still handsome, bending with interest to gaze on the artwork over the walls; he abruptly straightened when he reached a row of Lorrie's nudes. My friends were mightily impressed by his physical presence. Todd, wearing one of Lorelei's robes, offered him tea, which he icily refused. He regarded Todd severely, unable perhaps to distinguish his sex, then turned to Lorelei, who was lovely in her Turkish turban and slippers, holding aloft a cigarette.

Enchantée, said Lorelei, offering her free hand. Sorry it's so drafty in here, Viscount—we haven't paid the coal bill, yet, have we, Doll?

Her eyes sparkled wickedly.

They spoke of the ongoing conflict in France, and my father, deigning to sit on her brothel-red sofa, though still wearing his coat, told stories. He was very charming, of course; I had forgotten how charming he could be. I was proud of his charm, and also confused by it. Turning to Gary, who wore a uniform of uncertain provenance, he asked, And what is your regiment, sir? To which Gary could only emit strange noises in his exotic accent, so that we giggled.

You would do well to enlist in the RAMC, my father informed him. It is fairly safe and the exercise will do you good.

Enlist! cried Gary, suddenly stricken with speech. And have my spirit broken forever? He declared grandly, I am a pacifist and will not murder for anyone.

I was hoping, Lorelei interjected cunningly, that I could become a Tommy.

You would make an admirable Tommy, replied my father.

And Doll, she went on undeterred (for she did like to goad people), wants to be employed as a chauffeur.

You select odd trades for yourselves! cried my father, unable to contain himself. A chauffeur! And how will Doll hear the motor horns behind? She will have to have trumpets sticking out behind the motors.

I cringed at his words, and took out my red notebook tied with string. I sketched him briefly. He suggested I take the train to Flanders and work in a medical field hospital, as other women volunteers were doing. He offered a clerical job in the War Ministry. I thought of Lorelei's words about my inability to type, my inability to do *anything*, and bitterness filled my heart. I sketched his profile sharply—it was an admirable profile, any way you looked at it—and then I told my father that I would stay and *see it through*.

You don't understand or you deliberately ignore the fact that I am an artist and like artists from all ages choose the least comfortable road, I recited, having memorized this speech in the hours before I could fall asleep.

You are not the first artist I have known, my father informed me mildly.

I can't just sit down at my easel and paint what I see, I said, gaining momentum. I have the history of art behind me.

My friends agreed that this was a very good assertion.

And because I haven't been to the Louvre I am considered a freak.

Let's take her, said Todd to Gary, nudging each other.

It's wartime! retorted my father.

Your critical, unsympathetic regard toward me is highly harmful to my painting, I continued.

My father regarded me with astonishment. I see I had better get back, he declared, rising stiffly.

Oh don't do that, protested Lorelei. Your daughter needs your help and sympathy—she could have said financial support: I knew what Lorelei was thinking.

I'm afraid our Doll has looked further afield for sympathy and appreciation and does not regard her family's wishes any longer, replied my father.

My friends understand me, I insisted wretchedly, and Todd put his arm around my shoulders. Just those friends who are interested in me as a painter and are interested in my painting in regard to real painting are the people who keep me alive, I uttered, in stupendous confusion, feeling terribly isolated and alone.

These are barbaric times, declared my father, taking his leave of us. There are more pressing concerns in the world than self-absorption and self-glorification!

And he was gone—leaving, nonetheless, money on the mantle in an envelope marked *Coal Bill*.

Vera lay on her bed and pondered. She smoked and read her German novels carted across the ocean in her satchel. I felt her watching me from her window in the morning when I dragged out my mattress and beat it in the sunlight. I didn't like the smell of it; I suspected something was gnawing at it when I slept. I gathered the ashes from my hearth and swept out the hard-packed dirt floor. I dragged the ashes in a bucket to the alfalfa field, just beyond the homesteader's cabin and past the towering pine tree; I passed Abe, seated under the tree with his knees drawn up, his notebook flat in his lap. He was bent nearly double, scribbling fluently, utterly absorbed in writing his sermons, and he didn't look up. His hair and beard shone coppery red in the sun and I stopped and stared. I felt a surge of relief as I watched him in his silent, absorbed way, and I was content to inhale the odor of pine and hear the now-familiar sloughing through the trees. I let the sharp, morning light clarify my thoughts. Abe's intent posture and fastidious habits assured me that everything was as it should be. It was right that we had come to this new land. I scattered my hearth ashes over the alfalfa field, ignoring Vera's daggerlike gaze at my back. I returned to my shed with a lighter heart. Later she spoke to me as I hammered at the loose step on the back porch. She had asked me to fix it, since the wobbly step irritated her every time she stepped outside. She stood at the counter, whacking at vegetables with Janie's cleaver.

Do you know, she said, shouting through the open back door, that we almost separated, back in England?

I held up the hammer. I wondered whether Abe was back yet from trying to catch Sylvie for milking.

No, I didn't know, I muttered.

Back in England, during the war, she insisted. We had met you. You don't remember?

No, I said, automatically. In fact, I did recall an incident in my flat when Vera challenged Abe and he smashed the tea things with a poker before raising the rod to her. Violent, crazy marriage! Why hadn't they separated, instead of putting their friends through such frightful scenes? I wanted to ask—but what was the point of bringing this up now?

I think you would remember, she continued. He threatened to kill me.

Then why did you stay with him? I snapped.

She had the cleaver in her hand. She hacked at the root vegetables, her high, flat cheekbones suffused with color, her big body quivering with each stroke. She turned on me savagely.

Why do you think? she cried. I had left everything for him! I had left my children, my home, my husband! I had nothing but Abe—no job or money of my own. I worked for *him*, I edited *his* papers. I had no life outside of him!

Vera, I replied evenly, taking a step away from her cautiously. You are a strong woman. You could have left him.

She turned back, beating the dirt turnips, hard as pebbles. She flailed at the cabbage leaves, and I felt her anger subsiding. I knew she wasn't angry *at* me—her anger was much larger than anything I could have inspired.

You're right. I could have left him. The truth, she snarled, was that I loved him. I didn't want to leave him. He was coming back to me from Mexico, wasn't he, he was coming back to me, and so I received him.

I hammered at the sagging step, making the depression worse. Vera dumped the chopped vegetables into a pot of water heating on the wood stove. She bent and blew hard into the flame and it flashed up. She clattered and banged at the stove, and I stood up, shaking out the splinters from my hand.

And now? I wanted to know.

Ha, now! she cried. Now you can have him.

I mumbled, No. . .

Doll, why not? What are you afraid of? A man and a woman are attracted to each other and should make love. You have my permission.

We're friends, I murmured in confusion.

Friends! she cried. Men and women can't be friends without passion.

I don't agree.

I think you want him, she said, bending toward my ear.

It's not up to me, I said feebly.

Ach, so you do. She picked up the cleaver and wiped both sides of its blade flat against her apron. Then she looked hard at me, her eyes narrowed. She held the cleaver as if weighing the blade and the memory of the knife in Abe's trembling hand suddenly came back to me in all its horror.

You know what he wants? You know? *Ja?*

I shook my head. I was ready to bolt down the steps.

He wants to be a god—a *god*. He thinks it can happen here on this new soil. That anything can happen here. And Doll, she mouthed, grabbing my arm. Doll, he'll do it if we let him.

Now I'm old, older than the biblical Abraham, or rather Sarah, his wife, who wasn't supposed to bear any children at her advanced age, let alone enjoy orgasm. She laughed at the thought. I'm *supposed* to be old, in years. Hollywood movies declare this by featuring smooth-skinned, baby-faced actors, and newspapers quote citizens of "retirement age," and pep books declare how young you can *still* feel after forty—forty, already an age ago! But Akbar doesn't know anything about the weight of years and doesn't see me as old. He doesn't read newspapers either, or watch television, except superhero cartoons from time to time, and so when he comes to me, dismounts from his trees and appears in front of me at my easel with his erection showing through his pants, I take him up instantly. I'm not about to look a gift horse in the mouth, as the Americans say. I suspect, by his intensity, by his crazed, blue-grey, slightly crossed-eyed gaze through his rectangular granny glasses, that he is a bit off in the head, and a parolee from prison to boot. I might have taken fright twenty years before, thirty even, but he appears like a mirage to this thirsty old woman. At this point in my life I haven't got anything to lose. I won't be getting pregnant! And I'll take my chances at getting a communicable disease. He drags his knit crown off his head, loosens his massive hair. I kiss him full on the lips and knock his glasses off. No, I *French-kiss* him and knock his glasses off—he has never French-kissed before. He asks, soberly, How do you do that? I show him: Open your mouth and give me your tongue. This he loves. Where has this boy been his whole life? In trees. I wear a loose blouse and trousers—I've abandoned finery like knickers because the sun in the afternoon is always strong in New Mexico and I don't have the patience for fussy layers that need washing. My breasts are heavy, pendulous, always in the way—Akbar presses and kneads and finally unbuttons my raggedy blouse with its mismatched buttons and then unpadlocks my sad, armored brassiere that I detest but by common decency should remember to wear, and there they are, my big moonlike bosoms announcing themselves between us. Akbar goes to work and I am surprised that I like it—enjoy his mouth at my nipples, tugging and slurping. What a big kid, I think, what a cute boy, then he bites me. Ouch, ouch, I whoop, and tell him to be gentle, Lord, I'm made of clay! Then he is thrusting against my leg like a puppy and we move to the sofa that serves as my bed. I don't like the bedroom, never liked bedrooms because I don't like to be enclosed in the dark. I prefer the front room where the windows are and where I can watch the sky and who's coming and going on the highway. We fall over the sofa in our clothes. Akbar is modest and doesn't undress readily. And suddenly I see him—so absolutely fine and smooth and ready to take me, I am out of breath, completely turned on by the sandalwood smell of this man, by his perceptive fingers and sensitive mouth. His locks fan around his shoulders like the mane of a lion—exactly so. I don't even wonder if I'm wet—women are supposed to be wet, or aren't supposed to be wet, at my age—but I know I'm ready because my nerve endings are alive, from the tips of my fingers and tongue to my clitoris, with the feel of this man hard against my thighs. Then he's inside me and it feels so wicked and rockety that I lose myself—lose my usual paralyzing self-consciousness, my fear that I'm not doing something right. Akbar is not judging me, he is really *enjoying* me, I feel it, and this thought releases me to my own pleasure. I can concentrate on my own pleasure—the depth and fullness of this glorious, hard, eager body inside of me—so that before I know what's happening, I *come*, I achieve orgasm with a man for the first time in my life. I know so because I shout! Akbar smiles, pleased at himself, then looks shy, and gazes deep in my eyes as he pumps away, now that he can.

With the air bombings ended, we no longer had to fear hiding in the Tube or under the Arches on the Embankment. On my small allowance of £400 a year, we stayed in our flat, Lorelei and I, though by the end of the war and its forced privations she grew rickety and was diagnosed with tuberculosis that would eventually warrant her removal to a sanatorium. First, however, there was Marcus's party. On an early spring night that held a lingering winter rawness, we emerged from our house, testing the air, which smelled sourly chemical and colored the sky a rather unnatural mustard tint, and gingerly we crawled to Café Royal. Marcus had secured a private room for the birthday party of his wife, although she was not actually present. That is, some of the guests later swore Mrs. Willoughby had been present, but I don't recall seeing her, and anyway we drank a lot of wine and it didn't matter after a while whether she was there or not. We had heard she rarely went out of the flat since 1914, and it was not unusual to lose sight of people for a long period of time. People disappeared and connections were severed. Yet this night at the café we didn't dare miss. The prewar splendor of the place had sadly slipped past: the room was luxuriously threadworn, with plush velvet curtains we eyed covetously for the fabric of our trousers, and housed a warm, roaring fire. We toasted our backsides while sipping sherry. Some of our Slade cronies were present, like Natasha, and also Didier and George the handsome American editor, whom I would get to know better later on, and there was a frisson in the air because a special guest was expected. I couldn't ask directly, carting around my clunky ear device. I had a kind of stage fright about meeting intellectual people, because they talked so and I was immobilized in a noisy group. Eventually, the so-called special guest arrived, the slim, nervous philosopher I had remembered from Marcus's flat. He was the "prophet" with the red beard and direct, unwavering gaze. He stood awkwardly, holding his overcoat neatly on the crook of his arm, and next to him, stalwart and handsome, his large, purloined, and bizarrely attired German wife.

His quick, nervous gaze darted around the room—blue eyes, not black, as I had originally thought—then alighted, stunningly, on me. He held out his hand and came forward quickly.

You're the painter, he declared, and took my hand and shook it chillingly. I stammered and stared at his thin mouth.

We would be seated next to each other at the table. Vera, the wife, was placed to the right of Marcus, who held forth on the German painters. Vera seemed delighted, flattered, the firelight playing youthfully upon her fair face and flat, high cheekbones. With her blond hair, pulled loosely back, and light-colored frock, her solid frame and gutsy laugh, she lent a Nordic heartiness to our depleted English group, who looked altogether dour and beaten down by the war. Absorbed in her flirtations with Marcus, she never bothered to look our way, although Abe glanced at them from time to time and seemed to scowl inwardly.

I put down the trumpet squarely between us. Abe looked at it and laughed.

How do you make love to a woman with *that*? he asked, and I laughed with him, though shyly. From across the table Lorelei winked at me, coughing delicately into her napkin. Later she would explain the psychology of this curious couple to me, who needed to flirt with other people as a way of wooing each other, she said. Though I knew instinctively that this fascinating man, this brilliant leader and spiritual presence, couldn't be interested in me *that way*. Romantically. And yet he was terribly romantic, as I was to learn, about art, about love, about the destiny of the artist. He remembered my painting, he declared, and liked it very much.

What is it you are aiming at in your painting? he asked, in his abrupt, attentive way.

In my panic I tried to remember how Lorrie coached me to reply to this question. But it was hopeless, I would not impress this man. I backtracked and began to speak about what I knew: Light. I tried to explain how I used a kind of double lighting in my work. That is, I needed to acknowledge the public light of my subject, which is what we are all given to live in the everyday, the light by which one's parents and friends might see one, for example; and then there is the inner light, which is the secret of the subject, what one tries to hide, and feels protective of. . . Did this make sense? I asked him.

Yes, yes, he agreed eagerly, I think you are getting at the life of the work. Sexuality, I believe you mean.

Oh no, no, not that. . .

And there is so much which is dead now, he went on. These still lifes! Dead. The war has killed our painters.

Oh but, I demurred quietly, I don't believe painting is dead, not at all.

You don't believe that this illegal conflagration of nations has exploded art completely? That nothing new can be brought to it?

He was outraged and scornful, but I held my own somehow and he listened.

No, I insisted, I believe a great deal more can be done, especially now.

And what is that? he demanded.

Well, I began. Light is a form of truth, isn't it?

The war has eclipsed the light.

But we shall win the war!

There is no victory in bloodshed.

We can live free. The Germans haven't subjugated us.

As long as there exists poverty and economic slavery, there is no freedom. What can your pretty pictures do to change that?

I can change hearts, I murmured, and he nodded pensively.

We drank the wine that was poured continuously into our glasses. We ate food that was too rich for our empty bellies. We became very gay and loud in the fire-lit room at the close of the war. Abe espoused on the wildness he had witnessed during his travels to Mexico. He told us about the Indians, and got up impulsively to demonstrate the Indian dance step. He made a slow, serious tread in a circle—humming the Sun Dance song, he called it. We laughed and shouted and tried to imitate him, until he bent over suddenly, in a paroxysm of pain, and vomited on the rug.

He's been ill, said Vera. She rushed to him and held his head.

He fell to one knee. We drew around him. I took his hand and held it tightly. Vera moved officiously around the room while we stood rooted in horror; she gathered their coats. Marcus and Gary carried the sick man downstairs and into a taxi. Abe was driven away, dazed, speechless, and very pale.

We were sure he was dying.

Marcus began to pay attention to me after the birthday party. He took me to Hyde Park one early summer afternoon just after the signing of the Peace of Versailles and we sat on a bench and watched the equestrian practice. People passed in various guises: the maimed soldiers, the homeless dragging all they owned, the couples triumphantly reunited. Marcus held my hand, his face downcast and the furrows between his brows deeply foreboding. The war had sickened him spiritually and he no longer even took pleasure from his teaching. I knew that he drank a good deal; he smelled always strongly of tobacco and beer, even in the morning. He was lonely without his wife, who had been sent away to get well, though I don't think she ever did. He often took my hand when we were out, to galleries or to interview a potential portrait commission that he had secured for me, for Marcus helped me a great deal in my early career. He would press my hand between both of his when we parted in front of his Piccadilly flat. I wondered with a little thrill whether he was in love with me, though I suspected his sadness resulted from the despondency he witnessed in his wife and the necessity of caring for their children. What experience with men did I have with which to gauge his kindness? I imagined he believed me a promising young painter, but I suspected Abe Bronstone's attention had rendered me finally visible.

Marcus would tell me the facts of life. He lectured me on tone, and the attitude of the artist toward her material and how you can tell from the evidence—then abruptly he asked if I knew how men and women make love. I answered honestly that I did not. He explained it all to me. He was a married man and concerned about a proper initiation for me. He was afraid, he admitted, that I would end up in the *wrong hands*, he said. I told him that I had already ended up in the wrong hands. He was puzzled and confused: he believed I meant *him—his* hands. I told him about Sir Jeremy. I had never told anyone about Sir Jeremy before, not even Lorelei; I was sure that I could have done something to prevent his beastly mauling but I failed to do it. I was weak and dutiful. Lorelei, I felt sure, would blame me. I admitted Sir Jeremy's unconscionable behavior toward me when I was adolescent. Marcus cried out and tore at his hair.

Animal! he shouted, going red in the face. I should kill him!

He died, I told him. Sad and fat.

And you never told your father?

Oh no! How awful!

Doll, it wasn't your fault. There is evil in the world. Evil men, evil minds. Look at this war! How will you ever experience the beauty of lovemaking?

Teach me, I said.

Yes, he replied, a little distractedly, I think so, too.

We kicked along the neglected paths and crossed Bayswater, careful of the reckless automobile traffic. We pushed our way into a crowded pub he knew (and Marcus knew many pubs) and ordered ale. We couldn't hear each other over the revelers, so we gave up and didn't speak; Marcus drank steadily and I grew drowsy amid the smoke and noise. Several ales later I was nodding off, and Marcus said we should leave, as it was now dark. He was going to find a cab for me. Again we retraced our steps back through the park, but it was quite dark now. I suggested we stick to the main thoroughfares because of brigands I had heard about and other riff-raff, but Marcus scowled at the danger. He took my hand and led me deeper into the park, his lined face a study in concentration. I no longer knew where we were since there weren't streetlights then to guide us, only the solemn reflection of the Serpentine and the darker perimeter of trees against the bruised sky. From time to time I glimpsed figures moving between the trees, which startled me. Upon closer inspection I saw they were couples writhing together in the new grass. I held Marcus's hand tighter. Finally he found a spot near the trees and stopped. This will do, he said.

I must have stared at him, completely at a loss.

Well, Doll, do you want to learn or not?

He meant lovemaking, of course. I nodded eagerly. I put down the notebook I was carrying. After a moment sizing me up, he stepped in front of me and kissed me on the lips, pressing me back against the trunk of the tree. As we kissed he scrubbed himself roughly against me. He considered for a moment how to touch me, then seized my most obvious attribute, my breasts. He felt for the waist of my trousers and fumbled for an opening, and when he couldn't find one he seemed to grow discouraged. I helped him. I wondered whether we should lie down in the grass. But he was doing all right, pulling at our clothing until our flesh met with a little thrill and grinding himself against me to get himself revved up. He attempted penetration. It didn't hurt me, his penetration. At the time I didn't know that men's penises could vary widely, and had a mind of their own. I concentrated on the angry knot of his forehead. When he lost steam, I grabbed him under the flaps of clothing, too strongly because he cried out in pain. I was paralyzed by self-consciousness—my breasts spilled out of my blouse and the presence of them embarrassed me and seemed to embarrass Marcus, too. He kissed me quickly and rummaged a bit and I think the deed was achieved, although I'm not sure I felt anything.

We hastily buttoned up. I found my notebook in the dark and we fled the park. We were relieved to get away from the spot near the trees. We hardly spoke. Marcus found a cab for me and sadly waved me off. I think he wanted the experience to be tremendous for me, though I did not feel tremendous. How did other women feel after their first time? It was my only knee-trembler. At least I wasn't a virgin anymore—and already well into my thirties!

I have read that the land of the American West holds a lotus charm: the magnitude of natural elements such as light, heat, and space dazzles the human spirit and quickly derails the perfectly sane individual. Add to this organic spell the lack of water and human contact. The early miners and trappers learned this. The land is scarcely habitable, and if the light doesn't disorient you, the unrelenting exposure to the weather breaks your spirit. We were like the Pilgrims at first, newly arrived in this strange land, overwhelmed by the unbreakable surfaces and the cruel, cruel beauty. The grotesque geometry, the vastness of vista. The eye sought variety in forms, and grew blinded by the unrelievedness of it all. The thin air tended to constrict our breathing and make us tired after only a little exertion, and the thirst, after working a few hours on carpentry chores or digging like badgers, was monstrous, all-consuming. Our own fragility frightened us, rendered us impotent and our efforts futile. We often had to do a task over again, such as building parts of the shed for the animals—our orientation was faulty, lines ended up crooked. We accused each other of altering the work, corrupting it. We removed our hats, walked around and around the structure, swore out loud. We watched each other, looking for signs of disorientation and madness.

Though at first we *were* charmed. The morning light just breaking the Sacred Mountain filled me with exuberance, and I left my shed swinging a scythe with a light, singing heart. Soon the circle of valley just below us was carpeted on one side with the fresh golden blossoms of the flowering sage, while the other side, as if tidily cut down the center, displayed the mint green of the summer fields. Above us grumped our modest hill, Lobo Mountain, though the apex was obscured perennially by the dark masses of juniper and piñon. They hissed and spat their fragrant sap. Beyond the towering pine where Abe worked in the mornings, and the alfalfa field just beneath it, filling out in rich, shaggy grasses, rose the primeval Mountain herself, smoldering in the morning air as if after a night of violent, disquieting eruptions, and prepared to stew a bit over the early hours, and grow cool and paler until noon. Then the rich azure of the afternoon sky lent the mountain a darker and more solid cast, so that the landscape was drawn to it from hundreds of miles away, sinking into it, kneeling before it (Abe had pointed out the *toes* of the mountains), until the next savage ejaculation at nightfall, when the monolith sundered all light and the whole landscape broke up again into vaporous shapes. Day after day I watched the drama of our mountain and painted it a hundred changing ways. I was never satisfied.

Why can't you see? Abe said to me. I challenged him stubbornly. What did he mean—what could I not see that he could?

You want to contain this space, but you can't contain it, Doll. It's bigger than you are, grander. You cannot possess it.

I don't doubt that, I told him, your grander, bigger notion, but I'm a painter, aren't I? I have to contain it within the frame of my canvas.

It's not complete, he glowered, as I followed him out to the fields day after day, to hoe, to dig, to paint. He sat down on some pine roots and scratched his scalp under his hat. He was thinking, his eyes squinting, taking in the terrible midday sun that leeched all shadow from the horizon. The mountains were layered one behind the other like humpback whales galloping over a vast sandy ocean, chased by the long, perpetual stretch of dun-colored earth. We could never carry enough water with us, unless by horseback, but Abe was tired of running after the horses. So we hiked, came alone, and walked far through the pine forest, blazing our own paths. We often sat under the cool, fragrant trees, putting aside our notebooks, simply pondering for what must have been hours. Time wasn't told precisely in this land.

Eventually, I gave up—that is, I gave up on the notion that I could contain this uncontainable landscape and I stopped trying. I couldn't do it, I admitted to Abe. It was too vast, too big for me, and the task left me feeling powerless. Instead, I began to inhabit my landscapes with people, small and insignificant at first, such as the stick figures of ourselves Abe and I had inserted together (also Vera and the chickens, at the last moment), then larger, more central characters. My humans were Indians, the Old Ones who had made this land speak. It happened this way.

I had accompanied Domingo on an errand into the reservation. It was a feast day of one of the saints. I lay in the back of the cab and stared at the dome of sky—a great cloudless blue that in the tower of my deafness seemed to be *humming* with the day's impending heat. When the aural and visual combined seamlessly at such moments, as when I reclined gazing at the sky in the back of Domingo's cab, I imagined with perfect precision how death would feel. I knew exactly how I would execute my next painting. But this humming grew louder and more distinct as we climbed the road to the reservation, nearing the great mountain's base, and I sat up and sniffed the air. I smelled burning piñon—the smell from the hornos heating up the day's bread. And still the strange, heaving vibration, breaking up as we neared the reservation into a staccato, rhythmic pounding of drums, and as I looked, the ground around the tiny pueblo seemed to rise and fall in rhythmic waves of color. I was watching the bobbing headdresses of a thousand men, naked to the waist, their flesh painted garish, festive colors, and badger fur and cockle shells were tied around their ankles and wrists. Some carried water jugs upside down. They wore soft beaded moccasins or they were barefoot; many wore shaggy skins around their heads and shoulders like buffaloes. The clowns had their heads shaven, while the warriors' hair was carefully plaited and ponytailed. Together they made their slow, circular tread to the incessant beat of the drums. They circled the Plaza in front of their adobe houses, a mass of hot, rhythmic bodies, and on the flat roofs of the houses around the central pit there were the women and old people, squatting and watching silently. The sun beat down without mercy.

For a while I forgot I was the foreigner in the midst of the Indians and needed to hide myself. The sight of this epic dance was wondrous, and the vibration of hundreds of beating drums and pounding feet elevated me, pulled me out of myself. Just then there was a pause in the drumming and the earth breathed, the men shifted position, and I came around and climbed quickly out of the cab and watched the procession from the shade of a nearby veranda. I wore my round-rimmed black sombrero and imagined myself inconspicuous—Domingo was there with me. He told me that the Indians were enacting the drama of the Yellow Woman—there, he pointed out a male figure at the center impersonating the kachina maiden who wore corn husks about her skirts and carried a water jar. In a myth borrowed from the neighboring Acoma, Domingo told me, the beautiful maiden is wooed by the daring hunter Arrow Youth, and they marry. One day at the spring where she goes to fetch water, Yellow Woman meets the imposing figure of the Buffalo Man—Domingo points out the dancing figure with the great shaggy buffalo head—and they fall into conversation. He suggests that she come away with him, back to his people north—for that is the direction that the buffalo move—and she agrees, abandoning her water jar and hopping on his back for the journey. Later, Arrow Youth finds her abandoned jar, turned upside down, and sets out to look for his wife. He finds her, rescues her, flees with the buffalo, and slaughters Buffalo Man. The meat he boils and feeds to Yellow Woman, who refuses to eat it. You still love Buffalo Man, Arrow Youth accuses her. Then die so you can be with him. And he kills her.

How horrible, Domingo! I cried, watching this drama of the buffalo and upside-down water jugs with new eyes. Why are they celebrating this murder?

Eh, no, he replied. Yellow Woman bring the buffalo here so we eat. And she no dead—Yellow Woman live at night, she go with the moons. The moons bring the harvest. Her water jug bring the rain.

And so I understood the dance was more a hunting ritual than a romance—a tragic romance, as they all seemed to be. I felt strangely moved by it. Their sacred dance on the saint's feast day was not meant for the eyes of gringos—a gringa, no less. But I loved these peaceable people; I felt safe among them. The rhythmic treading was again taken up. The bodies of the men glistened under the heat of the midday sun and the paint colors ran in streaks along warmed flesh. The women were preparing the food and bringing it to the mouth of the *kiva*. I could smell the sharp, nutty bread removed from the hornos. On the roofs of the adobes other figures squatted motionlessly, old women and children, and then I saw Kate and Ralph across the square, standing under the shade of a porch. Kate saw me, too, and her face brightened. Instantly she began to move toward me, pulling at the hand of Ralph, who looked over, startled. She moved quickly in my direction, maneuvering around the crowds in the dusty square, picking up the front of her skirt with an unfamiliar clumsiness as if climbing steep stairs. I detected then the soft swell of her silhouette.

I took her hand and pulled her under the shade.

Should you be here? I asked in a whisper.

Doll, you're a worrywart. I wouldn't miss the feast day for the world! But Abe didn't come? He could be Yellow Woman's father— she pointed toward the dancers—the old chief holding the prayer sticks, scolding and admonishing. She laughed.

No, we rarely leave our mountain. I turned to Ralph, who hovered shyly and pecked at the dust with the toe of his boot.

Hello, Ralph, I said gently. It's nice to see you.

He smiled and didn't reply. I turned back to Kate expectantly.

You see, Doll, she cried, smoothing the fabric down the front of her belly. You see how Yellow Woman is favoring me.

I stuttered, confused.

Doll, I'm going to have a baby. It's happened.

Oh. . . Kate! When?

December. Abe's birthday, she added with a quick look at Ralph. He was watching the dancers and seemed to have forgotten about us.

Has Doc Hams come by to see you?

When the times comes, I'll send word, Kate uttered brightly, and squeezed Ralph's hand.

When the times comes, I repeated, feeling troubled. I thought of the women on the frontier who had to give birth without doctors and midwives. What did we know? What if Doc Hams couldn't get to her in time in his ridiculous old-fashioned horse and buggy?

I'll tell Vera, I added.

Vera knows, said Kate.

We watched the dance resume with the solemn tread of the men. The drums droned incessantly, the movement of the dancers was serious, hypnotic. The earth shook under a serene sky. Yet I had lost the moment of solemnity—of reverence. I could only feel a sense of foreboding as I watched the traitorous dance of Yellow Woman.

The Indian women leave the tribe and give birth on their own, out in the wilderness, Kate said in my ear, as if reading my thoughts.

You can imagine how many don't come back.

Why? Kate asked suddenly, biting her lip. She turned to look in my face. Why not? she asked sharply, and I instantly regretted my words.

I'll make you a portrait for your baby present, I said quickly.

Will you, Doll? she cried, delighted.

I knew then just how I would paint them: Kate as the Madonna, smiling beatifically in her high-necked frock and cap, like one of the first saints on American soil, and cradling in the palm of her hand, manlike in miniature, the Christ child. He looked, to my mind, remarkably like Abe.

But what I painted that summer was this: Abe held *me* in the palm of his hand. His face long, thin, and bearded to a point, framed by a kind of mosaiced nimbus that could also be a garland of leaves. His eyes sharp and satyr-like, a hint of a smile on the pale, pale face. And resting on his upturned palm: a childlike figure with eyes like great dark pools, clad all in white, and sporting gossamer wings. She looked like me at my most adorable comeliness, when my father still loved me for my beauty. I loved this painting, worked on it in secret and kept it in the privacy of my shed. At night when I couldn't sleep I hung it over the bed. I felt safe with it there, protected from harm. In the morning I quickly took it down and hid it.

A Mexican arrived with two horses to sell. I was very excited. I wanted my own horse, and I was wary of borrowing Vera's big-bellied Betty, which really belonged to Janie, who could reclaim it capriciously whenever she liked. I flew into Abe's cabin to tell him about the Mexican horse dealer. Abe was in bed with a sore throat and couldn't get up to see. He instructed me to ride the horses in front of the bedroom window, and I mounted each in turn and paraded past his vista. One of the horses was lively and black with a beautiful, sleek head; the other was nobly ugly, quiet, and brown. The Mexican scrambled under the brown horse's belly and between his legs to demonstrate his quietness. In the end, we decided to buy both, the black one for Abe, of course, and the unpretty brownie for me. But ecstatic I was, since finally I had my own mount. I named him Reggie, after my father.

In a week when Abe felt better, we rode to Lobo Canyon, several miles down into the valley, on our new horses. Abe called his Libertad, and I rode Reggie, which proved over time a tractable creature, as well as loyal. Vera was handsomely astride Betty. We gathered very early in the silver morning, just past sunup, still bundled in our blankets. It was a rare outing for Vera, who never wanted to come riding, then accused us of excluding her, but I knew she agreed this day to come because of the presence of Johnny Copper, an artist who lived in town. Johnny was slight, with thinning hair, little round glasses, and an earnest, blinking air. He had arrived by motorcar from California with his lover, both penniless and struck by the light, and when the car broke down on the road to Taos they decided to stay. That was some years before. In time, Johnny started a local paper, *The Rattle*. Since learning about Abe from Janie, Johnny Copper had been waiting for Abe's arrival, in this town where little happened over a great expanse of time. He finally had something to write about in his paper, and the messiah's arrival also lent him new justification for his own presence in this forsaken outpost of the lawless West. Now it would be a real artists' colony, he declared triumphantly in his pages. Blinking myopically, lightly perched in the saddle of a fine blond Palomino, he rode next to Vera, who liked to talk as she grew warm with the ride.—Marvelous! she cried. Wunderbar! How I can feel the thighs of this animal!—I trotted ahead of the two of them, behind Abe, and couldn't hear her go on. I was happy to calculate the changing light on the peaks. Abe rode in the lead, intent on looking at the ground.

Why don't you look up? I asked him, at a lull through the sun-speckled pine forest, when our horses bumped along side by side. The tall ponderosas rose on each side of us, their canopy of tufted heads filtering out the sun that we craved to warm ourselves. Across their rugged barks I noticed the claw tracks of bears that had trolled territorially through the area. Our horses trod softly on the bed of shimmering needles. Soon we would skirt the open valley.

Look down and see for yourself, Abe beckoned me—and I recognized the wildflowers that he often had strewn about the cabin. They populated his paintings and were etched into the wooden furniture: gentians, nettle, columbines, bluebells, harebells, herb honeysuckle. He relished seeking out the shadowy domiciles of these shy wildflowers, which had no real scent, and from time to time I watched him ahead on the narrowest path leap from his horse and bend to the roadside to pluck them. The flowers were never to be placed in vases for decoration; no, he packed the specimens like a good botanist carefully away in his saddle pack, and once back at the cabin he would remove each flower delicately and hold it by its stem close to his face for a long while, turning it over and over, occasionally sketching with his free hand its various components, and labeling it with care, before tossing it lightly on the table or dresser top to dry up and remain forgotten. And once again he shamed this painter for her lack of observation, as I had been looking and not *seeing*—had hardly noticed the small gems sprouting at our horses' heels.

Why, you're looking down to see the flowers! I exclaimed, though he had gone ahead and didn't hear. Behind me I detected the buzzing of conversation—*love*, I thought I heard over and over— were Johnny and Vera discoursing on the nature of love? But it could have been *above* (I looked up to admire the sheer white faces of the cliffs rising on each side of us, the indomitable flat-topped mesas), or even *mud*, which is the material from which the local houses were made. I didn't listen, as usual didn't need to hear what people said to know what they meant. I looked back and noted how the two riders trotted side by side. Vera astride Betty, her skin alabaster smooth under her wide-brimmed hat save for a slight cast of pink at the cheekbones, and eyes and teeth glittering madly; and Johnny riding the sand-colored horse, his slender skull turned toward Vera in a posture of profound attention, spectacles flashing. Vera was flirting, happy, engaged, and for miles I could concentrate on the swiftly changing scenery. For with each hill we circled or crevice between boulders we penetrated, the landscape was utterly transformed, like a house with innumerable rooms. The deeper one explored, one room inside the other, the more preposterous and elaborate the furnishings became. Having cleared the aspen forest to wander amid the open valley, we gazed across an expanse of golden green space, then wended our way through the intricacies of the canyon, closed in by devilish rock formations and treacherous horse trails. The light kept changing from dark to light, light to dark. The horses' hooves sent up flints and we covered our faces with kerchiefs. We had fallen in single file, with Abe far in the lead, then me, then Vera, followed in the rear by Johnny Copper. I heard the latter two laughing and singing some snippets of German—first Vera's strong clear voice:

Knupper, knapper, kneischen
Wer knuppert an meinem Häuschen?

To which Johnny responded in a mock Germanish baritone:

Der Wind, der Wind,
Das himmlishche Kind!

And the two would shriek hilariously. I wondered whether Abe could hear—his shoulders sloped in a stiff, truculent manner. When the trail bottomed out more evenly, and we reached a stretch of soft ground, he took off in a gallop, and one by one we gid-dyaped after him. But suddenly Abe twisted in his saddle to look back, and then I became aware of Johnny's distress whistle. I turned to see Vera lurch from the saddle of her running horse and fall into the scrub at the side of the trail.

We reined our horses around. Johnny was already dismounted and crouched at Vera's side. Her saddle had come undone, slipped out from under her. She pulled herself to her feet, sputtering angrily and shaking a fist at Abe.

Idiot! she shrieked. You did this! You rigged my saddle!

Vera, calm yourself, said Abe, riding over to her. I told you not to touch the saddle, when you don't know how to do it!

I didn't touch anything! she cried. You rigged it on purpose so that I would fall! She added some venomous-sounding German words we could guess the meaning of.

Vera, said Abe quietly. I don't see any broken bones.

He rode over to where she had fallen, caught the hanging blanket and saddle, and threw them over the back of Betty.

I'm not all right! Vera cried. No, not you! You are not touching my saddle!

She insisted that Johnny do it. She accused Abe of trying to kill her, and he scoffed.—If I wanted to kill you, I'd have found a more efficient way! Falling off a horse only makes you madder, Vera. Then he tore off at a distance in disgust. Johnny stood help-lessly, unused to hearing the battles between this man and wife. Vera brushed herself off, smoldering; she picked out the pieces of long grass stuck in her hair. We decided to stop there and break for lunch. We sat on a cluster of boulders under the shade of the pines, spacing ourselves warily from one another. The sun at the base of the canyon was warm at last, and it felt good on our skin. We watched the scuttling of a roadrunner. Vera, shaking, white-faced, taut, wouldn't address Abe or me, but only acknowledged poor Johnny, who was gallant as he handed out the sandwiches, but at a loss to mend her mood. I lay down and covered my eyes with my hat. I knew the afternoon was ruined.

Dark and light, light and dark. The desert chiaroscuro. We plodded homeward into the afternoon shadows cast by the precipitous rock faces. I recognized the strange furnishings of this house. The sky had deepened to a regal blue, the clouds softly scumbled. Johnny and Vera rode ahead; we'd lost sight of them and were glad to be alone.

Most people shut themselves up in houses and no longer have any real contact with the earth, Abe declared sullenly. The only way to live here is to possess nothing.

He turned in his saddle so that I could hear. I could watch his face. This was a good sign—that he wanted to talk, and needed to talk to *me*.

Here the sky claims you, I told him. You can't ignore it. If I could, I would live in a house without a roof and see only the sky, night and day.

You would go mad.

You go mad anyway, out here, I said, and Abe laughed.

Do you like it here, Doll?

I do, I said firmly. He could not question *my* resolve.

Even if I weren't here? he asked.

What do you mean? I cried, alarmed. Why wouldn't you be here? We couldn't stay without you. You are our leader.

It's just a question, Doll.

Your questions have teeth.

He laughed. Doll, I'm an old man.

I'm your age, I reminded him.

A sick man, then.

Not so sick. The climate here will make you well.

Aye, he replied. And Vera, he added—then stopped himself. I waited.

She's stronger, he considered.

Stronger than? I asked.

But got no answer. Abe rode ahead, gazing down at his flowers. We didn't rejoin the others until well into the pine forest.

→ Part II ←

Akbar's mother, the doctor's widow, questions his long absences from her. She wonders where he is spending his hard-earned cash. He makes an hourly minimum wage pruning trees, some days for ten hours, other days, when Lucky Tree Service's '57 Chevy truck breaks down, not at all. She reminds him that he needs to buy new gloves for climbing, a hard hat in case he falls, new boots. The ones he has are riddled with holes, the bottom tread worn well away, perilously slick on tree limbs. His mother still asks him when he is going to cut his hair—by now there are silver streaks in it, for Akbar is neither young nor old. She wonders where he is spending his nights. When is he going to get some proper sleep? How can he climb trees when he is yawning his head off? She suspects he is sleeping at my forsaken little adobe off the highway, on Avenida Mañana. She suspects that he is spending money on me. What can he be buying me? She suspects we are traveling together. Where can we be traveling? She wonders whether we are traveling to New York to sell my paintings. She worries he will catch evil germs in the big city. She asks about his wages and suspects that he is skipping days of work. (He does—he oversleeps.) She begins to fret. The hairs on her head turn whiter. What will become of her if her son leaves her for another old lady? Who will take care of her in *her* old age?

In his indifference—oblivion, perhaps—Akbar brings his mother's questions to me. He does not know how to answer his mother, so he lays the questions before me and lets me worry about them. Of course I will worry about them. If I worry then he won't have to get blue, and I can't stand to see my boy despondent. When he brings me a complaint from his mother, such as why he would spend good money on food when she cooks every night for him, I ask him a series of questions that allow him to cast off his worry and buck up.

Akbar, have you ever traveled outside the state?

Nope, he admits, has not. Parole restrictions.

What was your crime?

Larceny, says he. Akbar stole a car, did his time. He adds with a melancholy air: Akbar wanted to get to Mexico. Never made it to Mexico.

And your parents—they used to travel?

Oh yah, traveled a lot. Traveled all over the world, he tells me proudly.

Was it your father's work as a doctor that took them to all those places?

Yah, says Akbar. China. India. The world.

Why, I persist, did they not take you along also?

Too much trouble, replies Akbar.

But how else does a child learn about the world?

Too much trouble, repeats Akbar.

No, he has never been anywhere, not even to a fancy restaurant in Albuquerque. I ponder this injustice. The boy has been brought up like a zoo animal kept in the closet. I decide I am angry at his mother because she does not appreciate her son the way he is, a little shaggy, a little lost, but nonetheless lovable. I resent his mother. I decide there's only one thing to do: invite her to dinner at my house on Avenida Mañana.

We will make a dinner in the horno, I announce.

Spo-dee-o-dee, says Akbar.

It is late summer. The desert sun strikes warm during the golden afternoons and the wild lavender bushes in front of the house still kick up a good scent. Akbar brings a handful of dry kindling and crouches low at the small door of the beehive-shaped oven in my backyard. He gathers more wood, pungent sage, and piñon, and arranges it skillfully inside the mud oven. Then he sets the contents on fire. We savor the smell of the desert. He peers inside the horno for a moment, singeing his eyelashes, before stepping back swiftly to close the small oven door. He wipes the soot from his face with relish. The boy loves to light fires, no matter the occasion. He looks happiest splitting logs in my meager backyard at the base of the mountains and stacking the wood neatly on the side of my house. After the fire has raged hotly for some time he rakes out the embers and half-charred sticks with a long wet mop and waits for me to insert the food. We are having a whole chicken cooked in beer. Roast sweet potatoes and corn on the cob and fresh bread. It will feel like Thanksgiving. I hand Akbar the pots of food and he arranges them inside the hot horno, then secures the door. And we wait, seated on lawn chairs, watching the sky. He smokes a fragrant cigarette. The traffic on the highway passes. Soon it is time to pick up his mother and he leaves in my yellow woodie because his own car, unaccountably, has run out of gas.

The mother arrives. A small frail old lady with iron-dark hair pulled back tightly at the base of her skull, her face a mask of contained fury. She carries a small warm plate and rids herself of it when they come in. A bean-squash-potato dish. Her fine nostrils are a key to her state of mind; I notice they flare when she is alarmed, and they flutter delicately as she glances around the untidy room. I usher her inside the studio—only when I have guests do I actually note the state of where I live: paintings line every inch of wall space, banked in corners and behind the worn furniture, tables of paint and brushes crammed in tins and tins everywhere, the smell of turpentine thick as incense. She's wondering how a body can live like this (I think of my father paying me a visit to our wartime London flat), and briefly I wonder, too: why does Akbar want me? It doesn't make any sense, I want to explain to her, as I hand her a plate of cheese cubes, which she declines, staring at my hands. I take back the plate and glance at my hands—I haven't been able to remove all of the paint stains, especially wedged in the nails. I don't wear polish, I don't wear rings. My hands are a ravaged battlefield of liver spots and erratic tributaries. What did she expect—Jackie Kennedy? It doesn't make sense, I want to tell her, as we seat ourselves carefully on opposite ends of my worn sofa, and Akbar takes up behind his miniature loom, stashed in a corner on the floor. He used to make a living as a weaver, before the calling of the trees, and I have been astounded to see the intricacy of his rugs and other handiwork. He carefully lengthens out a stretch of yarn, brings it close to his eyes where he can see, and begins to feed it into the spindle, a strand of yarn so near the color of his own bark-brown locks, I marvel that he doesn't accidentally weave it into his beard. I laugh at the thought. The two consider me in silence.

Akbar smirks, then bows his head to his spinning. He is not going to help, I can see; he is incapable of being gallant. He is going to step back and let the two of us hash this out. He can't show his favor for one or the other; he has to play it somewhere in between. But his mother isn't saying anything, either. I wonder whether she even speaks English, but then I remember the hostess housekeeper of her husband's office, the same lady who silently welcomed the patients and took their coats. I try to remember whether she has ever spoken to me.

Akbar tells me you have traveled a great deal, I begin, smoothing my offending hands in my lap.

Neither looks at me. Neither responds. We listen to the *ratcha-ratcha* whir of the loom.

I persist, in my most English accent,—Have you ever been to England? When they don't reply, I continue gaily: I'm from England, haven't been back for many, *many* years—because when you leave you're like a ghost. They don't want you around. And I'm not ready to give up the ghost yet.

Not a peep from the guest. She looks vaguely strangled, flaring her nostrils.

I went through the war in London, I continue, can you imagine? I don't suppose you've ever been through an air raid? A blackout? A hospital of wounded convalescents? It's dreary, grim, to be sure, ma'am, not for the fainthearted. I'm as stout as they come and still I felt squeamish. Lost my mates in the war. Lost *many* people I loved dearly. Slaughtered, all of them, in the trenches of Passchendaele and Ypres, and as far away as British East Africa. You don't hear those names anymore. Then I came here to start over. Start fresh, start from scratch.

Akbar nods approvingly, intent on his weaving.

Mother asks suddenly,—How many years?

When? I ask, interrupted in my long-toothed reverie. *She's getting at my age, I know it.*

Since you're here.

Oh, on Avenida Mañana, some years now. . .

I mean, Taos, she snorts. *Here.*

Thirty-five, I say, glancing at Akbar. Give or take a year.

Ah, says she at last, in a firm, slightly accented English that demonstrates her fine Spanish schooling. She's satisfied and deigns to regard me directly for the first time, frowning at my colorful getup, turban and polyesters—I'm here seventy, says she. Brought here from Puebla, Mexico, when I was ten. And I've seen *wars.* Lots of wars. The Americans take everything and leave nothing, not even schools.

Yes, I agree, pleased she is older than I am.

Which war? she asks suspiciously.

My war? I ask. *Now here it comes,* I think—but the alarm rings for the horno and I jump up with wonderful spryness, not lost on Akbar.

The *Great War,* I tell her.

At table she sniffs at her food. She detects something in the chicken and can't quite place it. She demands the ingredient of her son, who muffles a reply with his mouth full. He has gathered all the food on his plate into a big bonfire, and lights the top with generous shakes from the hot-sauce bottle. His locks fan around his shoulders—from this angle I see how broad he is, how narrow his torso. My manly kouros. I'm proud of him. I smile at him. He doesn't look up, busy piling up his vegetables. Mother repeats his answer and I can see her nostrils flare. She does not approve of putting beer in chicken. She wonders why I use an old-fashioned horno when I can cook more efficiently in the gas oven.

But doesn't it taste good? I ask her. When she doesn't respond, I tell her I learned how to use an horno many years before, when there *were* no gas ovens around.

She looks suspicious again and narrows her eyes at me.—The Spanish brought the hornos, says she, and they taught the Indians.

Yes, I reply, people think it's the other way around.

But you're not Spanish, she sniffs.

No, and I wasn't around when the Spanish arrived either.

Akbar snorts, nodding at my score. Then he breaks into a cough like a hyena because the food goes up his windpipe. He's terribly uncouth, my lover. His mother glares at the boy.

Who taught you? she demands of me.

To cook in an horno? An Englishman who learned the ways of the natives.

Now Akbar has recovered and is interested.—Where did he go? he asks.

The Englishman? To Mexico, I say.

Didn't you go, too?

No. I heard he died and I stayed here, and that's when my life really started.

Akbar gets it, bats his eyes at me.

Taos, 1924

At dawn I detected the pounding of hoof beats on the bitten ground and peeked out of my shed. Junior rode up the hill on his immense black stallion. He was magnificent. He wore a blanket of two colors draped over his broad shoulders and tied to his saddle were his tackle bag, bow and arrow, and fishing poles. His hair hung in two long black braids laced with light-colored ribbons down each side of his dark, glowing face. I dressed quickly and snapped on my knife. I emerged into the cold morning and we saluted each other, touching forehead, heart, then fingertips. Junior's facial expression never altered. He didn't smile, didn't need to. I could read his moods in the subtly changing hues of his mahogany irises. He was happy to see me. I ran to the stable to saddle Reggie.

We rode to Red River, down the other side of our valley into the canyon. The day already promised a sharp, blazing sun, for it was well into the summer months. We adjusted the tilt of our hats. Junior rode swiftly on his tall, gorgeous mount, and I scrambled to keep up behind him on my plodding brown Reggie. We didn't need to speak, and this is why I loved being with Junior. We understood each other by hand gestures. Junior fancied our signaling to each other, because it was like the sign language of the Old People. Maybe they were deaf like me. He spoke his own native Tewa, I knew, the language of the pueblo, as well as fluent Spanish, because I had heard him making negotiations among the traders in the village. English he spoke haltingly and didn't like to. And if he didn't have to speak, he preferred not to, just as he preferred not to alter his facial features—needless energy expended, better suited for important tasks like fishing. He loved fishing, as I did. If he didn't speak, he was spared conversing with Janie's friends from the East, who were afraid to address him, anyway. Junior could ride away for hours and be a solitary Indian. Next to him I didn't have to be the white English lady and certainly not the white Englishwoman riding out scandalously alone with a redskin. I would become a solitary Indian, too.

We made it down into the canyon after a few hours. The horses had lathered and we let them drink from the galloping river. Junior chose a spot he called Laughing Waters. The spirits were propitious here, and we would have good fishing, he asserted with some significant gestures. The river's spray caught our faces, refreshing us. I was already hungry, ready to fish. I set up my pole that I had whittled myself and dug for grubs we could use for bait. But Junior didn't need bait. We fanned out along the banks of the river that had cut a deep gorge through the canyon, flanked on both sides by high, plunging, striated rock. My boots made clattering sounds as they struck the shale. The trout sway-finned seductively just underneath the surface of the chuckling river. They were long and fat. If we waded far enough, we could scoop them up with Junior's big net. But Junior sat placidly on a rock, his pole anchored in layers of shale, and rolled a cigarette. He sat on his rock and watched and waited. He was in no hurry. When he felt a tug on the pole, he yanked at it leisurely and brought the line up and grabbed the fish before tossing it into a pool he had fashioned behind him. He moved efficiently, without hurrying. Just before flinging it behind him into the pool, he brought the fish to his face and looked in its eyes—I even imagined he would bite into it, as if testing its worthiness. But I learned he was inhaling its last breath, inviting the spirit of the fish to enter him.

I was hungry and couldn't sit still like Junior. I blew up a small fire on the bank and took out my knife and gutted some of the fish I had caught. I used a pan Junior ferreted out of his saddlebags and I fried up the fish. The smell of fresh frying fish nearly knocked me flat, especially after innumerable tasteless stews from Vera's kitchen; I burned my fingers and tongue trying to stuff the soft white flesh in my mouth before it cooled. Junior laughed. I wondered what he thought of me—not a creature to be housed like his wife Janie nor like any of the tribeswomen he knew, for I had heard about his previous Indian wife, and his mistresses. But I was another category of human altogether, neither male nor female. And that was good, I thought, it made a friendship easy between us. We lounged on the rocks and ate, then tilted our hats when we got sleepy. The warm sun brought out the enormous dragonflies prancing on the water's fiery surface, their wings like iridescent fans of Japanese maidens. When Junior fell to snoring, I took out my sketchbook and found many things to observe, especially his solid, mahogany profile.

The sun was past meridian, the shadows slanting harshly against us in the canyon, and the trout weren't interested in us anymore. By tacit agreement we packed up our saddlebags stuffed with fish and headed out of Laughing Waters. The air blew hot and still once we moved away from the river, and I let Reggie amble behind Junior's stallion and ceased paying much attention. I was thinking of Abe and his happy face when he'd see the fish. Once we began to ascend the hills it grew cooler, more pleasant, and I revived and looked at Junior. He seemed to stretch higher in his saddle as if listening. We were entering the odiferous pine forest. He was turning his head slowly from side to side, his posture alert, watchful. I wanted to call—What was up?—but there wasn't any point in that: Junior's body movements told me to watch, to wait. I turned in the direction he was lookng and then I saw it: a black bear crouched at the base of a fir tree, scratching industriously at the bark. He was young and fat, busy at licking and sniffing with his long sharp snout at the dirt roots of the tree—maybe there were insect mounds there—and he glanced over at us reluctantly, cautiously, not wanting to be interrupted in his food gathering. Not wanting to *share*. But there we were, unmistakably, two riders on horses—the bear turned to face us. His snout was twitching frantically, catching our smells with new interest. I thought of the fish in our saddlebags and groaned in dread. Junior was already reaching around to remove his bow and arrow: he carried it always. My first instinct was to flee—to pull Reggie around and gallop out of there, fling the fish at the bear, and run like mad. As if sensing my cowardice Reggie whinnied and made a backward dance, but I was rooted there in horror. I watched Junior for what to do. He slowly strung his bow, lifted it to his aiming eye, pulled back the bow with excruciating deliberation. And the bear, sensing danger, raised itself on its hindquarters, becoming an immense shaggy giant that sent the horses rearing in fright. Then Junior released the arrow.

I couldn't be sure in what order things happened next. The arrow hit true in the neck and the bear fell back with a loud bellow that shook the woods. But then again it dropped to all fours and began to shuffle toward us baring black-rooted teeth, and Junior was out of the saddle and running for it. His blanket slipped from his shoulders, his knife flashed in his hand. The two were engaged like ferocious gladiators, as if having prepared their whole lives for this moment of mortal combat. I grabbed at the rearing stallion's bridle and yanked its head, pulling the trembling horse to a distance. I couldn't make out where Junior was, whether he had been pinned under the enraged, wounded beast. There were horrible snarling sounds that reached even my ears. The scuffle raked up primeval humus smells from the forest's depths. And then he emerged from under the body of the animal, incredibly, unscathed, at least as far as I could see, his limbs still intact, his braids swinging as he stepped over the great fallen monster. Junior lifted something high in his bloodied hands. I couldn't see, I couldn't look—what had Junior taken from that tremendous force of nature that had commanded the forest to thunder only moments before? Junior held it high in his dripping butcher's hands. He came near, he held it up to the gods, his face shining triumphantly: the heart. The heart of the bear, still beating. I thought I would fall. Junior shouted, "*Ai ai ai!*" the first words from him that I had heard that day. Junior began to sing.

Winter hadn't let go and the days in London were raw and bleak. The war had finished, exhausted the land and scattered the survivors, and the few of us left picked up our lives and moved forward. Many in our group like Mrs. D perished in the influenza epidemic that coursed through post-war London like the black plague. Our circle had been punctured when Marcus moved back to Fife to live within the bosom of his wife's family. There his children could move freely in the country and he would find employment at a boys' college. Others had left us for pursuits in Madrid or Paris. Gary and Todd led secret nocturnal lives down at the docks and we saw them rarely. There were others who came: George the American editor, who seemed to know everyone, and the hoary-headed ladies Fran and Mike who were really a couple (Lorelei had to point this out to me), and Didier the skinny Frenchman who was a painter like me and very poor. He was always bringing interesting pieces of trash from the street with which to make collages, and together we inspected his treasures of tins and refuse and broken toiletries. With these artifacts we made little shadow boxes that were the rage for a season.

We held Tuesdays; sometimes we ended up playing mah-jongg with the table set up near the bed where Lorelei reclined like

Mata Hari in her silk getup. She was sick and getting sicker but we pretended that she wasn't. Gary was passionate about the game, having learned during his stint in Singapore, while I had learned in the nursery of my childhood, and we taught the others how to manipulate the white bricks. But after a while I withdrew to sketch and didn't bother with the conversation. Or, I tried not to bother until George the handsome American editor challenged me:

What's that you're sketching so mysteriously anyway? he asked, looking up briefly from stacking his bricks, one eyebrow cocked suspiciously.

At certain awkward or embarrassing moments I had found it effective to hide behind my deafness, and here was a fine opportunity. I ignored him.

I say, George pursued more loudly with mock British airs. I *say*, you there, Doll! What *is* it that you scratch in that red notebook of yours? I think it's only fair of you to show us. Anyway, your mysterious scratching is like whispering behind someone's back, isn't it? And surely even you aristocrats know that's rude. My grammy back in Detroit told me it's rude. So go on, let's have a see.

Now I had to respond, or George would start to bellow. He bellowed whenever he had too much to drink and then he'd recite some lines from Longfellow or some such. I wondered how much the players had already drunk. George had a bullyish streak I didn't like much, which came easily to people who were handsome and entitled, also American and incapable of restraining from drinking to excess. I didn't know where George got his money, from Grammy back in Detroit maybe, but he was a good editor, everyone said so, and he was trolling London for talent to bring back to the New York magazines.

No, thank you, I told George. It's my notebook and I don't care to share.

Doesn't care to share! bellowed George. Now is that fair!

He whined and enlisted the help of the mildly amused Natasha, who sat closest to me.—Snatch it, Natasha, please do! I think old Doll there is scratching about us behind our backs. And I for one would like to know how Doll employs her leisure time in that ivory tower apart.

They all laughed. *Ivory tower apart!* I sat a little straighter in my chair and pulled the notebook shut with a smack. I was furious. Lorelei was no help, lying back against the pillows with eyes half-shut like an opium smoker, a faint, otherworldly smile playing at the creases of her sadly thinned mouth, and Gary at her feet only tittered and clattered greedily at his playing bricks. I suspected, by their lack of interest, that they already knew what my red notebook contained. Only Didier came to my defense in between puffs on his cheroot.

I would not, warned he with a canny Gallic smirk, narrowing his dark eyes.—Heed the great La Rochefoucauld, who said: The greatest effort of friendship is not to show our faults to a friend, but to let him see his own.

Now George's curiosity was truly piqued. He had ceased playing at mah-jongg and eyed me shrewdly.

Is that right, said he poisonously. Then, more forcefully: All right, Doll, out with it.

The laughter subsided in titters of embarrassment. They were all looking at me bemusedly, a little surprised by George's dare, wondering what I would do. How fragile was I really (a gentle-woman)—should they intervene? I no longer believed this was a joke. George was after me and I, for my part, feeling disgusted and angered by the violation of my privacy, would give him what he wanted.

Now, *Doll*, began Natasha, with a condescending sigh, but I silenced her with my upraised hand. I opened the red notebook to a page that would interest George in particular and turned the book over and held it up for all to see. And there was George, unmistakably George, feet turned slightly in, big handsome head crowned by a coxcomb, strutting and preening like the rooster he was. There were other caricatures of him as well, six pages, I showed him, leafing slowly through the notebook, six whole pages devoted to the self-important specimen who was George, carnivorous eyes always on the lookout for something new to devour, chest thrust out, mouth open and ready to shoot. I had sketched him over many Tuesday evenings at mah-jongg. The real George was appalled, and silenced, I noted with some satisfaction as the others snickered behind their hands, because he simply hung his head over the table cluttered with white tiles, and glowered quietly and did not ask to see more. Only later did he cite a bit of Longfellow on his way out, and in a small, dry voice that was not at all in the timbre of his usual bellowing:

> *How will men speak of me when I am gone,*
> *When all this colorless, sad life is ended,*
> *And I am as dust?*

But George the American editor reappeared another season and did this: he announced he would bring the famous incendiary revolutionary Abe Bronstone to our studio, along with his blond German wife. We were honored, Lorelei and I, a little flustered, even Lorrie, the girl about town, who didn't know what to wear and tried on a hundred outfits to set the right tone. Together we pulled the round marble table that had once been at Tilney Street near the fireplace. We set out tea and cakes I fetched from downstairs. Then Lorelei fell over her cushions in exhaustion and let me fuss, and I complained we didn't have any flowers for the mantle—we always had flowers to disguise the shabbiness of the walls! We had run dry after the cakes. She suggested I make them.

Make flowers? I demanded. Gawd, Lorrie, I'll just pop down and dig up some of the royal daffodils.

They'll arrest you—or are you aiming to test your diplomatic immunity? Just stir up some plasticine, Doll, don't you remember anything from the Slade? We've got all that. And you can paint the flowers and make them quite lifelike. Abe Bronstone, she added, would be *charmed*.

Her eyes shone particularly bright; I wasn't sure what medication she was on, something for the pain, I surmised, whatever medical supplies Gary or Todd found that had fallen off the hauler during their furtive nighttime rendezvous. But she wasn't going to help me, I could see that, so I brought out the plasticine and tubes of paint to appease her, and then forgot about the project when our guests arrived.

George disdained drinking tea, went right for the hard stuff, though it was just past four in the afternoon when they all shuffled up my stairway, gazing around the studio like a troupe of stunned, lost campers. Vera the wife stashed her small hat in a corner and sat quietly knitting just out of the light, a cigarette perched between her lips, and George and Abe set to deriding English authors. Abe wore layers of woolens he did not remove and he carried a ghastly pallor. They had been traveling over the winter, apparently, and he had been ill. He insisted on pouring the tea. George was hoping Abe would come up with some good writers he could secrete back to New York, but Abe scoffed and announced that England was dead and there wasn't any future here.

—But surely, Lorelei intoned diplomatically from her sofa, if you remain here, England is still worthy soil?

I won't stay in this country, Abe asserted impassionedly—not after the withdrawal from bookstores of *The New Man*. I have created an individual who no longer cringes in the face of patriarchy's bloodletting, who won't participate any longer in the butchery of nations, and can withdraw from the world, create in solitude if he wants, live with a lover without the conventional burden of marriage—and I am raked over the coals by the British authorities as being anti-social, misanthropic, unpatriotic! They have the power to remove my books, destroy my livelihood, and poison my reputation. I cannot stay in this hideous country, Abe concluded.

Then come to New York, by all means, declared George pompously.

Never. It's a city gripped by greed and lawlessness. It will destroy itself, too. New York is new, it is modern, but it isn't humanity's answer. No, said Abe, I shall go west.

Where, west? cried Todd breathlessly, bursting in, as he had just sprinted up the stairwell to our flat, his head sleekly oiled, his face freshly shaven, carrying the silken look of a mink newly emerged from its burrow eager for the night's fun.

Abe was eyeing the plasticine I had left lying around. He ignored the others and turned to me, suggesting we work at it together. He sat close, mindful of my hearing.—What were you making? he asked, and I shyly told him (not looking at Lorrie) that I had been making flowers for our mantle. Well, Abe knew about flowers, and instantly began to fashion some catkins he described from his recent stay in the countryside of Sussex. He hummed as he worked cleverly with his hands, and I sat nervously next to him, afraid I wouldn't catch his words. We painted our flowers in pretty pastel colors. And then he said:

I want to gather twenty or so souls and leave this place. Leave this planet, Doll, and sail away from this lost world and establish a place of harmony and good will—a new colony for humanity's redemption. Do you see, Doll, how it can be? It's finished here, there's nothing left after the war. With a collective good will and hard work and a little money—it won't take much. What do you say to that?

Why, it's grand, I replied. Though what I was thinking (and didn't utter to Abe) was what my father would say, and whether I could take my inheritance with me?

We will establish a society without money or class, continued Abe.

Surely that disqualified me? I wondered.

Without church or hierarchy, he continued.

Absolutely, I cried.

I can't find anybody, confessed Abe sadly.

Nobody will come with you? I asked, then blurted—But I will!

Would you? asked Abe. You are brave. I knew you were, from the first painting I saw.

I added daringly, I would go anywhere with you.

Ah! cried Abe, bowing his head to work the plaster with his capable hands. He nodded. Yes, I was the right kind of stuff. I blushed modestly, and tried to hide the trembling of my hands. Abe calmly rested his hand on my wrist.

Doll, you will paint, he said in that way he had of making it instantly so. In New Mexico you will find your subject. Not *this*—

he stammered, indicating with an accusing sweep of his hand my narrow, conventional flat. Not *these*—he took in my particular, arrogant friends—

But what is *your* subject? I asked.

He glanced over at Vera, where she had been sitting with quiet, venomous energy in the corner, smoking cigarettes. She had set down her knitting in order to lean closer to George. They sat closely and gossiped, and she threw her head back at his ridiculous bluster, offering her big, hearty laugh. I saw then what Abe noted as clearly as if Vera had declared it out loud: Vera had lovers. I sensed the pain surge through his thin, tortured frame. I felt him knot and buckle, then tear at the delicate flower in his hand.

I observe the eternal dynamic between man and woman, Abe said. I don't find an answer, Doll, but only a kind of violence of the natural world. The West will suit me. This is my adventure.

We rode down into the canyon, to fish or find Sylvie the cow that had strayed. Sometimes we would roam over Lobo Mountain to reach the reservation, and visit Junior or fetch Domingo for an errand in town. Vera remained alone in the cabin, reading. She said she preferred to stay, but then she wasn't there when we returned at dusk, hungry and saddle sore, and Abe cursed and tore up the kitchen to find something to eat. He had made a meat safe, carefully measured and cut to perfection, and hung it up in the trees to keep the animals from getting into it, but it was empty, sprung by what could only be human hands.—She's taken the meat! cried Abe, in a kind of furious bewilderment. I poured him a nip of rotgut brandy to calm him down. We made a fire and roasted beans and potatoes from Abe's garden and warmed the bread he had made some days earlier in the horno—she hadn't taken *that*. For a while we discussed the plans for the front porch that we would build and we had ceased worrying about Vera, when she came in.

Kate needs care, she declared, removing her hat and gloves. She looked tired, grim, and dusty.—A bloody long way, that, she added, when we didn't reply.

You walked from the farm? Abe asked.

Of course, I walked, replied Vera. Janie wasn't going to drive me, was she? Anyway, Janie stayed with her and kept that nut-house of a husband from setting the place on fire.

I sensed the tension growing in the candlelit room. Abe asked,—He's not better then? Is the baby all right? Has something happened to it?

I don't know, announced Vera. She seemed satisfied and watched the answer register on his confused face. Then the strain of her day seemed to flood her, and she exploded angrily.—I don't know! she cried. The girl's alone up there, and anything can happen suddenly, overnight, especially with a first pregnancy. She doesn't have her mother to take care of her. A girl needs her mother close by. Don't I know? Wasn't I full with child three times, and I lost my own babes—left them for someone else to bring up when their own mother wasn't there to care for them?

But the reference to her children had the opposite effect of convincing Abe: he hardened. He sensed she blamed him. Abe was impatient with her outburst, her sentimental tears. He said, accusingly,—You took the meat, then?

You can only think about your blasted meat, now, man? cried Vera savagely. They have nothing, not even bread. A few hard kernels of corn is going to give the woman strength to push out that baby? Do you have any idea of the perils she faces, isolated out here, pregnant, malnourished, and with a husband who could cause harm by his sheer incompetence? Do you think one doctor can take care of an entire mountain?

She dropped her voice and hissed at him: In the end you don't care if we live or die out here. You don't care what happens to us—humanly. We are only experiments to you.

She was disgusted. She hadn't even regarded me. Angrily, she gathered the scarf she had thrown over a chair and stomped into the bedroom, slamming the door behind her. She startled the cuckoo out of his clock. I quickly got up to go and slipped out the back door, casting a backward glance. Abe had sunk his head into his hands, the empty glass in front of him. A study in misery. Our plans for the front porch were spread out in front of him.

Sometimes I heard them. I couldn't help but hear, with the windows flung open in the summer months and my shed a few feet downwind from their cabin. They didn't bother being quiet, since I was deaf as a doornail, wasn't I? But I *did* hear them late at night, or sometimes early, very early, because Abe was up and out before dawn. Sometimes I detected her big, robust laughter in response to something he had said—emasculating laughter, and it made me uneasy.—Ha, ha! she cried, so that's how it is?—I didn't know what she was referring to, I didn't want to hear. In matters sexual I didn't care to know, being rather naïve, and practically still a virgin. (Did the knee-trembler in Hyde Park with Marcus count?) They were wrestling under the sheets. But Abe's voice came next, and he was cursing.—A woman can help her man, can't she? And she laughed again.—That's the best you can do? she asked. I was shocked: what kind of wife was she to Abe, and why did he tolerate her scorn? I heard him swearing again, more angry curses, and then Vera, her voice muffled, deeper, cried out in what sounded like pain. I pulled the pillow over my head. She moaned and Abe howled. After an interim of roiling, bickering, and snapping, she lit into him.—You animal, you brute! she cried. You disgust me. You're obscene, you're not even human! Objects were hurled, smashed, and there it usually ended, with something striking a hard surface, shattering into pieces—a door slamming.

But then there were quieter moments, and the candlelight flickered in their room, and I glimpsed shadows bundling together. Only Vera's strident, plaintive cry reached me over the moon:

What am I supposed to do with my passion?

In fact, I didn't hear any of this, surely, for how could I without my ear trumpet? Abe's dark countenance the next morning hinted at nocturnal unpleasantries—and dents in the walls, detritus on the floors. He was hollow-cheeked, distracted. I couldn't look him in the eye.

Janie came to stay. Her shiny black motorcar appeared like a vision rising from the morning mist. We were already at work sawing and hammering at the new porch. We wanted to finish it before the first snows. Some of Junior's relatives had been enlisted to help us cut and strip the wood. They were hard-working people, the Indians, wonderfully strong, and didn't seem to need much food or water, unlike us pilgrims. They never complained, and toiling next to those young workers, male and female, shored up my own stamina. Then Janie emerged from her brand-new chauffeured Chrysler—it was going to give Ford's Model T a run that season—as if she were stepping out on Park Avenue, and we marveled at the small, neat figure disembarking from the commodious backseat, carrying parcels, her short dark hair framing her boyish face. She drove up from Kate's farm, she said, where she'd brought some provisions.—Have you seen Kate lately, Abe? she called in her flutey East Coast tone. He straightened from his labor, and lifted a hammer in greeting.

You need to go down and see her, said Janie, making herself comfortable. She asks for you, and she's sulky and restless.

They spoke about Ralph. They didn't trust the poet husband, and discussed moving the animals up to the cabin. Vera stepped down from the back door, a cigarette crammed between her lips. She lifted a thick, bare forearm and brushed the strands of hair from her eyes. She looked hot and angry; the sweat had darkened the fabric under her arms. She had been cooking, and hated being disturbed by visitors when she was cooking. But she spied Janie's parcels, and behind her the motorcar, and the women moved together into the house.

We worked all day on the porch. We ate Vera's cabbage and carrot soup for lunch, with hunks of Abe's bread, some hard cheese, and bacon Janie had brought, and rested in the shade of the pines midday. One of the Indians had been relieved from the carpentry tasks to set up Janie's wigwam because she would stay the night. Her relatives would make it comfortable for her, bringing her bedding and kitchen supplies, she would see to that, or Junior would hear about it. I admit I never warmed to Janie, and felt ill at ease whenever she was among us, on account of her ambitions for Abe. Clearly she didn't love me because I didn't have the artistic pedigree. She appeared only when she didn't want to miss something. By late afternoon the thunderclouds gamboled across the mountains, frowning menacingly over the pine forest, and we sought shelter from the driving pellets of rain. Abe motioned to me and we slipped inside Janie's wigwam. She lay on a mattress with a compress over her eyes.

I hate these storms, she said, without looking around.—Is that you, Abe?

Yes, he replied, and we sat next to her, cross-legged. We listened to the battering against the oilskins.

Let them in, she said. Let them all come out of the rain. And the tribesmen, her relatives, moved inside, seating themselves around the small space layered in thick, colorful blankets, so that we appeared to be watching over the recumbent body of Janie.

At length Abe asked, Why did you come here, Janie? To New Mexico. Does this land suit you?

Oh yes, replied Janie. Back East I left two husbands and a fabulous culture. I was a sought-after woman. I traveled and held a salon where artists from all over came to exchange ideas. But it was making me sick. I wasn't happy in the city. I was famous and bored. I was adrift, purposeless. There was something I missed—and I have found it here. A spiritual stirring. I found it in the land of the Indians. And I found Junior.

How did you find Junior?

He built my house! She gave a girlish giggle.

There was a soft rustling among the relatives. Janie moved her head, listening. They were silent—eyes hooded, feigning sleep.

Spiritual health, murmured Abe, more to himself. I pretended to close my eyes, as the others did.

We get along, she murmured. Our cultures work side by side. You see that, Abe. You see how we have made a harmonious life.

I don't see, retorted Abe, with quiet vehemence.—I see the distinct preservation of an old-world class system. I see a hierarchy of power at which you are the head. You have not imagined a collective body—

You only see what you want to see, replied Janie. You made up your mind before opening to our life here.

I don't think so. You can't find spiritual health outside of yourself, said Abe.

Yes, said Janie tightly, deeply wounded. She had pinned great hopes on Abe and his ability to acknowledge her unconventional life.—I know you think so, Abe. You think I am only posing as a new woman. You think I am not authentic.

He didn't reply. The pounding of the rain intensified the silence within the wigwam. Obstinate and perverse, he refused to give Janie an inch.

And then, she said: Do you know Vera is plotting against you?

Abe snorted.

Vera. She's working behind your back.

Come.

She will harm you, said Janie. Tonight at Open Mouth of Bear. She's told the women to be there. She's organizing the women.

Janie confessed like a vindictive child. I wasn't sure whether Abe would laugh out loud. I peeked under my lowered lids and saw the twitching at the sides of his mouth. He condemned Janie for her mighty sense of privilege—couldn't she open doors anywhere with her name, her marriages, her family's money? Had she come out here to marvel at the wilderness, marry an Indian, and flaunt the conventions of a society she had grown bored of? And had Abe been duped to come at her request? What did she want from *him*, the miner's son? I saw the battle raging within him—the scorn in his eyes, his bitter disdain. He hated her.

Why are you telling me? said Abe at last. Aren't you a woman? A *new* woman, he added.

A disciple first, Abe. A woman second.

I closed my eyes tightly. The men were resting. The rain battered the oilskins.

Abe asked me if I had ever been in love. I replied that I didn't know. He laughed and said, How can you not know?

Just that, I repeated. I didn't know.

We had felled a tree. My job was to strip it of its branches and pare the trunk with my knife, and then we sectioned it with a long saw we worked in tandem, mostly in silence. Abe relished the task of chopping wood; he loved the violent release, the absolute, concentrated act of bringing the ax down precisely, the satisfaction of feeling the metal cleave true. He had surprising strength, for a slight man, a sick man, sicker than we knew, and endurance well beyond my own. He was in a lather, the sweat in his beard caught the sun and gleamed like bronze. He declared that a man displayed his mettle by the act of chopping wood.—Don't you love it, too, Doll?

I agreed that I did.

It was midday and very hot. We had been out for three hours at least, our wood making a tidy pile. My back was breaking but I wouldn't admit it.

But today Abe wanted to talk.—Didn't you love Marcus? he asked, slyly.

Marcus? I asked, feeling my face burn. I was humiliated at the thought that Abe took an interest in knowing about me *that way*— differently from the comfortable working friendship we had developed, side by side, chopping wood.

Come, we all knew what the other was up to, Doll.

He was hard to love, Marcus. He was a bit—distracted with other concerns.

Aye, his wife, said Abe. The wife who cut her own throat in a mental asylum.

He considered how to dissect the tree's harrow, which had the weird, lovely shape of a classical torso—a woman's.—A strange bird, the wife! he cried. Rather bloodless. Her only passion was for her painting, and he killed it.

He? How?

Children, Doll. He gave her all those bairns, made her give up her work—somebody had to look after them, didn't they? An artist cannot be a parent to children at the same time as she conceives her true progeny—her art.

I don't believe a word of it, I retorted, thinking of Vera—was the man heartless?

Then give me an example of an artist who could.

George Sand, I piped up, remembering an author my mother liked to read. She wrote at night when her children were in bed, I told him.

And she had to hide behind a man's name! Give me a first-rate writer. Rather Rousseau, who gave away his children.

Only a man could do that. Anyway, I said, when he didn't answer: Marcus didn't love *me*—I sounded more petulant than I intended.—Isn't that a necessary part of love, to feel one's love returned?

No, not always. Look at Marcus and his wife. In fact, some of the sweetest love is unrequited.

I don't see the sweetness! Only the pain. Marcus was in pain. And how do *you* know? I can't imagine your love ever being rejected by anyone—any woman.

Nonsense, Doll, said Abe. He piled the split logs onto a sled he had constructed for Libertad to pull back up the mountain. He piled neatly, meticulously, as he did everything with the care he had learned as a child helping his mother, the collier's widow.

You mean, in your youth, a woman rejected you?

Of course, but not only then. I loved several women before Vera. And it all ended in a smash-up.

You're too particular. What were you looking for? Why didn't any of the women suit you?

Maybe I didn't suit them.

I can't imagine, Abe. You have no idea!

What do you mean? he asked, looking up from his chopping. He frowned curiously at me from under the soiled brim of his hat.

You could have anyone you set your cap on. It's not like that for most people—for me, it's not.

Ah, but you hold yourself apart.

I don't.

You do. You have your deafness to shield you against the world of men.

I could love any man who loved me!

Not true. It doesn't work. . . conveniently.

Then how does it work? I asked—and weren't men always trying to explain to me the facts of life?

Abe considered, axe poised high.—Love cleaves, he said, and with a grunt brought the blade down with a resounding *thwack*. The log split cleanly, the sides falling to each side perfectly halved, as if split by lightning.

Cleave works both ways—to separate, or to bring together, he continued. It's an act of being struck down the middle by lightning, by the axe. It severs all former ties, transforms one, establishes a whole new being. A *coup de foudre* is what the French call falling in love—being struck by lightning. It's an irrevocable change—a spiritual severance and also communion. You have no choice when it strikes.

And that's what you found with Vera?

Aye. He sighed.

Again: I don't see the sweetness. Only the pain. The struggle. You always fight.

We are locked in struggle, yes. It was worse, in Italy. She defied me at every turn. We had to attend dinners with publishers, academics, organizers of the union who had read my books. She hated my being in the spotlight and grew loud and disruptive at these dinners. She claimed to be bored out of her mind. She broke out in German drinking songs. She tried to seduce my hosts! So I punished her.

You made her wash the floors to your rooms.

She told you that? Abe gave a wry, twisted grin.—Actually. . . yes. But in other ways. Ways between men and women. Abe glanced at me. The conversations in their cabin I had imagined I overheard in the wee hours flashed in my mind. I quickly yoked the sled of precious wood to the horses' harness, and turned away.

We can't carry any more, I said. The horses are restless.

He plucked a blade of sweet timothy and gnawed on it, tipping down his hat against the sun. He fell into thought, ignoring me. What did his sly look mean? I didn't know, but I felt sorely irritated, because while I thought of Abe, he was thinking of Vera, or whatever she represented—the stroke of lightning. And love for me had always meant loving a man who had other things on his mind.

I am an old woman. Silently I paint in my sunny studio every morning, facing the northern light on the Sangre de Cristo. I correspond occasionally with some of the old ghosts around here, who've lived in Taos since the early days—Janie and Junior lived well into old age, then spooked, but Johnny Copper is still around. I watch the mountains subtly changing shape with the moving light. I inhabit a world of solitary industry, mindful concentration. Sometimes I take off in my woodie to watch people at their work. I watch Akbar prune the trees. I capture him in the living light. From time to time I sell a painting, usually the smaller ones featuring picturesque scenes of flowers and Indians because people like to buy reminders of the pretty landscape of the West. Selling these potboilers, I call them, pays for my house and the unplanned bills such as the one this winter for the busted hot-water heater. There are always numerous unplanned expenses—supplies, repairs, a dinner out for my dear boy. The larger paintings of Indian ceremonials take more time, and I relish the work. I rarely sell these. Once in a while I show them at a gallery of an old friend in town. I expect no more from life than this. To paint. To gauge the light. To watch Akbar in the trees.

Akbar announces one day that I need to show my paintings—that people need to see them. I am astounded by this announcement. Why? I ask. People need to see, he insists, gesturing at the banks of canvases in my living room, and I suspect he has to prove something to his friends—to his mother—that I am an artist of some standing. I feel a sharp dig of sadness, knowing the end is near. I don't want to disappoint him, but I don't tell him that I've been around the block before and have already exhausted the sale of my paintings. Everyone in town knows who I am, knows where to find me. But times change, asserts Akbar, and people don't know your work no longer. *No longer.* What does Akbar know of the passage of time? But I forgive him—he's the head of the family now, his father dead, the sole caretaker of his aged mother. He has to look out for their future. I indulge him, agree to prepare a portfolio of snapshots. And off he trots to peddle my wares.

He drives a dusty grey Olds his father discarded years ago. Akbar never cleans this car. It contains detritus from early geological periods he does not bother to excavate. My lion's pride is his music, and he has noise always blasting from the AM radio—hippity-hoppety be-bopity rock-and-roll and twangy gee-tars and love-drunk voices howling to be put out of their misery. He turns it up for my benefit, his deaf ladyfriend. He has affixed a bumper sticker of Buddy Holly to his back window so that people honk whenever he drives in traffic. He drives with one hand, leaning his other arm out the window to dry his newly washed locks. He weaves perilously through traffic. When he stops for gas on Paseo de Perlalto he buys only a few cents' worth at a time—it's all he possesses in his wallet. He rebuffs my offers of money, but I refill his car on the weekends when he's sleeping off his bite of the black dog.

Akbar has friends, he tells me. Akbar finds you a gallery. I accept only because I've never seen him make a plan and execute it, unless it's a limb that has to be removed and he's calculating the ascending distance and climbing difficulty from the bottom of a tree. I'm astonished at his industry. In a few days he returns to me and holds out a business card. He smiles triumphantly, bearing black-gummed teeth he doesn't bother to brush because, he declares, Akbar has natural immunity.

I read: Gallery Smallhorse.

What's this? I say. Never heard of it. A new gallery in Taos?

Yah. They sell your paintings.

Jolly. Says who?

Says Akbar, and he clasps me ferociously.

We haul the paintings in my old woodie. Akbar is antsy when I drive him in my car because he has no patience listening to the tinny Spanish tunes I prefer on my own radio. He drums impatiently on the dashboard. His bony knees graze the door to the glove compartment, tricking the lock, spilling the contents of maps and wires. I drive slowly through the adobe village, quiescent at the base of the mountain like an ancient Bethlehem at winter's edge. We appear at the address on the card and enter the bright space and meet Miss Smallhorse, who is a diminutive young lady Akbar knows from the Indian school. She moves briskly, without smiling, her long jet hair swinging like a solid curtain, her hands gesturing decisively within wide, fringed sleeves. She is not unattractive, but rather hard-edged, and barks orders I can't make out. Today! she claps. Success! I think she exclaims. We cart in the paintings and she stops us with a forceful movement of her hands. She and Akbar exchange words.

These are not the paintings, Akbar says to me.

But these are the paintings from the portfolio, I say.

Nope, insists Akbar.

I retrieve the portfolio and open it to photographs of the ceremonials. Miss Smallhorse shakes her head vigorously. I leaf through the pictures in confusion and then I see what I have done inadvertently: I have inserted at the back some snapshots of the paintings of Akbar that I have made in secret—Akbar in trees and Akbar sleeping and Akbar naked. I have diligently photographed my paintings, as per habit, aware of my own mortality, aware that when I die someone will catalog, sift through, and select my work. Has Akbar seen these pictures? Miss Smallhorse notices which photographs I have come to. She jabs her finger, nods decisively.

Those, says she.

Not those, I say. Those aren't for sale.

Those I selected, insists Miss Smallhorse.

Akbar, I begin.

We get them, says Akbar, shrugging.

But Akbar, I say again.

He's out the door, returning the ceremonials to the woodie. He is ready to go and won't hear another word.

But dear boy, I try to tell him all the way back to Avenida Mañana. My dear boy, she wants the paintings of *you*.

Ai, ai, cries Akbar. I told you Akbar would sell your paintings! Why do you argue?

He's never snapped at me. I'm nearly in tears.

I don't want to sell these paintings, I wail. These I made of you. I want to keep them!

Gallery Smallhorse sells your paintings, says Akbar severely. We made *deal*.

He can't understand my sentimentality. I ransack the house for the paintings and he helps me drag them to the station wagon. He glances at one briefly, halts so that his coils of hair gyrate about his shoulders alarmingly. I weep and wring my hands. I cover the paintings protectively with a sheet and start up the woodie again. Akbar sits stonily, slumped against the door, twisting his locks. He broods. We head back to the gallery in silence.

He *thinks*, said Vera, in her German-accented English, with barely disguised disgust—he thinks that we have come here to this new land for therapeutic chastity and solitude. He *thinks*, repeated Vera, that this fine, thin air is going to elevate our minds and expel the baser elements of our nature.

She arranged her buttocks with comfortable plumpness on top of Open Mouth of Bear, that hideaway strangely named by Yellow Woman.

Our nature, she continued, meaning women's nature, which are lustful, base, and dirty, and always drawing men back to bed.—The women laughed.—He *thinks* this is the new order of the land.

The women assembled at the rock didn't disagree. They clutched their sheets around their faces illuminated by the bonfire. They reassured babies in their arms and laughed easily. They had learned much from Vera Bronstone, who exploded among them like a hailstorm, inviting change and chaos. She scorned their superstitions, taught them how their bodies really worked, told them where babies come from—and how to avoid getting pregnant. The women were serious listeners, Indian wives and the white pilgrims like me, sitting apart but close enough to thrust my trumpet up to hear. Janie wore a shawl over her head and shoulders, so that from the back she appeared small and modest, and could be mistaken for any of the other wives there. This evening I admired Vera, who presided with the sun edging down behind her, framing her handsome pale face in a shade of soft rose.

Friends, she called with a lusty laugh. I have always been considered sinful and unclean! I have a big fleshy body that has always attracted men, and I have welcomed the attraction. I grew up to consider my robust body healthy—vital and spirited and strong. My German mother encouraged me to eat! I was an athletic girl, always running after balls, chasing other children, and pursuing games. I wasn't ashamed of being physical. As I grew I brought that love of physicality to the men I loved—two husbands, some lovers. The first husband I fell for as a young girl—I loved him for his brilliance and his fine mind, and he wanted to make babies with me. That's what I wanted, too! Three baby girls I had, who brought me more joy than my marriage to that brilliant man who nonetheless had begun to alienate me from my physicality. He was a little overwhelmed by my demands in the sack, I think.—Giggles from the assembly.—But I was not unhappy, that is, I didn't recognize I was unhappy until I met Abe who convinced me of my unhappiness in my marriage. He convinced me that *he* could make me happy, bring me back to my healthy robustness, which is really my sexuality, is it not? Abe had awakened my sexuality, and he startled me into coming alive to my nature. He was the student of my husband, and it was a terrible scandal. We made beautiful love, ladies. Ah, well, you all know the delicious communion of first loving your man.

There were collective sighs and murmurs. I wished, however, that the earth would crack open and swallow me up. Instead, the sun dipped precipitously, the rosy light was extinguished, and I sensed the first tremors of the night air.

And my friends, Vera went on, I became truly alive in a way I could not with my children, and I even left my girls, because Abe told me I had to leave them in order to be with him, and I would have died if I couldn't be with him. It was like heaven together: the love we made kept us alive. I did not miss my children, until Abe began to get sick—then we couldn't love any more. Our physicality weakened—he was ill, and we couldn't share physically. We couldn't make love like we used to. How do you think I felt? I felt disappointed, of course. I felt a failure. I felt weak and humiliated. I loved Abe, but I couldn't love Abe, because Abe through his illness began to transform himself—the bile of sickness altered him, and he emerged as a being who no longer needed to love the way we used to. He no longer needed my physicality, my flesh, which had once kept us alive. So we came here, to this land of pure, high, thin air, to heal Abe, yes, but also to live in purity and chastity. This is Abe's vision, his choice, not mine. For me this purity and chastity he speaks about—it's death.

The women nodded sympathetically. They hummed. One figure stood up, her long dark hair creeping out of her shawl. The woman had a baby at her breast. She tried to speak, but too softly, and the others around the fire pit shouted at her to speak more loudly. She looked startled, then angry. I watched her lips as she spoke:

My husband, she cried, thinks I don't do it right! And I'm afraid he's finding other women who *do*.

Now we had heard her and we were outraged. We stamped our feet. Vera raised her hand to speak.

Is this his baby? she asked.

The woman nodded, readjusting the swaddling of her infant.—The last of six.

More shouts. Vera nodded sternly. And you've been faithful to him all along? she asked.

Yes, cried the woman.

Where's the justice? said Vera. Another woman stood up and shouted:

What is it he wants?

Everyone spoke at once, and some people laughed, then stopped at the serious, injured face of the first woman with the baby at her breast.

He wants me to. . . cried the woman.

There were instructions I didn't hear. I glanced at Janie, who was leaning forward, her mouth open in concentration.

Figures! shouted someone near us. We work for them all day, we make the meals, do the washing and cleaning, and they want a circus at night in bed!

Aren't you tired, poor dear!

I *am* tired, admitted the woman, glancing down at her sleeping babe.

Somewhere another voice emerged—too quietly. The assembly hollered for the woman to stand up. *Her* husband never wanted her, she said. He was disgusted by her. After the drudgery of cleaning, cooking, and taking care of their children, she was worn out and dirty, she admitted it, and he wouldn't come near her. Wasn't she worthy of a little bit of comfort? Didn't she love him when he came home stinking of sweat and horse manure?

There was an outburst of sympathy and protest. The small woman who had spoken staggered under the volley of shouts. She appeared as if she would burst into tears. Vera quieted the crowd, raising her white fleshy arms:

You love your children, said Vera.

Yes, replied the woman.

And the daily work you do makes a comfortable home for them and your husband?

Yes, she nodded.

And he won't touch you? asked Vera.

The woman shook her head.

Ach so, said Vera, shaking her fist. Be grateful you won't have another by him.

Other women spoke, wives hot with injustice. I knew what they were saying by the simmering of tempers in the crowd, by the wide shouting mouths. The women were tired and they were angry. Their men vanished for days to hunt and the women knew nothing. The men wouldn't include the women in their powwows. They were excluded from the religious ceremonies in the kiva. The men treated their women like slaves. And yet they weren't: the women kept the tribes together. This wasn't justice, said Vera, the wise white woman who had traveled to the larger civilizations, worlds destroyed by men's ambition and insolence. Vera assured them of what was coming. The men would destroy everything by their war lust, even what was dear to them—the women and children.

It has happened already, she told them. I have watched the destruction of the old country by war. Everything is ruined.

It can't happen here! came a high, searing voice. It was Janie, pulling herself to her feet in a passion.—It can't happen in our country, Vera. This is an artists' colony. We don't treat each other with violence. We are not warlike people. We are humane—humanitarian!

Janie, we must educate the people, Vera replied quietly. We must tell them the hard facts of life.

You are indiscreet, retorted Janie.

This is no time for fine manners.

We hold Abe in high esteem, insisted Janie.

We hold all our husbands in high esteem! someone shrieked from the crowd. Others chimed in boldly: We're all the same here. We're wives. We're mothers. And you? they asked Janie. What makes you any better than we are?

But we all knew the answer: Junior. Her tall brown husband. Janie was protected in a way the others were not. She was a white woman, she lived in a two-storey house. The women jeered at Janie. They touched her and she drew back, offended. Janie knew better: she used her money for the betterment of the community, building schools and hospitals, and wasn't going to stay and let them heap scorn on her head. She gathered the blanket around her and moved out of the circle.

Vera clapped her hands for order. The torches were lit. I slinked away, a betrayer to my sex. The women stayed and figured out a plan.

Vera hadn't got up that morning, and Abe had to put out the tea things. I watched him through the windows as he made a fire in the stove and toasted the leftover bread, then spread it with plum jam from the orchards in town. He chewed absently, staring out at the shy morning dampening the pine trees, and gulped the last from his tea cup. He grabbed his hat and slammed out the back door. Presently he was seated under the backyard pine, writing on his drawn-up knees like a schoolboy at his desk.

Are you sick? I asked Vera, blowing my whistle under her window at lunch time, as she had instructed me to do. She didn't like me barging in on her, she said, didn't like me anywhere near the house, the more agitated Abe became, the more estranged they grew. Her flushed, cross face appeared at the open window. The late-morning sun ignited the pine tips like tiny flames and caught the pale hues in her hair. Abe was out—it was safe to call at the cabin.

Not sick, she said. Thinking.

She had a pensive, dangerous look, her fair, flaxen hair blown haywire about her face. I stood below her, at the window.

I'm thinking about my children, the three of them, she declared solemnly. Not children anymore. I left them when they were very small, and I was full of them, day and night, and couldn't do anything else but chase after them, though I employed a Kinderfrau— and I thought, how can anyone manage to run a household with three children underfoot? They drove me crazy!

She laughed, a deep-belly rumble that heavy smokers possess, joyless to hear. I tidied the pebbles in Abe's neat flowerbeds with the side of my boot.

But then you never know a house so silent as when children are absent. I learned too late. Or rather, too early. The silence of such a house has haunted me for years.

She was terribly downcast. I didn't know what to say. I wanted to say I was sorry about her children, but I simply stood, awkward and speechless.

She went on, It's not fair what he's done. I waited, and she continued, more firmly: What he's done to my life. Then she turned back inside. After a while at the window I leaned in and asked if she needed me to bring something to Kate. I aimed to ride down and see how she was getting on, and I wanted to paint her while she was still big with child.

Is Abe going with you? Vera asked sharply.

I hadn't thought to ask. . . he's working. . .

Then don't.

Right-oh.

You should have stayed, she said. And then louder, not sure I heard: You should have stayed last night! We made a plan. And we're going to stick to it.

She laughed—that loud, diabolical laugh that meant she enjoyed humiliating me. I still heard her chuckling as she ducked inside to retrieve something, then reappeared at the window to hand down some loaves of Abe's bread.

Ach, Kate will tell you!

We would sail on the *Charlotte.* It departed mid-March, an auspicious time for ocean travel, Abe said. We stood in line to buy our tickets at the office in Waterloo Station. Abe was in charge, soberly taking my money and buying three tickets—one for Vera, one for him, one for me.—Do you think anyone else will come? he asked anxiously. Who, I wondered, did he expect to materialize at the eleventh hour—Marcus? Natasha? Lorelei? He gazed around wildly at the milling crowds. I knew they wouldn't come. They could not change their lives as I was doing. They believed me naïve. I *was* naïve, blessedly so. They already knew something of the world, and they were wary of this transatlantic voyage to start a new life. Lorelei suspected Abe was making it all up: the Indian dances, the artist colony we would found, the benevolence of the natural habitat. She worried that we would die of exposure and animal attack. Marcus could not leave his children, though he promised to visit. (He never visited.) Natasha would go as far as New York, though not on our ocean liner. The others were enmeshed in the artist's life—it was London or bust.

Only you, said Abe.

Only me.

I didn't delve too deeply. Here was a man who had decided my destiny and I had followed him, like a bride. Except that unlike a bride, I would meet freedom for the first time in my life. I was terribly proud of myself, wild with excitement, having broken with my family, my past—and I was exceptionally timid. Abe was proud of me, I could see that, as we strolled upon the magnificent vessel that would convey us across the ocean. I had never been aboard such an enormous boat. We had arrived by train in Southampton to await our berth, just as the Pilgrims had done. I reminded Abe of this fact, and he laughed delightedly.—How very like the separatists we are, he said. We're facing the unknown, Doll. We're separating ourselves from sin and spiritual collapse, and looking forward to regeneration—renewal. Are you afraid of your new adventure?

Oh no, I replied gravely. I've been waiting for this all my life.

(I said *this*, not *him*, too shy to admit the truth, even to myself.)

What if you hadn't met me? he asked. What would you do with the rest of your life?

I would always be looking for you.

He was pleased by this reply. He leaned against the polished railing of the ship's deck, crammed with voyagers waving madly across the moat to their loved ones, dangling streamers and doffing hats. The day was bright and cold and held a hard festiveness. Abe was wearing his smart brown suit. There was no one to wave us off. Vera had instantly taken refuge in her room. She was already a bit sick, and needed to lie down, calm her nerves, and smoke. Abe and I would see her seldom over the voyage on the great-breasting *Charlotte*, and take long strolls along the decks together, despite the sometimes vicious Atlantic winds. We spoke about our respective childhoods, or we spoke very little. I preferred this companionable silence, and he was relieved to share it—tired of showing off, of showing *up*. We trusted each other: we were becoming dear friends. From time to time he would venture again the question:

What if you had never met me?

To which I responded unwaveringly: Then I would never have lived.

He was satisfied, though a little apprehensive, and only later (there were terrific storms on board—he wasn't always feeling well) did it occur to me that he was worried for my safety—worried that he was taking me away from the protection of my English home. Had I brought the right clothes, warm garments, solid shoes?

I'm an adult, I said. I'm your age.

You're an innocent, he replied.

And Vera?

Vera's fallen. She has nothing to return to.

His face closed up. He looked weather-beaten—life-beaten.

But, I persisted, don't we all wait for that moment when someone we care about tells us: Come. Come with me. And we know it's a moment to act on because it will never be offered again.

How do you know this? he asked me.

Don't I know something of life? I'm your *age*, I reminded him again. For we were no longer young, nearly middle-aged.

Yes.

And Vera, I said.

What?

She met you and you said, Come. And she came.

Oh, I don't know, he mumbled.

Yes.

Doll! he cried suddenly, arrested by the shouting around us I couldn't hear. He grabbed my arm, spun me around to look out into the sea. We were plunging through turbulent, beryl-green waters, and straight on, he pointed—a vision.

It's New York! he shouted. We'll make history.

I was painting Kate as Mother Earth. Tall, raw-boned, ruddy from the sun—she was careless about wearing her hat—standing with her hand on her high, protuberant belly, she reigned amid the filthy chaos of her house. Ralph was mucking about in the stable; she didn't bother about him now. If he disappeared she knew one of us would be up to see her shortly, and how far could he go?

She didn't feel like sitting in the garden, she didn't feel like sitting in the airless kitchen, so I set up my easel in the dusty yard with the chickens racing around me. The two cows thrust their heads between the wide broken slats of the fence, staring like disgruntled neighbors. Kate came out and leaned against the kitchen door with her forearm to her cheek. She cocked her head and regarded the sun through the crook in her elbow.

Fall soon, she said simply, like an old farmer's wife who had been watching the skies all her life.

The land had changed her, as had the pregnancy. She was no longer an eager-to-please, quick-to-smile Boston bride. She had become attuned to the changes in light, wind, and sound. She knew, for example, what Ralph was up to at any moment by the clattering he made among the farm's ruined machinery. She didn't bother with an apron, she wore no hat. I set to work. The cows gave an exasperated lowing and the fluffy white chickens took off around me like scampering children in their soon-to-be-soiled Sunday frocks. The slow-munching cows were part of the family and Ralph was a kid, too, dropping the farm implements he attempted to sort in the barn and making a racket at it. What a big clumsy teenager! A child-man, he couldn't father a child, that was certain. Then Kate moved back inside, restlessly, and I tracked her through the open windows of the house. Her bright form appeared like a sleepwalker, picking up objects, putting them down elsewhere. She moved things around but nothing got tidied or changed. Finally, she came out again and squinted at the sun.

Would you like some tea? I asked at last, and put down my work.—I can toast the bit of bread I brought.

Oh that would be lovely, she replied.

I went in. The kitchen stood in disarray; I didn't know where to start. I rooted around for some wood on the side of the house— Abe must have brought it, I recognized his small, tidy axings— and on the third attempt I started the old stove. What was she thinking, bringing a child into this nest of rot? The dishes were filthy, exposed on the counter to all manner of vermin. How did they live? But there was tea, a box of biscuits, and even a jar of plum jam. I studied the label and gazed through the cloudy glass, wondering how old the jar was.

Vera brought it, said Kate, reading my mind. I turned around. She must have shouted.

She came last week.

I nodded.

Does Ralph want tea, too? I asked.

Yes, he'll be in, she assured me. And sure enough, like clockwork Ralph appeared, sat down, and proceeded to wolf down bread and jam with blackened hands and long, grubby nails, all the while humming as if we were having a marvelous conversation. He tossed back two cups of tea sweetened with honey. Presently, he got up, tipping his hat at me, and vanished through the kitchen door.

They're moving you out of here, I told her.

Yes, she answered absently.

Don't you get lonely?

I have visitors.

That's good, I said.—Feeling all right, are you?

Just fine.

Anything you need?

Oh no, she said.

We sat in awkward silence. I wanted to get back to my painting. She had already forgotten why I had come.

Abruptly she said: You were there, Doll. Last night, at Open Mouth of Bear.

Yes, that's right.

You're celibate, aren't you?

I beg your pardon?

It isn't my business, but you are, aren't you? Because it's all of our business now.

I don't follow you, Kate.

Last night Vera said that in order to teach the men a lesson, we must all be in this together. And we all agreed.

What did we agree on?

To be celibate.

How does she propose to enforce this decree of hers?

All of us agreed. It won't work unless we all agree.

She's declaring war, is what she's doing.

Yes, this will change everything for us. For me, though. . .

She trailed off and pushed herself from the table. Although her arms were thin, she looked strong, hale, the way that nature inevitably fashions pregnant women, enlisting all of their corporeal attributes to nurturing the baby to full term. She brought her cup and saucer to the counter, then turned to me, her face grown alarmingly red.

He's not the father, she said.

You think I didn't know?

I suppose so. He's been so sick, she said, nodding to the yard where Ralph could be seen bent over a furrow, oiling its dull blades.

You wanted a baby.

It wasn't planned. We didn't think. . .

Does Abe know?

I imagine he knows Ralph is not the father.

But haven't you told him?

No.

Don't you think it's the right thing to do?

She shrugged. I'm afraid he'd be mad. I told Vera, though, she added.

Vera!

She says it's good, the baby will be healthy. The reservation will accept it, that's their way.

The reservation? I echoed, with a creeping sense of dismay.—I don't understand.

They welcome the bastards—what we call them, the Indians don't. And Junior has others.

Junior!

Yes, Junior. The father of my baby.

He doesn't tickle me anymore. I don't ask, Akbar, will you stroke my head like you did in the beginning and make me feel like a little girl again? He used to scrape his fingernails gently along my scalp. But if he doesn't do it, then he doesn't want to do it, and you can't make someone love you. You only recognize when something's not the same between you when you start thinking about it—you never had to think about it before—the joy, the naturalness of being together. You start thinking about being together, but what you really mean is *not* being together, the *un*naturalness of it—the lack. The lack is all you're thinking about, and you're miserable because of it. You wander around in your misery, hoping he won't notice, hoping it's not the same with him, but he feels the lack, too, that's the way it is, the two of you work together in your unraveling. In your misery. You don't meet each other's eye. You move from the bed, spiraling away from each other, and dress awkwardly, apart, and with a kind of shame. I have never felt shame in front of him, but now I do. When we move apart from the bed I slip quickly into my clothes, eager to cover myself, my ridiculous body grown old and obsolescent. How can anyone love such a ridiculous body as mine? What was I thinking, imagining he would love this soft old body, these sagging bosoms like cow teats, my big appalling bottom? These thoughts make up my misery. He spirals away from me and I can't blame him. I can't be angry with him. I can understand and feel shame for him for having loved me at all—ever.

I watch him dress out of the corner of my eye. I ask if he wants breakfast before work and he says No, he's late, he'll take a cup of coffee at the diner. He wears his dusty jeans from the day before, his unclean Lucky Tree Service shirt he pulls from a heap on the floor. He is still damp from his shower—I listen to him in the bathroom with a sinking heart—he usually bathes when he comes home in the afternoon, dirty from the trees, and rarely in the morning. The thought of his not bathing in the morning would cheer me, since I think of him out there among the world wearing the scent of me from our love nest, and I am happy to accompany him this way. But he has washed off the scent of me this morning, donned his dirty clothes reeking of yesterday's tree sap and smoke. His locks are leaking over his flannel shoulders.

He dresses, his face gathering shadows from the cave of our room. He throws items into his rucksack, grabs some stray fruit off the counter, a ball of soft cheese from the icebox, a tin of crackers. He refills the big canteen of water. He turns swiftly, brushes my cheek with the rough side of his finger, gently, a bit sadly, and heads out into the light. He holds the door for a second to keep it from slamming—this he has never done before.

There's a café across from Gallery Smallhorse on Bent Street and I push inside when it rains and sit at the window, a little recessed from view, and watch the goings and comings at the gallery. There isn't much. Indeed, the figures in my paintings pose sensuously for no one. The gallery door flashes open periodically, but I only spy Miss Smallhorse ensconced at her desk. She is occupied at typing and shuffling papers. Certainly no Akbar in the flesh. Still, I wait. The proprietor of the café, Mona, knows me by name and knows what I'm watching. She brings me a cup of black tea even if I forget to order one. She's a big lady, very short and wide, and moves with difficulty between the small tables, sometimes knocking to the floor with her ungainly hip a loose menu. Then she bends with enormous ceremony and laughs a little bit at herself, though I try to pick up the menu first. She asks me how's it going, Dolly, how's business, and have I sold some paintings? She leans in to shout in my ear, knowing I'm deaf—she can't remember which ear to shout into. I haven't got on my aid but I reply, just to be sociable, Yes, yes, it's going, and I *have*. And so sad about it? she persists, as she always does, out of kindness. I tell her that I don't like the rain which reminds me of bloody England I left forty years ago and don't plan to go back to—not ever, thank you. Mona gives a little indulgent nod. She's trying to sympathize, but she has no idea what I'm talking about. She lumbers away.

I'm the only one left in the town from the old days—me and Johnny Copper, that is. He's old but not even my age yet. But here he comes, of all people in Taos, there's Johnny, entering the café, setting off the little bell over the door, and looking *good*. He's very tan and scrawny—he shrank a lot, though he never was a big man, like Junior was—and nearly bald. He removes his hat, his skull mottled like the hide of a Guernsey cow. Wizened and lean—old men have the luck to be skinny like Johnny. For a second, just a second, it occurs to me to hide, but where can I hide myself? And in these bright polyesters? I'm nearly the only one in the café this morning, nursing my tea and feeling sorry for myself—feeling like crying—sad to death that I've lost my absolute last chance at finding a splinter of love in this lousy desert of a world. I sigh and watch Johnny and wait for him to distinguish me through his milky retinas. He does, ballyhooing so that Mona turns to look, grimacing at the effort. He plucks at my cheek with lips that don't quite make the target, then slides in next to me. Well, now I have to plug in my aid and my box.

By god, Doll, seeing you always snatches me a day out of my grave! cries he.

You're looking pretty good, Johnny.

Ha, for an old bag of bones!

I'm older, I say, which is true.

Are you now? Don't look a day over. . .

Seventy?

Nah. . . hey, what'cha doing here? You don't get out much from your place up the highway, do you?

I'm a homebody. A shut-in. But I've got a show across the street, Johnny. Have you seen it? I ask a little anxiously.

Not yet, Doll, I will, though, I *will*, and I'll write it up in *The Rattle*.

No, don't bother! These paintings. . . they're nothing like my ceremonials.

Oh yeah? More planes?

No more planes, Johnny, that was the Second World War! Those are gone, some teary-eyed lady in Nebraska bought those and carted them away—said they reminded her of her husband, a pilot. My planes in lovely flight—B-24s, Flying Fortresses, Lockheed bombers and Lightning planes, Douglas bombers—I loved watching those take off and land from the Albuquerque airport during the war. And I remember the woman came to my show in Santa Fe, wildly excited when she saw the planes, and wondered at the symbolism—well, the bloody war was going on! She wondered if *I* knew what I was doing. Can you imagine an artist being asked that?

Johnny shakes his head.—Moons, then, Doll? Won't you give us more moons? He adds tenderly, You had a passion for moons.

Ah Johnny.

Now the tears do come, and I swat at them angrily. Why did he have to go and say that? He cocks his head, and his trembling brown-speckled claw moves haltingly over to my side of the table and grips my hand. I sense in the fragile pulse the quavery ticking of his biblical heart. I smell the vinegar on his skin—he's been cleaning. He owns an old inn out on Paseo del Pueblo Norte, and since his partner died he does most of the work.

I shake my head reprovingly.—You know old people are supposed to forget things.

I don't forget. I remember writing those very words in *The Rattle.* For my first show.

That's it, Doll. All those moons! New moons, full moons, Indians wearing war bonnets and singing under crescent moons. Sad blue moons.

I painted them when I heard my mother had died. I painted them while remembering—everything—the war, our war, Johnny, the life out here, the ideal community we tried to build. . .

You're not still beating yourself up about it all, are you, Doll?

I don't know, Johnny. I still wonder whether any of it could have been helped. Did we realize how sick Abe was?

We didn't know about TB then, just that the lung disease would get you in the end. Some people gained more time, but you had to rest, and rest completely, and that wasn't Abe's way.

But the air here is salubrious, sacred, the finest—as fine as in the Alps. It should have cured him. He was on the mend.

Vera had it in for him.—Johnny adjusts his little round glasses. He says the name—*Vera*—which always sets me trembling a bit. The word still has that power over me.

Her spirit lingers here, I say.

What happened to those paintings, anyway? asks Johnny, when I grow thoughtful. He slurps shakily at his tea.—The moons?

Janie bought them. Lock, stock, and barrel, and took them all away, back to Italy with her and Beny—the next husband? With the money, I could afford to stay. I never saw those paintings again. I wrote to her, then to her husband, and he assured me they were in a gallery. I know they exist because I've seen them in books about me. But I'm not going to Italy at this point to find out, am I?

Johnny is having trouble bringing the hot cup to his lips. I'm afraid he's going to spill the contents over the table. I wonder if I should help, but I decide he won't care to have his muscular control questioned out of pride, so I look away, and watch the comings and goings of the gallery across the street. There still isn't much.

Johnny, I say, surprised how good it feels to talk: She was the one who summoned Doc Hams. She didn't want him to die.

He was furious, probably popped a pulmonary while screaming at her.

Abe hated doctors.

He was *afraid*—the doctor would have told him the truth. He was already a very sick man. A goner.

He was never afraid, Johnny.

He told you?

Yes, he asked me that summer what I would do without him there. Whether I could follow *her*.

Horrors, says Johnny.

We sip in silence. It's a companionable silence, made secure by years of having shared the same history. We're the last of it. It was our time—doesn't matter good or bad—just our time, when we lived our best and fullest, maybe our most daring, and it makes us happy to place our shared memory between us, testing its contours, fondling it, tweaking it into a recognizable shape.

Doll, you haven't told me what your new paintings are about. Johnny jerks his thumb in the direction of Gallery Smallhorse, where the prim, businesslike figure sits behind the front window.

Adult matter, Johnny. You're too young. What's that, son? Sugar you need? I'll call the waitress. Mona's a friend of mine.

Sometimes, after Junior washed his hair, he would sit before the fire in the Great House combing it out in long rivulets between his knees, his white sheet falling loosely over one shoulder, and he would groom himself like a woman. The Indian temperament is exquisitely calibrated between male and female so that a fine young body could appear either way—the bared torso of a young warrior had the lithe silhouette of a supple aspen tree. Also in the hands, as I liked to sketch them: the hands of these young men were brown and smooth, the fingers elegant, long, and narrow, while the women's hands were often coarsened from work, thick and calloused like white men's hands. The women grew disfigured by the work they did, bending and stooping, squatting and digging, so that by middle age they were unrecognizable from their early forms as lean, nimble trees that bent only for the wind. But the men ran—they ran and they threw and they rode horseback without saddles, and they grew hard and erect and unbending. I loved to watch Junior—yes, he was exotic to me, so magnificent in his height, his self-contained grace, and silent bearing, and also when he sat cross-legged by the fire in the Great House and combed his long black hair down in rivulets between his knees.

I had come to the Great House to meet Domingo so we could ride into town for provisions. We needed iodine for a flesh wound on Libertad, some corn meal, and sugar, and we had been instructed to tote a mattress belonging to Janie up Lobo Mountain to Kate's farmhouse because she didn't have a proper bed. It was still early when I arrived at Janie's ranch on the edge of town. The sun hadn't had a chance to warm the front rectangular courtyard where the tiered pigeon houses were perched like watchtowers on either corner and kept up a constant riot of birdsong. I tied Reggie up in the shade of a cottonwood, climbed the wooden steps, and entered the cool interior of the two-storey adobe. I slipped in, without knocking, and sat watching Junior for a while, who was drying his hair by the hearth in the main room. He greeted me with a nod—how can a man who doesn't speak seem more aloof than usual? By the resigned way he relaxed his head as he combed, first to one side, then the other, by his drifting gaze, by his singing sighs. He ceased when we heard Janie. She was speaking sharply in Spanish to her maid upstairs, then she descended, stolid, square, and pugnacious.

Doll, make yourself at home.

I was surprised to see her down so early. I knew she dined in bed, which accounted partly for my early arrival. I had hoped to be on my errand without having to encounter Janie, or even Junior, for that matter, whose secrets I kept uncovering without intending to. I felt I was invading his privacy. But Janie swooped down the stairs in a simple white short-sleeved dress, which she wore like a schoolgirl, and no makeup. Her face looked pinched and unhappy. She glared at Junior as she stood in the middle of the room, as if undecided where to sit or stand, and finally trailed into the dining room to give instructions to Rufina. And Junior, gathering his heavy, lovely hair, tossing it back so that it swung around his back, got up and followed her slowly. There was no way she could win an argument against this man.

I sensed the pressure of doors slamming and feet clattering over the kitchen tiles. A maid came running through the main room where I sat, then dashed out the front door. I detected voices I didn't recognize; perhaps there were other guests. Maybe there was shouting, but I didn't think that Junior would shout. More doors closing, and pounding of feet. I looked out the window and saw Junior, mounted on his stallion, galloping grandly across the hard earth, toward the reservation. The house fell silent.

Domingo appeared in the courtyard, head lowered, his face dark; he was leading Reggie. He moved quickly and said little. We hooked up the wagon with my horse tied to the back, and together we dragged out the mattress intended for Kate. We headed first into town, clattering along the road lined by scrub bushes, fruit trees, and precipitous gorges into neighbors' hedgerows. Beyond were the wild, aromatic undulations of the valley and the dominant mountains. The sun stepped higher in the sky.

Domingo, I shouted at last, seated up next to him, what's wrong with everyone today? I pulled out my trumpet and thrust it under his chin.

He snapped the reins against the horses' rumps and clucked his tongue. Glancing at the contraption I offered, he reared back with elbows flapping.

Not good, not good, lady, he replied miserably. Home is rough, very rough.

Your home? I asked. Is Rufina not well?

Terrible, terrible, he cried, turning pink in the neck. The wives have all cracked up!

Cracked up, really? What a curious expression to use, Domingo—did Abe teach you that? I laughed, then stopped at Domingo's dejected face.—Well, what's wrong with her exactly?

Domingo blushed and stammered.—In the bed, lady, he shouted, making sure I heard over the clop-clopping of the hooves, the rattle of the wagon. No action, very bad!

Oh, I see. And Janie and Junior—no action for them, either? I pointed behind me.

Junior is mad, and Janie is tired, Domingo signed in emphasis.—He hangs around, Janie not happy. She can't stay in bed all morning or Junior won't go away.

Mercy, Domingo.

The women make trouble, he said.

What do you think they want, Domingo?

Trouble.

They want better lives? I suggested.

We have good lives, said Domingo.

Yes, I agreed. I think so, too, but I don't have children, and big meals to make, and washing to do for a household, and gallons of water to haul on top of my head from the river.

You're not one of them, he told me darkly.

No. But I *am* a woman.

A woman without a man doesn't count.

Domingo! How *dare* you.

I stared at him. He faced forward, unflinching. I could have lifted my hat, my vilified hat, and swung it at him. But I had never struck anyone in my life, not even my loathsome brother Abel who teased me mercilessly, and I loved this gentle soul. Yet here he confessed what he thought of me truly.

We plotted along the knotty trail. I brooded and sank into myself. The day was poisoned for me: I couldn't stop wondering whether everyone here believed the same about me as Domingo did. What did I care, anyway? Abe valued me the way I was. But still I felt abject. We entered town and I swung down before the horses had halted fully in front of the grocer's. I had a list of items we needed; Abe and I had worked out the list together. I tore the list in half, and thrust the bottom half into Domingo's hand. The list of heavy items. I felt a delicious sense of malice as I handed him the foreign paper and watched him stare at it in confusion. I rushed away, calling orders.

I knew Domingo couldn't read.

The traders had set up early under the verandas of the Plaza. They arranged their wares on blankets spread over the ground— silver tools and jewelry, items of hand-carved wood, rope-soled shoes, blankets, beaded accessories, soap, pipes, trinkets. The traders lounged in the back along the wall, in the deep shade. They eyed me as I did the shopping. The women were absent today, and I felt conspicuous; I pulled my hat down around my ears. There was a trader I knew well by name, Sandor, who sold basket weave, and though I mostly dealt with his wife, she wasn't there, either. I needed a broom, since the rats had been sharpening their teeth on my old one, and I approached him. We greeted each other as per the custom, touching forehead, heart, and fingertips. Sandor was my age, maybe older, though it was hard to gauge these faces lined deeply by a lifetime of squinting against the sun, his eyes black, polished, and sharp. He asked me what I needed, and showed me the brooms he had, all solid but made for what seemed like midgets. I fingered them with a few sweeping motions, then asked Sandor after his wife—not sick I hoped? He shook his head and scowled.

Bah! He cried. She has her own ideas!

I gathered from his fulsome replies that she was home, and that all the other ladies had stayed home to do the washing this day, even though washing day was usually Saturday, and it was only Wednesday; they had all taken it into their heads to wash everything in their houses, splash the whole place down, and get rid of every lick and spittle of their men. This I gleaned more or less from the angry discussion of the traders, who pressed close to hear Sandor's tale of woe, feeling free to add details whenever they felt moved, by gesturing with expressive thrusts of their arms and miming the action. I understood nothing, and yet I grasped the whole story: The women had wrestled the blankets from the pallets in the morning, scenes of near battle the previous night, and some still encased with sleeping spouses, and they crammed baskets with whatever garments they could carry, hauled them down ladders from the pueblo, and headed toward the stream, hollering in loud gusty singing all the way, and dragging their children. There was an unnatural gaiety among them, intimated Sandor, like witches aiming to make mischief. The men's voices grew louder, almost menacing, and I sensed that they were truly unnerved. They believed a kind of collective madness had overtaken their women, and they were baffled. They were feeling more hurt and powerless than angry. But that would follow—as I sensed from Domingo, a gentle soul with a dark depth I hadn't fathomed. Their anger would surely follow.

I needed to find Abe.

Abe laughed.—A modern-day Lysistrata, that's what she thinks she is! She's banding the women together to save Greece against Spartan forces—she's going to force peace with Athens' neighbors by getting the wives of all the soldiers to renounce sex! They're storming the Acropolis to bar entrance by men. Well, then let her! He spoke mockingly, in disgust, and knocked back his hat to wipe his forehead with the side of his palm holding the knife. He sat in the sun at the side of the house, whittling.

Why? I asked. Why would she do this to us? We came here to keep peace, to live in harmony with the tribes. This is a dangerous precedent.

I squatted near him, resting my backside against the fence. I pawed at the dirt impatiently with my knife. I liked the smell of the fresh virgin pine he cut away. I watched his expert fingers as he whittled, fashioning the legs to a chair he was making for the kitchen. The designs were fanciful, like the floral detail on the headboard of the bed and mirror he had carved and painted for Vera as a kind of homecoming gift—coming *here*, to their exiled home. He held the wooden chair leg up for a moment, and I admired it. But his face contained a storm, his hat falling forward, casting his face in shadow.

The men in town—I began, cautiously. I wanted to tell him about what I had learned.

—Don't concern me, snapped Abe. They can attend to their own affairs—their own troublesome wives.

They blame her.

I blame her.

What will happen? I asked, before I could stop myself, because I had to know—Abe would know what to do.

Open yourself, Doll, was all he would say.

We were waiting for Vera, without admitting that we were waiting for her, for it was well past midday, our usual meal-time, and like all laborers we were creatures of habit. When she appeared, through the dark curtain of pine, I felt an absurd spasm of relief. She carried two heavy buckets of water, her straw hat askew, her strong, square shoulders straining from the effort. Abe glanced away quickly, but made no move to get up and help her—he never helped with hard tasks of burden, a kind of tacit admittance to his lack of ox-strength, which Vera had in abundance. I ran to help, relieving her of a bucket, sloshing some water over my boots. She hissed at me—how careless I was, and here she had come all this way from the stream without a spill! Miserably I followed her inside. We cast off our hats, scrubbed our hands in the sink, and silently laid the table. We ate leftover pea soup, the three of us, without having to speak, mopping up the broth with thick slices of bread, and drank the fresh water gratefully, and there were some new plums to suck on. We waited for the cuckoo to emerge. When the silence grew too much for me, I took up my hat, and, hoping they wouldn't notice, tiptoed toward the back door. But it was Vera who spoke sharply, breaking the spell:

Have you decided, then?

I turned, blankly.

Come, now, Doll. This we discussed. When Abe will come to you?

I froze.

This house is closed, she sneered. We won't sleep together again. And since I doubt you're going to join us women—are you, Doll?—since you won't make a move without him, without his consent, and always take his side, never against him, I assume you're with him and not us. Is that right, Doll?

I mumbled, and glanced at Abe, hoping for a sign. But he remained immovable and I couldn't read him.

Then he will come to you tonight and you can have a go at him.

Vera, that'll do, Abe lashed at her.

I bolted from the cabin.

A cover charge is written: fifty cents. Seems a bit steep to me, though Akbar has instructed me to tell the door attendant, Charlie, that I'm a friend.—A friend, I say, happy to be in New Mexico where people won't consider me the oldest person in the room, nor even the strangest looking, in my bright turban and polyester slacks, when everyone else at Stella's wears dungarees and has floppy hair. Charlie, who's an old cat, knows me, and he smiles. He sports a little goatee and hipster cap.

Sure, sure, Doll, he says. How ya doin'?

I wave and shrug. The music is loud—*mambo-jambo, wooo-wa-wooo-wa!* I hear the affected chirping of the DJ over the jukebox, who could be Akbar, though they all assume the same moondoggy slang over the microphone—*jungle music in the house!* There's no way to talk, and who can hear? A music club is a treat for a deaf person, since the vibrations are especially soothing. It's a bit like being back in the womb. Akbar loves that line, says he feels that way when he's jukeboxing at Stella's, smoking his fragrant cigarettes and swaying to the beat he's crazy about. *Cha cha*, he croons. *Mambo!* He sways with the upper part of his body, a sinuous, feminine movement of the shoulders, and dips his head almost coquettishly, down and around, so that his locks spill and tangle, then throws his head back, all the while moaning sweet strains. The thought of him moving to this music suddenly makes my knees rubbery. I look around for somewhere to sit—other than the beatnik lads there are a few geezers at the bar, men with long greying beards who've dragged themselves over the desert for a drink, on hands and knees most likely, and sleep outside with their burros. The rest of the place is nearly empty, and smells humid and boozy. I seek a table near the stage, though I have to pass the jukebox station, where Akbar is set up behind headphones; he can't see me at first, as he sashays to the beat, then he does see me, and he nods slowly, and even gives a shy, tentative smile.

Well, now, his look tells me he didn't expect me. Why should he have? I don't often make it into town, especially in the evening when I don't like to drive. I can hardly see to drive at night. But we have been to Stella's together; in the late afternoon we wandered to the bar after looking at rugs next door in the import-export market. He works Monday nights as a record spinner at Stella's and often drops in for a free beer where they know him. I knew to find him here. And I've missed him. My look tells him so. He smiles in his slow, dreamy way, sways his slim torso to the music. I sip at the pint of beer that Charlie's brought, the last of the gentlemen.

Akbar doesn't feel he's a good spinner unless people dance, and there's not a body on the dance floor, but I'm feeling too self-conscious; I haven't had enough beer yet. Akbar can't drink—that is, he can't hold his liquor and gets tipsy after a few sips. He's out of practice from being in the clinker. I keep at my pint for a while, filling the tank. But Akbar is speaking into the microphone, sweet garblings I can't make out. He's dedicating the next song to *our sister Doll*, and he puts on my favorite number—my favorite song because it's his favorite, too, "Hully Gully Baby," which he's played for me at my house and mouthed for me in private moments. When he loved me. Well, I laugh, and now I have to dance. I get up, and get moving. It's lonely out on the dance floor by myself; nobody fancies watching a dippy old dame in bright polyesters. My breasts flop and flop. No one's moved from the bar. But then Akbar joins me, comes out from behind his station shedding his earphones with a graceful decline of his long, tree-spiraling neck, and a secret, pleased smile. We move together. It's joyous, just the two of us—no, it's desire, Lord I know it now—we move closer and we touch. He brushes against the front of my blouse, maybe accidentally on purpose, a thrilling moment. Oh love, I will hold him, I'll hold him tight. I've lost everything I ever loved because I never went after it—never claimed it as my own. How *chinless*. I've shown a namby-pamby constitution, I've been a pushover all my life, which is almost over, let's be frank. So I hold his gaze for the last few seconds I've got, and I squeeze his hand, until the sweet song my dear boy dedicates to me ends.

When the drums sounded I saw how the animals stiffened and pricked up their ears. The cow raised her head, listening. The cat—Abe's cat, given by Kate—arrested while cleaning itself, one leg high in the air. The tribesmen were gathering that evening. The men beat the drums and by a collective summons we gathered at the fire pit. I came by habit, and only when I had sat next to Abe did I notice there were only men there. Abe passed the pipe and I took it. I was startled by the fierce coldness of the air—so early in the fall—and remembered Kate's ominous words: *It will be fall soon.* I sat close to the fire. I had thought to bring a blanket, and as the others came with the setting of the sun I watched the smooth hills recede softly one beyond the other, toward the vast distance.

I relished the huddle of warm bodies next to me. The whole sky held an expectant glow, ready to receive an annunciation, it seemed to me, while the valley beneath us spread open in descendant shades of blue. I wished I had thought to bring my sketchbook. I was always thinking in terms of how to render what I saw, afraid of losing something. But I heard in my head the words of my former teacher Marcus Willoughby, who had reminded me that the brain could retain infinite information, especially impressions made by the senses, and I wouldn't lose the memory. I shouldn't be afraid to lose it, he said—exile was often the place where the memory of these impressions emerged without interference, and most strongly.

Abe was speaking. He reminded us all of the reasons we had come to this desert land: The world we had retreated from was corrupt and rotten; the center had collapsed, and we the survivors, the refugees, were scattered. Abe launched into his jeremiad—Where could we go for a fresh start? We had come here, where you welcomed us, Abe said, indicating the seated assembly, and there was a murmur of assent. We found one another, he insisted, in his trusting tones, and we worked together and you welcomed us, all of you. And again a murmur of approval rippled among us, though these were only the men seated around me: their wives had refused to come.

And while you taught us how to survive in this harsh land, persisted Abe, we brought our arts to teach you, and some knowledge that was good from the old country, such as carpentry skills and animal husbandry.

We agreed that we had all learned from one another. I thought of Domingo, and our lessons at perspective, and the way Junior taught me to fish from horseback in his effortless way. I thought of Abe's unique sense of fashioning wood and Kate's pottery she had learned from the Pueblo women, and again I felt a communion and safety among the tribesmen, my friends. Then Abe resumed, and a shadow fell:

Friends, speak now and tell me what has come between us.

There was an awkward silence. No one wanted to speak. I pulled the blanket over my head, hoping it wasn't me, the lone woman, who hindered the men from speaking. But hadn't I learned I didn't matter? *A woman without a man*—no one took note of my presence at all.

Your woman, said a voice, and I recognized Sandor, the merchant of basket weave from the market.—She brings new ideas to our women. She brings seeds to sow, but not welcome this season. She's like Yellow Woman, she works at night.

There was laughter.—You mean Vera, said Abe, my wife? He threw his head back. Ha, ha! he cried, laughing with the others at the idea. But beneath their uneasy laughter there was seriousness, because the men had pondered Vera's role, her blondness, her connection to the kachina spirit, and they were uneasy.

Another voice, more strident: The Yellow Woman is trying to change our wives. She brings trouble.

It was a cry of betrayal—they were questioning Abe's authority. He listened quietly, sobered, saddened.

Don't blame the Red Fox, said another, he can't control his woman—can we control ours?

More laughter.

Friends, said Abe, cautioning reason. People—let us not speak of *control*. Of *power*. These are odious words from the old country: they lead to war. They don't apply to us. We share the burdens of work and communal living, and also the joys, the fruits. We share equally with our women. Our households run smoothly on an equitable division of labor. Each partner attends to what best suits him or her. Why is it upsetting to you that your wives act independently of you? Don't you act independently at times from your women? Is there not trust at the heart of your partnership with them?

They don't want us anymore, cried Sandor.

They don't want our children, intoned another.

Men, they can't bear children every year and stay healthy, retorted Abe. Can a field continue to yield the same crop every year?

They'll find another sire, came a voice.

Really? replied Abe, astonished and aggrieved.—How can that be? Can you believe your wives' hearts so fickle, so faithless?

I spied Junior in the fringes of the pine forest. He raised his hand from the folds of his blanket: *Peace*, he signed. *Peace, and go safe.* He wanted me to leave, but I didn't want to leave. Abe was counseling no action at all; he urged the men to ignore their women, to let it all pass over, as if it were a common household row, and surely they would come around and all would be the same as before. Ignore them, Abe said, attempting a lighter tone; women hate to be ignored! But the tribesmen disagreed. They were afraid to lose their women, afraid their wives would leave them, and find rivals. The men were insecure without their women. Standing with them gave the men strength, and now they felt weakened.

We want her gone from here, said the men, by common accord.

Abe appealed to them. We are one, she and I, he said. We came together.

I signed to Junior: *No. Don't make us leave!* And emphasized *us*—the outsiders, the refugees. Junior's impassive face flashed in the white heat of the fire. With a few strokes he indicated *Her* by the blondness of her hair, the curve of her shape.

Yellow Woman.

The old mother I recognize in the hardware store: fragile frame, proudly poised, slate-silver hair secured in a crisp bun. She wears a grey straight skirt and sensible shoes, a coat that is too big for her—maybe it once belonged to the doctor, her husband. She has nice legs, I notice, shapely calves clad in thick, flesh-colored hose. (Probably *stockings*—with hooks and garters and all that rubbish I never mastered as a proper lady.) Something contained and diffident about her reminds me of the Queen—the young toothy one, that is, who clutches her square little purse where her ancestors once held a scepter. She's getting keys made, Akbar's mother: she hands an old-fashioned turnkey imperiously to the hardware store clerk to be duplicated. Puzzled, he turns the old relic around and around in the palm of his large calloused hand. He is doubtful. Childs is a big man with fat, clumsy fingers from plastering walls all his life—as his side business, he must have plastered most of the adobe structures in this town. *What the hell?* he seems to say, but thinks of a more polite way. He tells Doña Feliz he doubts he has such a key to compare it to, then disappears into the back-room. I contemplate exiting without her noticing—residual cowardice, I entertain—but she might already be tracking my progress in the shop, might already have seen me; I can't tell by the stiffening of the folds of the man-sized coat. She has a birdlike profile. I think of Akbar with a stab—and I'm standing there just behind her, near the packages of rat poison so that when I speak to her she has to crane her neck in order to clear her chin over the collar of her coat.

Hello, Doña Feliz, I say.

Ah. She nods and blinks with a grimace of pain. And how are you, Miss Dolly? she asks, a little too loudly, with the familiar flare of her nostrils.

Can't complain. And yourself?

Fine, fine.

Childs the clerk returns. We are relieved. He tells her he'll try to match this key, but he won't promise anything. This is an old one! he cries, holding it out in his plaster-thickened hands, and she nods, she understands.

My sideboard is as old as me, she declares. It comes from the old country, from Spain. And solid, very solid. No one can break into this furniture! Only my son will have this key.

Then why make a duplicate? Childs asks, churlishly, but he doesn't get an answer. Doña Feliz blushes, holds out money, which Childs won't take.—Wait till I can find a way to duplicate this, he assures her. And she turns to go.

He'll lose it, says Doña Feliz, when we are outside in the light. I hold her elbow as we step through the parking lot. I have forgotten what I came for at the hardware store. I don't understand who she's talking about at first—who will lose it? The key, she insists, he'll lose the key. Everything of value I have in the sideboard. So I'm putting a copy in my safe deposit box, just in case.

She means Akbar. She moves slowly, lifting her face to the sun.

That's prudent, I tell her. One can never be too careful.

And that boy is careless! she cries.

Maybe a little, I reply vaguely, sadly.

She catches my tone. She asks suspiciously, Are you still seeing him?

Why not? I ask stiffly. I saw Akbar at Stella's the other night. He was working, I say proudly, but I don't add: *We danced.*

He is busy, she announces, collapsing inside her coat as she folds herself into her ancient car.—He is working very hard in his trees to make money for his future.

Yes, that's right, I tell her, slamming her door. *His future.* I lean into the crack left in the window before she can roll it up.

We're traveling, I shout.

Traveling? she echoes, alarmed.

Yes, we're going to travel and see the world. He hasn't told you? We'll go to England, we'll go to France, to Spain! The old country. All the places he's never seen, but has dreamed about visiting.

Where you never took him.

He never told me he wanted to travel, she insists.

Maybe you never asked him!

On a fine, fall morning we rode down Lobo Mountain to Kate's farmhouse. We carried sacks of provisions tied to our saddle-bags. Abe rode in the front, looking gloomy with his battered felt hat sunk over his brow, gazing down and not inclined to speak. He didn't spur on Libertad to plunge ahead and lose us, as he did when the three of us rode together and he was feeling competitive and show-offy. Vera came next, plodding on big-bellied Betty, her heavy legs flapping from the sides, and I pulled up the rear on Reggie, hanging back. I felt skittish near the two of them, who hardly spoke to each other, and if they happened to collide on any matter, such as hoisting Vera into the saddle, a row broke out, and she pushed him away when she suspected his tampering with her saddle. She lashed at him and Betty shied, moving sideways and nearly stepping on Vera, and another nasty argument ensued. I helped her remount and we set out in sour moods, though the light was clear this morning and very beautiful in the hills, and I was sorry that on such a day we had to start badly.

We smelled the fire before we saw the house—the smoke curled invitingly from the chimney. I was relieved at the sight, since I couldn't get over a feeling of dread whenever I approached that farmhouse down Lobo Mountain, wondering what we would come upon: what had Ralph been up to? But I was thinking of myself when I saw the smoke trickling from the chimney, making the air fragrant with the piñon I loved—I thought of having a cup of tea and warming my hands stiff from holding the reins. We tied our horses to the corral fence and unloosened the sacks from our saddlebags. With arms full of packages of tea and bacon and rice, Vera and Abe headed toward the house; I poked inside the barn. A scrim of flies hit me in the face. The place smelled vile. The two cows regarded me expectantly and groaned piteously. They needed to be milked, and I could only imagine the state of the horse stalls. Had the animals been fed? I yanked some hay from the cage, tossed it into the stalls, and shook out some feed for the chickens that were dashing at my heels. The pet dog appeared at the barn door and sat on his haunches, watching me with a frankly uninterested stare, and didn't utter a peep. Weren't dogs supposed to bark at strangers? But this wasn't a normal dog—it wasn't a normal house. I was filled with a chilling sense of foreboding about this place.

I joined the others in the kitchen, seated next to the wood stove, which Abe was feeding with a kind of frenzy. Ralph wore a scarf and was reading from a book of poems, rather theatrically, in his high, feminine voice—the poet was Rupert Brooke, who had died in the Great War. Vera was swaying to Ralph's singsong with its flat A's like the Midwestern prairie:

> I have known the most dear that is granted us here,
>   More supreme than the gods know above,
> Like a star I was hurled through the sweet of the world,
>   And the height and the light of it, Love.
> I have risen to the uttermost Heaven of Joy,
>   I have sunk to the sheer Hell of Pain—
> But—it's not going to happen again, my boy,
>   It's not going to happen again.

—He's marvelous, isn't he? remarked Ralph of the poet, and we all nodded at the enthusiasm of this handsome young man with his dark shy eyes that never met your own.—We published several of his poems in the literary review. And Brooke died so young, Ralph trailed off, making the odd rotating movement of his wrist.

Kate patted the heavy front of her apron grimed with clay from her pots.

He was barely a man, said Vera. Yet he had to fight for his country.

I never cared for the poet, said Abe.

Too earnest? Vera asked, poisonously. I should think his innocence would have interested you.

Ralph went on, ignoring them: *There shall be*, he intoned spontaneously from his book of Brooke's poetry, *in that rich earth a richer dust concealed. . .*

Our graves, noted Abe, bitterly. We'll all die under an English heaven, won't we? The sun never sets on an Englishman, even out here.

A dust whom England bore, shaped, made aware, continued Ralph, rather disconcertingly.

I think it *is* a richer dust out here, I ventured.

A body of England's, breathing English air, Ralph droned. *Washed by the rivers, blest by suns of home.*

What can you grow out here? asked Kate.

Bones, said Abe.

We laughed uneasily.

Well, yes, said Kate, in confusion.

He means metaphorically, I added, for her benefit.

Abe agreed heartily.—That's the spirit, Doll. Metaphorically. What do we grow, she asks? We grow ideas, don't we Doll? We grow paintings, works of art—they sprout up all over the desert!

Vera puffed out her elbows, making impatient, restless movements like a disgruntled hen. And babies, she added.

Ralph ceased reading and we became aware of an awkward silence within the dingy kitchen. Vera spanked her pockets for her pouch of tobacco and headed outside to roll a cigarette, and we stayed and drank Kate's weak tea. Then Ralph was gone, too, drifting out the door with his book of poetry and his scarf tied with a Bostonian elegance around his neck, and we three were suddenly alone. I shifted nervously, made to get up, but Abe threw me a look I couldn't decipher.

How is it with him? he asked Kate quietly. She gave a kind of despairing shrug. He went on, more gently: It's going to be increasingly hard to live out here by yourself, isolated, and with the baby coming, Kate—by December?—She nodded.—It will be cold and you will need someone to look after you.

I don't need anyone to look after me, she cried. Do you think I should go home to my mother? Back to *Boston*?

No, Kate, not unless you want to. But you need to be among people who can take care of you. You need to go stay with Janie for a while, until the baby comes.

With Janie! Oh I don't think she'd go for that.

I think she will, when I ask her.

Please don't ask her.

I'm surprised she hasn't thought of it first. She'll see the wisdom, and she has many people there who can attend to you.

When the time comes, Kate said, employing the ominous expression I heard her use before.

It's coming, said Abe. The first frost hit last night. The house is cold. What will you do for fuel, food? How can Ralph help you? We'll take the animals and care for them till spring. We'll close up the house.

But what about Ralph?

He'll go with you.

To Janie's?

To Janie's.

I was making wild eyes at Abe but he wouldn't see. What was he thinking? Had he spoken to Janie? Did he think Janie didn't know—could he be so blinkered about those around him? He lay his hand on Kate's arm and leveled his gaze sternly:

Please do this, he said. For the baby.

For whose baby—whose?

When he speaks of poetry he doesn't seem so daft, does he, Abe mused as we sewed. He inclined his body toward the flickering candle, so that his back made a perfect arc, his fingers stabbing at the wool fabric nimbly, balletically. The light shone golden red on his beard, lightening his eyes to a limpid blue. A hank of Celtic hair fell over his brow. His concentration was marvelous. His clothes smelled like hay and pine, as he had been whittling earlier in the waning afternoon light, finishing the chair legs. I leaned toward him, nearly falling forward, to catch the sound of his words, the scent of his clothes heated by the warm stove of my shed.

Doll? he turned his head suddenly, and spoke so quietly I felt only the vibration of his breath. I started, leaning back so that my feeble wooden chair creaked in complaint. I took up my own sorry sock with its uneven seam and I yanked at the thread.

What?

You're preoccupied.

Am I? I hate to sew. See, look at this mess I made.

He regarded the zigzagged seam, took it up, and sighed. With a quick glance at me that was not unkind, he pulled out the thread and began to resew it straight—perfect.

What's the point? I asked, peevishly. No one will see the bloody sock.

Aye, but it won't tear again this way.

Yes, perhaps he was right, I thought, as I watched him, his gently sloped back, the patient hands. Things straight and perfectly sewn can't rip or tear—they fit, and what fits perfectly can't break apart. Seams, bricks of clay stacked one on top of the other, shards of pottery reunited in absolute flawless fusion. Nature's puzzle pieces. Unsunderable. And bodies, too, I thought moodily, bodies fit together the way nature formed us, the perfect soldering of two bodies in the act of love—sex—bodies fashioned for this purpose. And Abe's body—slender, angular—did it fit more perfectly with Kate's tall, strong frame, or against Vera's fleshy corpulence?

He looked up and met my gaze. I recoiled abruptly.

Such mean thoughts tonight? he asked.

The state of that barn! I cried, looking away to locate the moon in either of the windows. There it was, hanging east and slightly off-kilter, framed between the cheap cotton chinz of my home-made curtains.—You wouldn't believe the stench! And those poor neglected cows. What are those people thinking?

They are casualties of this isolated land, Abe replied. There are plenty out here. We grow smaller and smaller against this gigantic backdrop until we believe we don't matter at all—that our actions don't, individually. And we either must perish or join a larger, stronger body—the collective. The Indians know this. It's the way they live. That's the beauty of the collective, Doll, working together to whip the elements that otherwise defeat us individually. There's no way to survive out here on your own. Men have tried, men have failed, colonies founded, vanished, gone mad, disappeared, been devoured by wild animals, destroyed resisting the established tribes. The Indians know from centuries how to live in one magnificent body, opening themselves to the land, the cycles of seasons, the unrelenting sun, adapting to the landscape's cruelties and beauty. The tribes allow each member his or her own strength.

With a sigh, Abe ceased, and returned to his sewing, his face closed.

After a while, he added: We'll herd Ralph's chattel here, let them graze in the fields with the others. We'll ring the necks of those mangy chickens. And Kate will be comfortable with Janie, don't you think? The servants will dote on her.

Abe, really, what can you be thinking? I asked. Janie will be furious to have to take on responsibility for her and her baby.

I watched him. Why couldn't he see, why couldn't he read my troubled gaze?

It will be taken care of, was all he said.

We sewed in silence. I brought out some hard cider I had found in town—Prohibition reigned in this childish country, so you couldn't readily buy the stuff, though the traders all made it at home, homespun aquavit from currants or junipers or whatnot they grew in their yards. We sipped from my little tea cups. Abe didn't seem inclined any longer to speak, and I wondered at his change of mood after his lecture on the collective body. Or was it the thought of Kate, or Kate's baby, that troubled him? Then he stretched his stiffened back like a cat, and stacked the mended items on the small table that served all purposes in my shed—socks, a scarf of Vera's, a pair of his underleggings that had been full of holes from constant washing—and he tidied up the sewing supplies, placed them back into the basket, and returned it to its place in my cupboard. He bent over the stove and examined the contents. He threw in another log and took up the candle, absently wiping the soft dripping wax off the candle's lips with his finger. And he turned to me at last and said:

May I sleep here, Doll?

I nodded, dumbly.

He went out and I blew out the candle. He walked to the privy. The moon through the window lent a brittle, ghostly glow to my little room. Quickly I undressed and threw on my flannel nightie and leaped under the frozen sheets, kicking and turning to warm the bed. Then I lay still and listened. I felt his footsteps rather than heard them. He reentered, gently pulled the door to, and sat in the chair to pull off his boots.—Doll? he called. Startled, I replied, Yes?—You're in bed, are ya? He spoke in his Midlands drawl, and I said, Yes, I'm warming up the bed, and he chuckled in his quiet way. Soon he had stripped to his underthings and climbed over the bed, and I threw open the covers and made room for him. He was a slight man, extremely thin. I knew well his bony contours from watching him swim—I had even spied on him when he was taking a bath in the tub on the porch during a hot afternoon. I was afraid to touch him. I was larger than Abe, in most places, and he reached for me and pulled me toward him so that my breasts were pressed against his chest. It was an odd sensation, crushing my breasts against him, and I was flooded by confusion, for how was I supposed to be with this man—like lovers, like brother and sister? Was I a sexual partner or was I a mate? Men of my acquaintance seemed more comfortable in my company fishing or sawing side by side—but how did *I* feel about it, and did anyone ever ask me? They did not.

What happened was this: I closed my eyes, and then I opened them. Abe began to undress me. He took hold of the hem of my nightie and pulled the grannyish thing firmly and purposefully over my head. And there I was, sitting up, all of me, as plain as the hot moon that beamed like a stage light through the window of my shed, lighting up my ghoulish skin. That's when I shut my eyes—and opened them to see that Abe was naked, too, devilishly disencumbered of his long johns. He was lovely and pale, his shoulders narrow, his chest hollowed, cavernous from his lung ailment; as he moved over me, his red beard itching my breasts, I saw how impossibly slender his hips—how much smaller he was than me! And his manhood (what could I call it?) a tender stalk of perfect willing whiteness. He kissed my lips—we'd never kissed this way, only chastely on the cheeks—and he found my tongue, which embarrassed me; I couldn't help it. I still inhabited myself, for a while at least, until we kissed some more and pressed together and the bed grew warmer, the moon shut out, the wood snapped in the stove, and I moved my arms eagerly around him. I grew a little bolder, and explored his frail, fish flesh, sensing with my fingers his soft and hard parts, and I even dared to stroke his buttocks and find his secret crevices—such was my innocence of men! He kissed me up and down. His eyes had a wicked sylvan gleam, and I felt a delicious heat spread over my sacred parts as I lay back, in expectation of what women enjoy most in the act of love, or so I had understood from Lorelei. He hovered over me as I nestled down in anticipation, moistly uncupped, and then he went still. I felt the cold air on my exposed skin. He had ceased moving.

I peeked down and saw that his manhood had fled between his knees. A surge of childish shame engulfed me. What had I done wrong? He seemed stricken, anguished, his chest suddenly racked by coughing. Then he fell onto his side and buried his head in my pillows with a groan.

The moon intruded mockingly and I became horribly aware of my nakedness. I groped for my nighttie and turned to face Abe, who was coughing fitfully. I pulled the covers over both of us and waited, hiding there. We didn't speak. Abe spent himself coughing for a very long while.

His voice woke me out of my light dozing.

I can't, he began.

It's your lung disease, I said.

Nay. Sexual intercourse, he lamented. I haven't been able to. . . perform. Vera misses it, won't let me hear the end of it, can't do without it, and she threatens me. But I *could* satisfy Vera. I could bring her pleasure in coitus, when I was healthy. For years we enjoyed each other. But I am still unable, Doll. . . I can't get over. . . oral stimulation of the female body. . .

How's that?

Cunnilingus.

I thought that's what you said.

I've tried.

You've had other women.

Never could do it. It's like returning to the wet, dark place of the womb. It terrifies me to put my mouth there, to smell and taste my mother, so to speak, and I end up fainting away in a kind primordial disgust.

How does Vera feel about being disgusting?

Doll, you're angry.

I'm. . . just disappointed, I ventured to assert, then felt ashamed for saying it.

I'm sorry to disappoint you.

No. I mean. . . you can't disappoint me, I decided, resorting to my stoic English rhetoric. We don't *fit*, I said simply.

Aye, Doll. I'm old.

You use your oldness like I use my deafness, Abe.

Aye.

We're the same age, I reminded him.

I'm failing, Doll. We are facing mighty opponents here. Least-ways the women! He turned over as his coughing subsided. He stared at the tin ceiling.—I feel already defeated, and by Vera, he added.

You can learn.

What can I learn?

To love, I said. *To love me*, I meant.

Aye.

To open yourself, I said, using his own words. I touched the hollow of his chest and felt him tremble.

I stand under the cottonwood and look up at the hole-ridden soles of his boots. Holes that tell the sorry tale of a life of low-wage labor and lower expectations. I've never presented myself in full view of his crew, who eye me with interest. They smile, they nod, they offer me tea from their thermoses. Strange bitter tea, maybe *funny tea*, I wonder as I sip politely and watch them unload machinery, haul ropes, and pace back and forth. These men are kind to me: I wonder for a moment if they think I'm Akbar's mother—have they met Akbar's mother? It's chilly this morning, the tea feels good and warm in my throat. There is a black-skinned man on the crew with a massively muscular build, Sisco, who speaks with a heavy accent.—Hunee, he says, this turban you vair like Africaan laadee, and he smiles at me with great shark-white teeth. He unloads the clunkety '57 truck and kicks it when it won't start. There's the ruined old roué Murphy, tall with long blonded hair incongruous on a man his age (I think, but who am I calling old? he can't be fifty), sadly thinned at the top: I've seen him at Stella's once or twice hitting on the younger girls to dance. He has a thick hillbilly accent I can't understand, and neither can Akbar, who nonetheless loves the old sweet guy and worries that he's always being jailed for public drunkenness. There's the owner of the crew, Lucky, who doesn't bother to show most mornings, as he stays up late smoking herbal cigarettes with his girlfriend—I've heard about him, too, a big shaggy glad hand who's always drumming on surfaces. But Akbar is the one they send into the trees because he's in his element there, shimmying up the trunk like a mountain cat, dangling by the thread of a swaying rope, humming and stretching his sore shoulders and catching the sunlight on his freckled face. He's never once considered the danger. He's high up, hooked, sawing elegantly, really glorious to behold; he throws me a dazzling smile I'm not sure how to interpret—happy to see me, after these weeks of his not being by? Pleased to show off in front of his crew? Trying to throw me off his nights' taking pleasure in another laadee's arms? The thought chokes me in sudden misery. But I'm firm at my task, and I wait till he comes down, after an hour or so. He stumbles on sea legs and I steady him with my arms.

Hello, boy.

Hey.

He brushes my cheek. Paint, says he.

And you, I say, and indicate his own dirt-smeared face. We smile at each other. We walk a bit.

Akbar, I tell him. We're taking a trip.

Hey sure.

When can you get away?

Take zee Saturday, says Sisco, helpfully, we no work zees weekend. He winks at me, and Abkar shrugs.

No money, says he.

We don't need money where we're going, I tell him.

Whar ya'll goin'? calls Murphy in his melodious drawl.

Paris, I shout. We're going to Paris.

The men applaud.

Instead, we drive across a late summer's desert that looks like Stonehenge. Akbar, it turns out, is afraid to fly. How can a man who lives in the trees be afraid to fly? I don't ask him, reluctant to conjure subjects that will elicit non sequiturs, or worse, references to his sadly deprived upbringing. I've emptied my bank account, filled up the car. He lets his hand rest on my thigh as I whale across the desert in my woodie. I want to cry with gratitude, but I don't—I scarcely look over at him, intent on driving with both hands, and I can't bother with my hearing aid. We don't need to speak; we never needed to speak. Dear boy, he distrusts speech as much as I do. We don't need to pursue the paintings hanging in the Smallhorse Gallery—he knows they're not selling, just attracting some interested shoppers—my, my, they ask, who is *that* fellow?—nor why I haven't seen him. I'm driving hellbent through the desert between great slabs of prehistoric boulders. He's amused by the way I drive, lets his chapped hands catch the static of my polyester trousers so that we spark together, and we laugh. Doesn't ask were I'm going, just *south*—doesn't ask how long it will take—*longtime*. It's going to be evening soon; the sun makes a lovely encrusted *couscousier* tumbling down the horizon, and I suddenly recall seeing such an enormous platter made of burnished, battered metal at the market years ago and marveling at its provenance—such portions! Akbar spreads his thighs, releasing the pressure in his dungareed crotch, and rests his hands between them, turned slightly in so that the fingers with their long blackened nails form two fans tilted toward each other. He drops his head back, letting his locks cascade languidly down my Naugahyde seat, and he's asleep. So he won't see me squinting at the road, since I can't see well at night. But I'll get there. I'll get us there—I have to.

It was the cold weather that began to unravel us. We were used to working in the outdoors, chopping wood for five hours at a stretch, repairing fences, running after the horses through the alfalfa fields. We painted long afternoons under a flawless azure sky. Then the cold drove us in and we were captured. By late fall there were storms bombarding the tin roofs with hail the size of mothballs. We thought of London during the war. We took refuge inside the horse shed and painted together. Like Marcus, Abe insisted the best painting was done by memory—you didn't need to gaze at your subject; the feeling was *here*, he said, rapping hard his hollow chest. I wasn't sure he was saying this to cheer me up—he had his strong opinions always. So we re-created on white canvas our jewel-bright skies and meandering horse trails dotted with incendiary wildflowers. We didn't last long in the shed, however, where there was no stove to heat our frozen fingers and soften the tubes of stiffened paint. Abe threw down his brush in disgust. The hail smacked the roof, the wind threatened to uproot the work of our seasoned hands. We cowered like poilus in our self-dug trench. By November the snows had buried the confident traces of our labored boot prints.

Vera resented our presence in her kitchen, when we tramped in to warm our fingers; she shooed us out whenever we were underfoot trying to rustle up some tea. She was missing her daughters, and feeling edgy and irritable; she wanted to have them come out and live with her. They were old enough now, she said, and their father would allow it. The university professor had written to her. But Abe refused to consider it, refused to discuss it, decreed that having her children here was out of the question. Did she think she could turn back the clock? Hadn't she made the inexorable step of leaving and did she imagine she could rewrite history? But Vera couldn't see this clearly, and fought Abe point by point, and held her own savagely. The arguments between them were terrible, the words murderous. She hated him, she told him so, hated him for ruining her life, ruining her children's lives. She wished she had never met him, never set eyes on him in the Heidelberg library fifteen years before.—And to think I actually believed you, she cried, hysterically, actually believed that a new life could begin with you! But you have destroyed me, destroyed my love!

She laughed, her hideous laugh that left my ears ringing. I switched off listening. I didn't care how cold it was outside—I fled, tumbling blindly through the icy moonlight. Any place was warmer than near her. Sometimes I took refuge in the barn with the animals. I pulled the milking stool next to Sylvie and lay my head against her warm, beating flanks and tried to think.

In the evening Vera gathered the women to her at Open Mouth of Bear. They came gladly, sharing their collective travails. They bundled against the cold and trudged the distance from the reservation, and some stayed the night outside in temporary wigwams. She gave them lessons in menstruation, conception, and birthing, and showed them diagrams on the mysterious workings of the woman's body. At the cabin she fed them soup and read from her Brüder Grimm collection. They pushed in at the door, eager to learn, dazed by the light, swathed in blankets and headscarves, some hauling babies, and Abe, by tacit agreement, slinked out into the shadows. He often appeared at the window of my shed, signaling with a small torch, and we would hike to the pit and make a fire. It was cold and raw these nights, and we felt unwelcome and alone. Sometimes the tribesmen who had been hunting came and sat with us in companionable silence. Or they stood and stamped their feet around the shed. They were grumbling about this and that, about their wayward wives, and sneaking glances up at the lighted cabin, reluctant to lay blame in front of Abe for what they considered their wives' desertion. Their women should be home. They should be fixed at the hearth, in the minds of their husbands, who needed an anchor, a place to go. The husbands were at sea without their women. The men's faces were hardening, I saw it; in my notebook I drew in charcoal the anxious faces wrapped in white sheets. Their graceful, feminine hands were never still. Maybe they would plan a hunt, a great scouting party as in the warrior days. But no, they hadn't the heart. And Junior wasn't there; he hadn't come from the Great House. Their spirits had dampened. I could see the men were waiting. They smoked and grumbled, watching the mighty mountain, then they went away.

If it were too cold, or snowing, Abe and I sat in my shed and pulled the thin curtains closed, which I hadn't done before, never having felt self-conscious until now, and we sewed for a spell or read about national politics from the week-old newspaper. The news made Abe snarl and sneer. He hated politics because it brought out men's venality, he said. People talk endlessly about politics because they can't talk about their own life! Talking about politics allows them to take a stand on something when in their own home they pull the covers over their head and won't get out of bed. They prefer to go through their life with their head stuck in the sand, he said. I wasn't sure anymore who Abe was talking about. Who was sticking their head in the sand? The people in the greater world—or us? Or did he mean the tribesmen? Abe was raging inwardly, two red blotches burned on his cheeks that I hadn't noticed before. He railed with glassy eyes and wrung his beautiful hands.

Ha! he cried. What are we afraid of facing? Is it really our wives at issue or is it ourselves?

At night we slept side by side and he seemed agitated, as if he couldn't get comfortable. We slept like sister and brother, in our long underthings, hardly touching, thankful, however, for the spreading warmth of each other's body in my cold little shed. Finally, he fell asleep on his back, and snored through his mouth; I wasn't bothered, in my deafness, just relieved that he had found a moment of peace. I shifted, carefully, and fell asleep, too.

I don't know which happened first: he got sick and we received news of the birth of Kate's baby. Domingo rode up Lobo Mountain to tell us the next day. He had hitched up his cab to ply through the snow—the sky was leaden and opaque, threatening heavy precipitation. I think he imagined he would take all of us back with him; maybe those were the orders. I emerged quickly from the cabin, pulling my blanket close.

Very hard, he gestured to me.—Lady in much pain.

And the baby? I asked anxiously

Baby girl is perfect. Big girl, mumbled Domingo, embarrassed. Hungry and—he stopped with a pained, anguished expression.

What?

He made the sign for *black*.

Black?

Much black hair.

Oh. That's nice, I offered.

No, no, Janie is angry, very angry. Brown baby no good. She send for Vera. Vera must come. See, I bring the cab for her.

And. . . Junior? I asked, watching him carefully.

Junior take off. Junior gone to reservation with our tribesmen.

Why? I asked.

Janie very angry, he repeated.

Vera was ready to leave. She had expected Domingo. She came out onto the porch hauling her satchel from the old country. She wore her woolens and bonnet and glanced up dubiously at the blanched sky, pulling on the grey gloves with the red piping we had darned the previous evening. Abe must have left them out for her to wear—I felt a tug at the tenderness of the thought. He was nowhere to be seen; he must be hunting down Sylvie through the frozen fields or fetching water from the still-trickling stream. Heavily, Vera climbed up next to Domingo and pulled out her tobacco pouch. They lurched into motion. I watched the wagon rumble down the slope, wreathed in Vera's smoke.

Later I swept out the stable and picked the horses' hooves, a delicate operation Abe had taught me to do, though I didn't like to because the horses wanted to step on me. Near nightfall, just as the snow resumed its gentle, relentless accumulation, he appeared. He was chewing on a piece of hay, his face utterly pale, washed out against the frosted background, save for the two troubling red blotches on his cheeks. He looked worn out and half frozen. He had been down to Kate's farmhouse, he said. He had been reading poetry.

Reading Ralph's poetry? I asked, incredulously. Had he imperiled his health by hiking the mountain in this frigid weather?

He is a beautiful writer, Abe said. I didn't know.

Kate always said so.

He has a passionate soul. And he loves her very much.

I never doubted it.

We need to prepare our dinner, he said, and stiffly turned toward the cabin.

The baby! I called, almost forgetting. Kate's had a baby girl.

Aye. He nodded as if he already knew, setting through the drifts briskly without turning around. By evening he was in bed, coughing up blood.

He sleeps as I drive through the bum of Arizona—never cared for the state, the way they try to tame the landscape, digging up the dirt for irrigation in order to make it look like some place back East, with green lawns and deciduous trees and such nonsense, and I'm glad it's dark as I'm sieved through an immigration point at Nogales. I give the officials ancient papers I have unsheathed and a bit of a bribe to keep them from asking too many questions about my sleeping navigator. He wakes in the middle of the Sonoran Desert—Desierto Sonorense—and then it's too late to stop anywhere in civilization, or rather too early in the morning. There's nothing around but wildflowers sparkling like moon gems in the sand and Daliesque sand sculptures beckoning spectrally— I snicker to myself at this strange country I've brought us to, my secret little joke, but Akbar is stirring, yawning, and stretching. He wonders, what makes me laugh?

Oz—O-Z, I spell it for him: this place reminds me of the scene in the movie when Dorothy comes upon a field of poppies and they all start yawning and falling asleep. You know it, don't you? I ask, suddenly unsure how old the boy is—but now I'm yawning, too, at the thought of sleep, my eyes watering so that I can't make out the road. I forget I'm an old lady and need my rest.

Need to stop, says Akbar, and through his coils of hair I glimpse the first crimson rays of sunrise. He takes a long swallow from his oversized tank filled with electrolyte water. I pull off onto a dirt road that seems fairly level, in full view of mesas but providing little shelter for us. There isn't much else for miles and miles. The woodie rattles to an exhausted stop. The air buzzes dustily and we sit unmoving, stunned by the silence.

Mexico, says Akbar.

I nod. He grins and gets out to relieve himself. He disappears around the back of the woodie, and I feel the hatch open.

He's rooting around in the back. I'm too tired to see what he's up to; I lean my head back and feel myself sinking into the swelling of space that invades the car with the motor shut off, filling my ears. I feel the first warm surge of sunlight on my skin. My limbs are made of great weights, and it's not unpleasant to release them. Then I feel myself being lifted gently out of the car, and guided through the exquisite scent of mesquite. Akbar navigates me into the back of the woodie. The junk I normally keep there has been cleared away; how he managed I haven't a clue, and can't possibly think about now. I'm comfortably laid flat on soft blankets Akbar has spread for me, has thought to bring. For us—he's making room to stretch himself next to me. He crosses his arms behind his head for a pillow. He says, *Mexico*, contemplating the word. I scoot a little next to him. I feel safe like this, watched over. The air is delicious. Then he sniffs and drapes his arm over my face, adding a shadow, before gingerly, gently, stroking my head. The turban has dislodged and my white hair springs free. He strokes my aching scalp with his fingers.

Mexico, he says, marveling.

I rode down the mountain to get the powder he needed to soften his cough. He said he couldn't breathe. His fitful coughing frightened me, the gobs of black blood he spit up horrified me, and I needed to get help. I would ride down the mountain, because Abe was suffering, in bed with a cough he couldn't stop, and I was frightened. He didn't want me to go, he said the fit would stop, it always stopped, but I couldn't stay there and watch and do nothing. He was retching violently, exhausting himself. His face had assumed the slick pallor of the moribund. He was going to die. I assured him I would tell only Janie and she would give me medicine. Janie was the one who had medical supplies. And a motorcar. He didn't want the doctor there. Doc Hams was meddlesome, he said, don't go to the doctor! I said I wouldn't, but I would get medicine from Janie.—And don't say a word to Vera, he scolded me, heaving over the side of the bed, spitting black bile into the spittoon.

Yes, all right, I muttered, and stuffed another log in the stove. It was late evening already: I would be leaving him for the night before I—before anyone—could return. Was this wise? Should I stay in case he needed me? In case he coughed himself unconscious and fell out of bed—the room grown icy and still? For even the creatures hibernating secretly within the cabin's foundation wouldn't come near him. Would he freeze to death? What—*what* should I do? And while I paced and pulled on layers of woolen clothing, he coughed, ceaselessly, wretchedly, heaving up what sounded like his very lungs—what was the wisest course of action? I couldn't stay and listen to his death rattle (this decided me), so I grabbed some provisions and plunged into the night. It was cold but still: the snow had ceased falling. I saddled up Libertad, who was the swiftest horse we had, surest on the dark snowy ground, and hearty in the cold. He gazed at me with startled, nervous eyes. I tightened the girth, and I sensed his keen intelligence, his questioning look. Where is my master? his eyes seemed to ask. I quieted him, and stroked him, securing the bridle and bit, and we set out, with only the moon, at nearly full mast, to guide us. I pulled the blanket over my face, set to the biting wind. And with a quick glance back at the cabin—one feeble light shone in the bedroom window—I directed Abe's horse down the trail.

I urged him as fast as I dared—but what a beautiful night! The pine forest, engulfed by the recent snow, seemed to be holding its breath, the spindly branches like lacy sleeves beckoning to us bewitchingly. We were caught under the moonlight in a place of mystery and silence. The forest appeared like a room full of characters in pantomime who had abruptly frozen, in seductive poses, hushed and waiting, until the cue was given to breathe again. But the stillness was a ruse, because as soon as we moved on, and the hoofbeats of my horse were swallowed by the snow-padded tracks, the branches would resume their swooning dance, and the place would come alive. I looked back, with a wild pattering of my heart, to see what I could see: I knew then that trees *do* dance before the moon. I would paint it.

I hurried down the mountain because I was afraid. Over and over in my head I rehearsed the entry I would make at Janie's Great

House, and the careful wording of my pronouncement: Abe needed powder and would they drive back with me up to the cabin? But there would be alarm, surely, and questions, and how would I downplay the seriousness of Abe's condition? Would Junior help me secretly? Could he drive me back? But then I remembered that Junior was at the reservation. On and on through the dark snowy paths we trod, Abe's horse and I, and I justified the journey a thousand times in a thousand different ways, shaking out my stiffened fingers, and answering owl calls through the canyon, to keep up our courage. Except that all the raveling threads of my guilty thoughts wound at the same knot—*Vera*. Vera was there at Janie's house and Vera would know what to do.

But I didn't tell Vera, not exactly, and by holding back the gravity of Abe's condition I felt I was being loyal to him—and also hastening his decline. I rode into the Great House's courtyard in the wee hours of the morning, the delicate hour just before the edge of sky began to pale. The pigeons were silent, watchful in their houses. I was rigid with cold. A dog barked from somewhere inside—one of Janie's bull terriers—and I dismounted and led Libertad to the stable. He was trembling with exhaustion and I bedded him next to Vera's Betty, his companion he was happy to see; he whinnied a little, and I brushed him off and gave him some water and oats. There was a faint light in the downstairs window when I approached the house. Domingo's wife, Rufina, came out, carrying a candle. She pulled a blanket over her shoulders, her long black hair swaying loose, catching the clear light of the moon. I gestured in greeting, touching my hand to my heart. Then she recognized me, gaped at my sudden wild appearance at this ungodly hour. Her black eyes grew wider when I told her in a creaking voice that I needed to see Janie.

She dashed inside. I went after her. The fire in the great hearth had been allowed to die out. I kicked it up and blew at the embers, trying to warm my hands. A little flame blazed out and I nearly wept in relief, peeling off the layers frozen against my skin.

Doll? Janie appeared after a long while, waiflike in her dazzling white nightgown. She was appalled at my frozen condition, her face drawn, closed in sleep.

Is it Abe? she asked instantly.

I nodded. He needs medicine, I told her, working the muscles of my face with difficulty. Some powder to soften the cough. He'll be fine with medicine, I said evasively. It was strange to hear the sound of my own voice.

In the middle of the night?

He told me to come. . .

Damn it, Doll, would you tell me what's happening?

He's coughing, I declared flatly. He needs medicine to ease the lungs.

She turned and scampered with surprising sprightliness up the stairs, her white gown billowing behind her. After a few moments she reappeared with a box of vials and needles—I recognized the stuff because Abe had used injections before. Janie snapped a word to Rufina, who hovered anxiously, holding up her candle. She would fetch Domingo to ready the motorcar.

Doll, Janie said, turning to me, businesslike now. Do you know how to inject this?

I stared at her. And then behind her, Vera appeared, descending the staircase like a vengeful ghost. Janie scowled, then turned quickly to see what I was looking at.

Vera stopped at the base of the stairs.

Doll, said Janie, brusquely, turning back.—Do you?

I doubt it, came Vera's deep reply. You've got to give it in the bum.

I can do it, I said.

It's written by weight, said Vera. He doesn't weigh much. If you give him too much, you'll kill him.

All right, Vera, said Janie, resigned, tired.—Did you hear? she asked me.

I nodded. Then Vera called, more urgently, in her husky accented English: Is there blood? Should I come?

He's coughing, I muttered, wresting the box from Janie.

I glimpsed the flashing of headlights ricochet off the white-washed walls—Domingo was turning the automobile around. He was there, ready for me. I could fly back up the mountain with medicine for Abe. I could get back in a fraction of the time it took to get here.

I'll come, said Janie, as I made for the door.

I held up my hand. No. *He doesn't want any of you*, I wanted to tell them. I can do it, I repeated, more loudly, I can take care of him!

They followed me out. I'll come, they each insisted, as I climbed into the motorcar next to Domingo.

No, I said, he doesn't want anyone.

I signaled to Domingo fiercely. The women didn't stop us. We found the road with difficulty. I noted the lightening of the sky. And I realized I hadn't seen Junior—neither Kate nor the baby—hadn't felt them here. He was gone. He had taken her to the reservation. I felt certain of it. The realization weighed heavily on my already despairing mood. I carried back up Lobo Mountain the medicine box and Vera's parting words: *If you give him too much, you'll kill him.*

It appears that death is following us through the Mexican villages. From town to town we run into funerals: processions of somber townspeople wending through the dusty streets toward the parish cemetery. We inch the woodie along and have to stop for the desultory cortège. We watch the people carrying the casket—in one village, a tiny coffin of a child. We witness the terrible grief of the family, heads downcast and faces ashen and set as gravestone. The women cover their heads and mouths with black lace shawls. Our woodie does not elicit interest in these places. The townspeople are isolated in their collective misery, and unreachable. No one bothers with us, no one notices the gringos passing through, on their way elsewhere, reluctant witnesses. And yet we aren't—reluctant, that is. We have nowhere we have to be. We observe this spectacle of grief almost lovingly. Akbar becomes thoughtful, and speaks of his father, the doctor. I don't recall Akbar's speaking of his father before. Rather, he speaks of the absence of his father, which he felt acutely as a child. The father was away, the father had important business attending to sick patients, the father was constantly removed from the presence of the family. And so he became for the son a kind of idol, a superhero in his absence, which Akbar filled up with amazing feats on the part of the doctor. My father saved armies of soldiers fighting the Americans, Akbar tells me. My father saved people from burning buildings, airplanes, car wrecks, that sort of thing. I nod and sketch the procession of mourners.

Never knew my father, Akbar says. And now he's gone.

It's a pity he never knew *you*, I tell him.

You look at it that way, considers Akbar, leaning over the steering wheel as we stop for the sadly meandering procession. The townspeople file into the churchyard, the little pine coffin carried aloft, wreathed in flowers.—You are a painter. You look at different angles. But he don't like my hair, my friends, my grades in school, always at me, *cha cha cha.*

A shame, I say, wondering that my boy doesn't blame his mother. Abe always used to say that a son was rarely kind to his mother.—Parents are looking out for your survival in the big world. They want you to have success, I tell Akbar, not entirely comfortable with this conversation that brings me too near the generation of his father and mother—also my own. They want you to have *power*, I tell Akbar. I stepped out of my own family and lost a kind of power myself. I didn't marry someone of my class; I was an aristocrat, you know. I moved here to become an artist. Maybe your father didn't think you could be a doctor with long hair—a doctor like him.

Akbar can't be a doctor, he mutters darkly. Akbar climbs trees. Akbar can't heal nobody. Can't heal Akbar.

I love that you climb trees, I assure him. I knew he wouldn't be impressed at my aristocrat remark.

And you paint pictures, he says.

I feel my face prickle: I think of the pictures of him hanging alone and unprotected in the Smallhorse Gallery.

Oh darling boy, you're not mad about the pictures?
Nay, nay.
I did them in love.
I know, Doll baby, he says, and sighs.

We drive on through the desert and sense a change in the earth. Day has broken brightly upon the sand. The lay of the earth itself shifts, bent at the edges, as if the land is an iron bar that a great titan pulls down at the ends by his massive strength, making the center bulge somewhat and stand out. We stare ahead, a little uneasy, eager for what we will see, what will come next over the horizon. Akbar takes the wheel; he drives distractively, one arm dangling out the open window, scattering his coils to the wind. He sings to the meringue tunes we pick up on the Mexican radio. He has a sweet, high voice when he sings, and he moves his shoulders side to side in his seductive sashaying motion that thrills me so. Then he dons sunglasses and sits up a bit, gazing forward as we round bend after bend. The tires screech when he takes a turn at speed, the woodie's big back end swinging out into the meridian. Strange new birds career overhead. What are they? Akbar doesn't know. We scan the rocky vista; we sniff the air expectantly. The familiar salt odor precipitates a kind of tingling in my joints. I find myself salivating, hyperventilating in my seat. It occurs to me that I will have a heart attack from the change in air pressure, out here, at the edge of the Sonoran Desert, and Akbar will have to revive me. I imagine him giving me mouth-to-mouth resuscitation, pounding on my chest. I glance over proudly at my hero, who is sweating, scratching in his ear. He stares straight on. And then the earth plunges, my stomach collapses, and I gasp—the road opens up and there, before us, gleaming wondrously in emerald Technicolor—is the sea.

We shout together. Akbar yanks at the wheel, pulling over wildly, bumping out of control over the uneven dunes. His coils are tossed every which way. The car halts, he has to get out. The driver's door swings open, he falls out, and sinks to his knees. I run to fetch the tank of electrolyte water and hold his head in my lap. We cling to each other on a lip of tufted grass and peer down with vertigo at the white-crested waves breaking over the rocky beach below. Great jagged cliffs line the shore, skirted by the narrow highway. The place is deserted save for the brisk little sand scavengers bravely breasting the hard salt breeze. Farther out I spot a cluster of shrimp boats. The air is moist on our cheeks— I lift up my face to the wind and feel like a girl again. A girl in England! I used to play every summer on the Scottish coast at our country house, Dunwoodie. Has it been this long since I've seen the sea, half my lifetime? Crossing the Atlantic Ocean that dangerous spring with Abe was my last true glimpse. Yet how different this Sea of Cortez—the color of a swimming pool, benign enough for the fragile-looking fishing boats, nearly tame—nothing like the turbulent waters that vomited me upon the American shore.

Akbar, I declare, I was born on an island!

I regret we haven't studied an atlas together, and examined the lay of England. I've never shown him where I came from. I wonder if he will ask me. I rock him in my lap, lift his sunglasses gently away from his nose. His eyes are as translucent as the sea. He bats his lashes against the light. He is smiling

Why, he wonders, did you never have children?

Me? Ah boy. And I begin to laugh.—Children? Does the sea make you think of having children? Here the sea reminds me of my childhood back in England, and you're thinking about children, too!

Yes, many many children, he says. The sea is full with children.

Oh, my love!

Is he thinking of the funeral of the Mexican child? Is he thinking about the child I can't give him? Of course, I think, relishing the salt spray on my face and the sense of the massive water pressure pounding against the shore. My dear boy has brought me full circle from childhood to old age, and how I love him for it. What can I give him back, if not a child? How can I give him life, as he has given me? *Too late, too late,* the seabirds cry. *Oh lo lo lo.* And here the happiest moment of my life becomes the saddest.

I took one look at his slick-white skin against the bloodied bed-clothes and shrieked. He was drenched in spewed blood, lying halfway off the bed, and the cabin was very cold. Yet he stirred, opened his eyes in their dark sockets like purple bruises, gave the barest of smiles. Abe was alive when I returned with Domingo. Left alone any longer, he would surely have died. He looked like a specter, a ghastly jack-o'-lantern, and I covered my mouth in horror. Domingo set to work firing the stove, warming the room. In a pot on the stove he heated a bit of broth he had brought from Janie's kitchen. He carried it to the bed and we sat Abe up, changed his soiled clothes, and wiped the encrusted blood from his face and matted hair. I tried to spoon the broth into Abe's mouth, but spilled it, my hands shaking. Abe's chest convulsed intermittently; he was exhausted from coughing. Domingo took over. We huddled at the bedside.

The box, Domingo motioned at me with the spoon.

I pulled out the box of medicines and sat next to the bed and proceeded to read the weight instructions. Abe, reviving with the broth at his lips, coached me.

How much do you weigh? I asked.

Ten stone, he replied, the small, grim smile hovering at the corners of his mouth.

Ten? But that's how much I weigh, and that was back in the summer when we were eating chicken and lots of eggs and Vera made sachertorte. Abe, how much truly? You've wasted away. And what is that in pounds? It says here. . .

Stop the namby-pamby, fer chrisssakes. . . Just give me bloody vial-full, that's what Vera does.

But if I give you too much. . .

Vera hasn't killed me yet, has she? And not for lack of trying.

He instructed me on how to sterilize the needle, fill it with the liquid, knock out the air bubbles. He pointed spectrally to his hip and we pushed him over gently. Domingo swathed the delicate, nearly transparent skin of Abe's thigh with a cloth doused with some brandy and I shot the sick man, clumsily—it took a couple of stabs.

Ow, said Abe.

Sorry. I make a lousy nurse, don't I? My father always said so.

Nurse, hell, he murmured, lying back, his muscles beginning to relax. My angel. . .

He swooned away. Was he dying, then? I stood up, alarmed by the transformation of his features as the drug took over—he appeared nearly blissful. I paced about the bed out of my mind with fear, but Domingo, my knowing friend, tapped my arm and reassured me. He indicated the gentle rise and fall of the sick man's chest, and put his face close to Abe's mouth to feel the barest pressure of his breath. What if I had killed him? I wondered over and over, seated beside him for the rest of the morning, fretting and muttering to myself until I was displaced by Doc Hams, who blew as if by magic into the room, a rotund, whiskered presence in a grey woolen greatcoat. I was relieved to see him, and moved tearfully to shake his meaty hand, when I saw that he had Vera in tow. She removed her bonnet, placed it on the chest of drawers.

A massive hemorrhage, announced the provincial doctor, after a quick peep at the patient under the sheets. This man is very ill. Pulmonary tuberculosis, I have no doubt. Surely you've known?

Vera pursed her lips sternly. She seated herself where I had been sitting and took over with barely a bump in succession. She resumed her knitting as if she had only just put it down, her handsome broad brow furrowed in a study of classical gravity. As if she had never left his side. The couple had known of Abe's condition without allowing it to be mentioned.

The fool, she said, referring to no one, or to each of us—me probably. Doc Hams simply frowned in displeasure at the folly of us mortals.

I felt moved to speak in Abe's defense.—He'll be mad you're here, I said to Doc, and it sounded like a child's warning.

What! cried Doc Hams. He should be in a sanitarium.

He'll be furious, I pursued, angry at the country doctor's arrogance.

How can a man who speaks the truth about others be so utterly unwilling to be enlightened about his own precarious physical condition?

Exact, said Vera. She nodded at Doc Hams.

He closed his bag with a final snap, gathered up his greatcloak.

When he is strong enough to be moved, he must go where it is warm, said Doc Hams.

But the mountain air is good for him, surely? I began.

The winter in this drafty cabin will kill him.

I served Doc Hams two cups of tea. There were sweet buns from Janie's, a little stiff, but we had no butter or jam to offer. Doc Hams smacked as he ate, and wiped his whiskers. And without another glance at the patient, he departed with Domingo, satisfied that he and Vera were in medical collusion. I closed the door firmly behind them. I knew the news would travel fast. Indeed, in a few days the tribesmen got wind of Abe's condition. They heard he was dying. They didn't blame me, as they should have. They didn't blame Abe, the sick man. They blamed Vera—for casting a spell on Abe, for being absent in a moment of crisis. They blamed the Yellow Woman.

I imagined we could have made it through the winter, left to ourselves. I sat next to the sick bed of my cherished mentor and sketched nervously, restlessly. Abe lay in bed, propped up with lumpy pillows, and read his musty Puritan tomes. Mostly, he vituperated. He was very pale, his frame grown thinner so that the linen nightshirt hung dejectedly, but his chronic coughing had subsided for the most part, thanks to the nightly injections—he detested the sluggishness the drug imparted during the daytime—and he was sleeping better. Vera cared for him with a rough-handed solicitude, in the morning and evening, and cooked amid a fiendish clatter, scattering even the hungry cats in her way. During the day she was out, administering to the women of the reservation, and when I saw her ride off in the back of Domingo's cab, I could sneak back into the cabin without having to whistle my arrival and incur her wrath. Abe wasn't allowed to shout or grow red in the face—Doc Hams's orders—but he argued just the same—with his books and with Vera and with me, and then with the occasional visitor, such as Kate and her infant as brown as a forest nut, and a few of the tribesmen such as Sandor, the trader of basket weave. He brought with him magical herbs the *bruja* had ground for the sick man's recovery, and which Vera instantly threw in the rubbish bin when he had left. I knew Abe was truly better, and I sat with him and sketched in my red notebook. I was planning large projects for the spring, desperately looking forward, hoping the winter would slip by and no one would notice that Abe hadn't packed up to leave for warmer climes. He would stay right here with me.

Abe let his book fall on its spine in his lap.—We have forgotten our errand into this wilderness, he declared. What was it? What were we trying to find by coming here? To find riches? The fountain of eternal youth?

No, I answered dutifully. We renounced all that back in the old country.

We did. We had riches, we had comfort, and we turned away. What a corrupt society! The war polluted our origins, our homes, made a laughingstock of what we used to call national heritage and culture. But what have we found here? We sought health—alas, Doll, I have not found health.

We found *light*, I shouted, tapping my pencil against the sketchbook.

Aye, we have. Please don't shout at me, Doll. He sighed. He spoke quietly.—Yes, we have found creation, and put it to good use. But community, Doll? Didn't we come to share a unity of spirit with the natives, the tribesmen, who have been the brave stewards of this land for centuries and who've invited us to partake of its fruits with them? Have we not tried to forge a covenant with them, with the land, the Sacred Mountain? Our community, Doll; we had community, and it's broken apart.

He would argue with himself, and grow bitter and remote. Then Junior arrived, as if sensing just where this jeremiad about community was leading.

He filled the threshold, his blanket slung over his broad shoulders, his long black braids wrapped neatly to the tips. He touched his forehead, then chest, in greeting. We did the same. He waited, and Abe beckoned him to the bedside with a spindly hand. Junior sat in the chair I pulled up for him, a dainty blue chair whose legs Abe had painstakingly and ornately carved months before. Junior looked stiff and unhappy. He was clearly on a mission, having come when Vera was out of the house; I suddenly ached for the easy confidence we had shared while fishing away the afternoons in Laughing Waters. We hadn't needed to speak to understand each other. But now I had to hear him, and thrust out my trumpet in front of him on the bed.

I thank you for coming, said Abe.

Red Fox must get well.

I imagine what brings you, said Abe. And I'm sorry.

Junior nodded forlornly.

Sickness, he murmured, is bad.

Sometimes unavoidable, agreed Abe. But medicine helps.

We drive out sickness, said Junior.

Do you? How will you drive out my sickness? Or do you mean that you will drive me out, as old Doc Hams says? He laughed, though the sound was dry and forced.

No, said Junior. Not you. You didn't bring sickness.

Yes, Junior. I must have brought it with me from the old country. I carry the white man's sickness from the old country.

No, insisted Junior. Not the Red Fox. You light the way. We don't drive you out. Just the sickness.

All right. How does it work? In the kiva? You bring a medicine man, or do I go to him?

We take her.

Her?

Abe glanced at me, his eyebrows hiking up.

Junior shook his head slowly.—We take her out. And the sickness departs.

Her? said Abe, frowning. Out?—Not, surely—Junior, what are you saying!

Yellow Woman. We take her to Sacred Mountain. She is our sacrifice to sickness. And then the tribe is cleansed. The snows pull back. The sickness flees.

Junior, surely you don't think Vera is Yellow Woman—

Sacrifice.

Abe gripped the spine of his book. He might have laughed—I hoped that he would laugh at the absurdity of the idea, *to take her out* like gangsters in a dime-store novel—really, the idea! But he did not laugh at Junior. He was powerless in the face of this ancestral wisdom.

Junior placed his hands together in preparation to leave.

It's our way, he declared. The way it will be.

And he departed.

✦ Part III ✦

Domingo told me that in the Great Cosmos there grows a very large and beautiful tree whose leaves bear the names of all the people on earth. When the time comes for a person to die, the leaf bearing his or her name will turn from yellow to brown, then wither and fall off the tree. The Spirit of Death visits the tree every morning with his basket and retrieves the withered leaves he finds scattered on the ground. He reads the name written on the leaf he holds in his skeletal hand. Then the Spirit of Death sends down his messenger to the earth and summons the person whose leaf has fallen. And this poor soul must hasten and return to the realm of the Spirit.

And that, declared Domingo, is what is done.

What? I demanded testily, butting my head into Sylvie's shanks as we tried to milk her in the barn. She pushed all of her weight stubbornly against me as I leaned under her to draw the milk into the pail. She hated being milked by anyone but Abe. She rolled her great liquid eyes to the back of her head, nudged me against the stable wall, and would press me flat if I let her.—How I hate this cow! I cried.—What is done? Where did the leaf go? I shouted at Domingo.

It's fallen, he declared, his hands still at his sides.

Well, don't just stand there. Help me with this cow.

The snow hadn't let up for days. Everywhere on the mountain there gleamed a vast, naked silence. With each snowfall we felt like we were being buried alive. We were always at each other in small quarters, irritable and quick to snap. Abe was convalescing in the bedroom of the cabin. He read voraciously, scowling over the pages, muttering to himself. Vera stood on the porch, tugging at her shawl around her shoulders. She stamped at the snow and shooed it off the porch with her broom, the cigarette drooping from the side of her mouth. She lit another, sucking greedily on the butt in the manner of smokers who seem to puff themselves to combustion, then went back inside to start a cabbage soup. I stayed away, fed the animals, chopped the wood. Domingo appeared just at moments when I almost despaired, and he helped me haul water and wood; we brought supplies from Arroyo Seco and medicine from Janie's. He told me the news, too, such as reports from the reservation, where baby Fleet Bird was growing fat and she and mother Kate were ensconced in the bosom of the tribe. He told me Junior was scouting the mountain on his great stallion and Janie had had a party for white folks—I felt scorn for that world of society, yet peeved, too, that I hadn't been invited. More artists, Domingo said, from New York. Janie was always bringing out artists who wanted to meet Abe. But now that Abe was bedridden, Janie's ambition was thwarted—my sense of abandonment up here in the snowy hills was eased by this cruel thought.

We struggled to milk Sylvie in the barn.

And Ralph? I inquired. Has anyone thought of poor Ralph?

He scratches on notebooks in Janie's barn, Domingo indicated. Talk of returning home to Chicago.

Home to Chicago! But this is our home.

Then Domingo started in on the Tree.

What are you telling me? I asked him, stepping away from the milk stool so that he could give a try on Sylvie's hardened teats. I smacked her on the haunch for good measure. Domingo trained his dark, doleful gaze on me.

Whose leaf, Domingo? I don't believe a word of it.

He signed the Red Fox.

I dropped the empty pail, turned away so that he couldn't see me cry. I had been indulging a lot in secret tears. I only had to gaze out the window, watching the snow fall, and my heart revolted in my chest and the tears gushed from my eyes. A grown woman! I felt like a rejected, spoiled child all over again. Abe would be disappointed in me. But I couldn't see him, or he wouldn't see me, or Vera wouldn't allow any visitors until he was stronger—I was alone, absolutely alone in my grief and my sadness.

Domingo, how do you know these things? When did his leaf fall? How long before the Spirit sends for him?

It fell. The messenger of Death has been sent for.

No, stop it! I cried. Junior said he's going to get better. Junior told us so.

The spring, maybe. It's a long journey.

A long journey! Oh, but Domingo, there's so much to do.

He picked up the pail and took my place at the side of Sylvie. I heard the sound of milk squirting against the metal. I watched Domingo work his hands with a kind of magic energy under the body of the wretched cow, lovesick for Abe. I felt relief. There would be milk for Abe and he would be restored in body and spirit, and spring was only weeks away—maybe the Great Spirit was mistaken this once? Maybe the leaf could be returned to the tree?

Once a leaf falls, another grows in its place, replied Domingo, as if reading my thoughts. And the fallen leaf rejoins the earth to make it fertile.

I'm not comforted by that thought, I said. His leaf will fertilize the soil? Domingo, I want to have a talk with this messenger of death when he comes.

The snow suspended time. Suspended a need for making a decision. The tribesmen were waiting, and I sensed the fever beneath the inactivity. I sensed the doom like drumbeats just below my hearing's register. I couldn't sleep in my shed at night for fear of when they would come. I awoke at night with a jerk upright and looked instantly toward the eastern window, certain I would see there, framed around the points of the moon, the cluster of painted faces. They would wait for the snows to melt, I knew, wait for the route ascending the Sacred Mountain to be passable. They were watching the skies, calibrating the temperature; they were sending out scouts. I saw them in town watching the mountain. Their wives had rejoined them, stealthily and without fanfare—the women were back at their men's sides, beating carpets and arranging their wares around the Plaza for trade. They would be impregnated by spring. They didn't look at me. I watched for Sandor, a sympathetic face; but instead of Sandor at the trading post, I found his wife, a short lady, jade-eyed, holding her broomstick at the ready. I bought a laundry basket, thinking of Vera, who yearned to do laundry out by the river at the first sign of thaw, and I tried to speak to the weaver's wife. She muttered and I couldn't hear. She let my coins fall in her palm without touching my hand—she looked away from me. I had seen death, or maybe I even heralded death, and had become unseemly in her eyes. The men shaded their eyes.

I sought out Junior, or rather, he found me, his shadow spreading over me like the umbrage of a thick, shady tree from the eastern forest. I would study these trees later on trips east to sell my paintings—the mammoth red maple in the full splendor of summer. I was crouching on the ground, picking through the beaded wares, looking for an eye-catching palette, when Junior stood over me, offering his shade. He wore a white sheet over trousers and blouse, his braids wrapped in light blue ribbon and beaded at the tips, and around his neck was strung a necklace of massive bear claws. I was dazzled by the sight of him—the air was bright, the sun already intense at the beginning of March. The snows were retreating on the great mountain. I stood, joyful to meet my friend and fishing partner. I gave our traditional greeting, my hand at my head, then heart.

The baby, I asked, how is the baby?

He indicated the baby was well, being taken care of, growing like a weed. I laughed to hear it, though Junior's face turned rather sad. I wondered at his change of expression—wondered, but didn't ask. I knew one couldn't elicit information from Junior unless he wanted to disclose it. He turned his body slightly, away from the crowd of traders, and I moved with him, under the hang of the shop's porch, where we could speak confidentially.

His was the voice of the tribe. Though he wasn't the chief, he possessed more livestock than the others and he had the biggest house, and he straddled two seemingly incompatible worlds with grace, the Indian's and the white man's. I wondered whether he truly liked any of us transplants, besides Janie—tolerated us, perhaps, but he didn't really understand us and what we were after. I imagined he liked me a little, liked my drawings of him when we fished together at Laughing Waters. We had never spoken again of the bear, but his performance had inspired in me an enormous awe of him, and I think he felt it. He tolerated us, until we grew problematic to him, to his people. Now he stood stock still, towering over me, his mouth set in a grim line. My heart beat a little faster in my chest.

Abe's leaf had fallen.

It's time, announced Junior. He looked into my eyes. He indicated the retreating snow in the hills.

Only the flare of my nostrils signaled that I had understood.

He described the Yellow Woman—by the circular movement of his fingers, and graze of his face signing *fair, comely*, I knew whom he meant.

She won't leave, I said, lifting my chin a notch.

She must come, said Junior, nodding once.

Come? Come where? I asked.

He indicated the mountain.

What's up there?

She knows.

How?

A smart lady, she knows all.

It's true, I said, giving an awkward laugh. She knows all. What if she brings a bad spirit your way?

He scowled a little, unhappy with me. It's time, he said again, simply, and I felt the epic momentum to his words.

She's strong, I protested futilely.—She has enormous force gained in the old country. She'll fight you, Junior.

There was no point objecting. He had come to tell me one thing and it was said. He didn't look at me again. He turned away then, toward his people. He was most loyal to them always. He gathered his sheet over the broad shoulders, and in that movement indicated that we had finished.

Astride Reggie I stumbled back up the mountain. It was dark by the time I had unsaddled in the shed and looked longingly toward the cabin lights. My heart was heavy, bitter with despair—should I knock? Whistle? I dragged my parcels over the dirt. But then the door swung open and Vera appeared on the porch, her proud profile delineated sharply against the violet sky and framed by the pine sleeves. She squinted out into the obscured yard, unseeing. She wore her apron, her ash-blond pile of hair listing perilously. She wielded a wooden spoon like a weapon, and shouted to the goblins who would hear:

Doll! Where are you, then? Are you coming to dine?

She called heartily in her comical accent. She could have been hailing a cab on Lower Broadway. *Come on, Doll, are ya coming or what?* In her smoke-huskered voice she sounded like a sailor. I smiled, relieved. So she was in a happy mood! She sounded as she had before, when the days were still full of promising work, and we felt new in this land, and there was much before us. We hadn't let our arguments, our differences, crush our spirits. We were explorers, missionaries, pioneers—and we hadn't been beaten.

I'm here, I said.

Then come on—*ja.*

She turned back inside, and I followed, greeted by the strong aroma of basic rabbit stew. I'd given Abe my catch earlier in the week, and I knew we had a few potatoes left in the pantry from the fall, moldering, maybe a couple of stringy carrots, and plenty of sage, it smelled like, too. Moreover, there were other smells that startled me as I followed Vera into the warm, bright kitchen—baking apples, though where had she scrounged up apples at this point in early spring? I could only imagine Janie had something to do with it. Raisins, cinnamon, nutmeg—the smells of early childhood. Vera had made strudel, her favorite. How extravagant! I staggered under a cornucopia of smells, and the array of food on the spread table. And there sat Abe by the fire, dressed in clean clothes with hair combed and parted, inclined rather demurely forward in his chair, whittling. He looked up and winked at me mischievously.

I stood rooted at the center of the room, my mouth gaping in astonishment.

What's that you're giving us, lassie? He imitated me, sitting up and placing his hands on his hips, sashaying saucily.

Vera burst out laughing.

I shook my head, amazed and displeased by their hilarity, so misplaced, it seemed to me—had they no idea of the gravity of our situation?

Not funny, I murmured. Not funny at all. I began pulling out supplies from my parcels.—We're not through with the snows yet, by the by. We need to conserve through the spring.

Oh prudent, Doll, ever foresightful—is that a word? mocked Vera, glancing mirthfully at Abe. She took the bag of flour I offered and tossed it into the cupboard.

Should be a word, by God, Vera dear, said Abe.

Are you drunk? Both of you? Really, is this wise? The whole valley can smell your strudel, Vera. Listen, I cried—Abe, we are done for! We should pack. We need to clear out, and fast. We'll take what we can carry, and leave the rest, and Domingo can come back—

They were laughing at me, Vera the loudest.

Doll, she said, calm yourself. Don't spoil my dinner; see how I worked all day? My last supper. Sit down.

Her words stunned me. We scraped our chairs over the bare floor, and Abe, ghoulish in the candlelight, his eyes sparkling with a rare, strange fire, took our hands and intoned a brisk grace. Vera had smoothed her hair and put on a clean smock and looked pretty and alert. We tucked in and ate silently, and though I couldn't remember when I had eaten last, I felt increasingly heavy-hearted, and lost my appetite. The two ate lustily; I was repulsed by their hunger. Finally, after mounds of strudel, they leaned back, glutted and groaning. Vera lit a cigarette. I started to get up and clear, but Abe stopped me with a gesture of his hand.

Sit, girl, said he. Tell us the news from town.

You don't want to hear the news from town.

Vera puffed away thoughtfully.—You saw Junior?

I did. Vera—I began.

Ja, ja, she said. Janie's been here. Brought me apples, and we klatched all afternoon.

Then you know you haven't got much time to get away, I blurted.

Abe gazed at me reproachfully but I was too angry to give in now. I leaned forward and spoke quickly:

Vera, let's go then. I can ride out with you. I'll saddle up the horses right now. Abe is too weak to travel, but I can. We'll take the road to Santa Fe—leave a message for Johnny Copper—maybe he can set us up later and help us secure a place in Albuquerque. We'll go together, Vera, but we have to get going!

They looked at me sadly, the two of them. I knew the look—I was not unaccustomed to being regarded as a halfwit. I stared back at them. And still they said nothing. Finally, I sat back and let the ticking of the Bavarian cuckoo clock sink into my skull. I closed my eyes, pressed my fingertips into my throbbing temples, and waited, listening for a signal from the mountain.

So you are calm, said Abe, leaning into my ear. Now you will see at last that you can't resist the momentum of history. Of forces greater than yourself. Vera has seen this, and recognized her purpose, and grasped the role she must play.

What is that role? I asked. To be sacrificed on top of the mountain?

There are worse ways to go, quipped Vera.

You can't be serious!

Oh yes, I am very serious, replied Vera. Aren't I, Abe?

She is the earth goddess, said Abe, his face glowing. She united the women. Now she can be reunited with the elemental forces of nature.

I stared from one to the other. You've lost your grip on reality, I told them.

Vera will help reverse the misalignment in their worldview. She will ride to the top of the mountain and by her holy presence—

She needs protective clothing, I said.

Doll, you're not listening. Can you hear me? Abe spoke louder.—There's no point in resisting, Doll.

She'll get sunstroke, I insisted.—We need to pack food for her. She shouldn't eat what they give her!

Hysterical, murmured Vera.

She must be delirious from her ride.

They thought I couldn't hear them. They imagined my inflamed sense of self-righteousness had deafened me utterly. I kept protesting as Vera led me out. I told her to go, to flee. That Junior would kill her. That she would never see her girls again— her beloved daughters. I used the only argument I knew would arrest her. Finally, at the threshold of my shed, she listened. She pulled her shawl around her tightly, and shook me in the strong grip of one hand. We stood close, closer than we had ever stood to each other, and she shook me, not gently. She had a motherly smell of baked apples and cinnamon, and loomed in my doorframe, large and indomitable.

I'm not running away, she told me fiercely. I face what comes my way, I always have. You know this about me, Doll. I won't run! I'll go with these men and face their blasted mountain and say my piece. And the struggle of the wills will ensue, and the stronger will prevail.

It's you against the mountain, I said.

Ha! cried my Wagnerian friend. She dropped her hand from my shoulder. She jerked her chin toward the cabin.—You have to take care of him now.

He won't let me do that.

I did. Now he's dying, he has to.

Does he think of you?

Of course. It's my decision.

I didn't believe that, but I didn't protest.—Won't you come back, then?

No, she said. I've burnt my bridges. At a certain point you recognize there's no returning to the life that was.

But your daughters. . .

They have their father. They've lived all their youth without me. They'll marry nice young men, they'll do fine.

They'll remember you, I said.

Ah!

They'll remember you. They'll learn how you broke away from convention and forged a life of freedom—

She gave me a derisive smile.—Who will tell them?

I will, I said, confused.

You won't leave this place.

No. But they will come here. Some day.

Yes, maybe, she mused.—That would do.

We stood awkwardly. We gazed down Lobo Mountain, illuminated by the clear, cold light of the moon. Bats dashed pell-mell among the pines. Strange animal calls haunted the hills—my familiar nocturnal friends. I wondered if I should hold her, take her in my arms. But I was afraid, unsure in my body, which always felt puny next to hers.

That will do, she said again, absently. She acknowledged our mountain, the moon, and our small, insignificant situation here. Abruptly, she turned, having already forgotten about me in the fullness of her thoughts.

Goodnight, Vera! I called to halt her. She nodded, in handsome profile, the vernal moonlight dancing over the flat planes of her cheekbones. I watched her move away, somewhat sideways, picking her way over the uneven shadows, her form heavy and deliberate, and then she emerged on the steps of the porch. Briefly she called the cat, *Miche-miche*, and clapped her hands with authority, and the creature came bounding up the stairs. The door opened, the cat brushed past her skirts like a tumbleweed, and she disappeared after it into the light of the cabin.

The next morning she rode away.

I wonder whether he will leave me eventually, grow restless, and want to drive back through the desert, back home, to his mother. I like the little town on the coast we have found, the fleabag where we stay at night, and the bed we sleep in together. We sleep tightly bound, Akbar wrapped like a wandering jew around my torso. For safety and warmth, I think happily. Our joined weight creates a great gully in the center of the spring-shot bed and we sink together in the night, suspended, straitened. He hammers against me without mercy until the burrow we've made doesn't allow for an inch of leeway. I have to urinate toward morning, and gently extricate myself to get up, though I hate to leave him; it's physically strenuous as well to climb out of our pit, and I emerge stiff and stooped. I push open the window to the sea for a bit of air in the clotted room. I am thrilled to smell the air, gaze at the miraculous sight of waves upon waves dilating like shimmering sand dunes. I am continually startled and delighted by the sight of the sea. Akbar sleeps through the disturbance, and when I return we sink down again together. His arms entwine themselves trustingly around my gnarled frame.

But I can't sleep. I am too old to sleep this late—too old for the hungry sleep my darling boy snatches whenever he can. And the sea light, and sea smells, excite me. I wait, watching the gradual blanching of the walls of the room. The lighter it grows, the noisier it must be, though I sense the activity rather than hear it—the fishmongers begin to gather at the wharf, the nets are hauled in from the night, makeshift stalls set up along the strand. The fishermen hawk their morning catches to the housekeepers and restaurateurs who gather to buy supplies for their daily meals. Each morning the sky over the sea is remarkably blue—serene. Akbar doesn't stir; he can sleep through a war, so I haven't a clue how noisy it is really. Through the cracked window I glimpse the swoop and dive of muscular seagulls, and feel the first active gusts carried from the warm currents of the sea. With Akbar's limbs entwined around me I can close my eyes and smell the sea and be almost under-water—we are drifting mollusks, throbbing sea anemones. We are a floating island, self-sufficient, impermeable.

He is happy with immediate concerns satisfied—happy over our simple, abundant meals of fish stew and tortillas served by smiling Mexicans, content to bask in the sunlight and contemplate the unfathomable expanse of water under lowered sunglasses—unhappy when money is transacted and he pats down his slender wallet. Then he grows anxious and won't meet my eye. I imagine this must be true of human nature in general: that is, one is freed to inhabit one's true self once the spirit-killing concerns of finding the next dollar are met with dignity. I have told him not to worry about money, but he is loath to be dependent on me. I can't stand to see him patting down his chest, taking out his sadly beaten cloth wallet while frowning at the restaurant's bill of fare, then yanking open the torn sleeves to gaze incredulously inside its gaping chasm. Every time the dismal bottom presents itself, and every time he seems deeply distressed to see it. He plucks at the material with long fingernails, pulls on his locks. Then he looks everywhere around the room except at me. I'm afraid he will flee. I'm afraid he will return to his fallout shelter in the desert of New Mexico. I rest my hand on his forearm to still him. Secretly I refill his wallet with pesos. Then anxiety lifts from his brow, and he is light again, unhindered.

At such moments my heart constricts and I recognize that this boy is not an adult, probably never will be. He is eternally arrested in boyhood. We converse in a kind of parallel universe of mutually unintelligible concerns and memories—which the other can't share but understands tacitly. He knows nothing of responsibility. He speaks of thefts he has endured over the years, when the car was broken into, when his flat was robbed, when objects were stolen from him unjustly, removed without his consent. He couldn't be reminded to lock his doors, secure his music collection out of sight, ensure that a friend spending the night in his flat return his key. He is too kind, or thoughtless, or distracted. His mother rails about his carelessness. She warned him, didn't she? But he doesn't heed her. The theft remains to burn on his sense of self-worth: it is a betrayal of his immense trust in the order of the universe. He takes the theft of his things personally. He feels helpless. And it happens again and again, this bad luck, this betrayal.

You can take control, I tell him—I mean, of his life, his destiny. He hears without listening—nodding, humming. I can barely make out a word in the noisy seaside café.

Can't go to work without my music, he laments.

Did they fire you at Stella's?

Nah. He loses interest in his story. His eyes hidden behind the sunglasses, the skin of his nose freckled by the sun. He wears a faded khaki jacket, his locks secured high up in his white head-scarf, giving him the docile look of a Sikh provincial official. I imagine he will lose his job as a DJ. It's a good job, a job that lends him a sense of self-importance, and I want to shake him—maybe his mother wanted to shake him, maybe she *did*. Instead I tell him about a person I knew who took control of her own life. Who defined herself her own way. I tell him about Vera, the woman who rode away.

He cracks sunflower seeds between his strong teeth. Drinks a local syrupy version of orange Kool-Aid that leaves his teeth with a greenish hue.—Who was after her? he asks, skeptically.

The tribe was after her.

Uh-huh. He doesn't follow me.—The students, he says, where I live—they always looking to lift something to sell.

I nod. He speaks in non sequiturs. I'm not sure he's really listening, but I continue anyway, and tell him about the Bronstones, husband and wife, whom I knew a lifetime ago.—The Indians were experiencing unprecedented snowfall that year, I continue, and their wives kept having babies no one could feed. The wives gathered around Vera. She rallied them, taught them about their bodies and how to be true to themselves. She gave pep talks and raised their political awareness. As a result, the Indian elders believed she was the cause of their misfortunes.

Okay, says Akbar. He cracks his seeds, ruminates.—Was she?

The cause? I'm not sure. Actually, yes, she was.

How's that?

How? Well, she was blond, for one—he laughs—and big, buxom, attractive, loud, and a chain smoker, I say. Actually, she was irrepressible.

Crazy, says Akbar.

A man with a camera ventures to our table to take our picture. For thirty pesos, the nice young man offers, with a combined air of hope and defeat. I quickly decline, shaking my head, before Akbar can make a sad show of pulling out his dejected wallet.

Akbar leans his elbows on the table, moving closer.—Now this husband, he says, offering his attention. Was he also—irrepressible? He smiles at his use of the word.

Oh yes, I say. Abe was bossy and given to angry outbursts and not easy to get along with. But he never asked any of us to do work he wouldn't do himself. He was well loved. He was our leader.

A leader, says Akbar, and laughs.—Akbar needs a leader, he mumbles.

You don't need a leader, dear boy. You are your own leader. I'm very serious. Vera upset the universal order. And she had to set it right.

So they took her away.

Yes.

Did they kill her?

Sort of.

His eyebrows over the sunglasses lift expectantly.

They killed her spirit.

Ah, says he. He nods soberly. My dear boy understands.

I dreamed I felt their numbers surrounding the camp. I peeked out through my window curtain. The horses emerged from the trees, halted quietly, and waited in front of the cabin. Their riders wore wide black sombreros like mine that darkened their faces and woolen ponchos slung casually over their short, muscular frames. I strapped on my knife with trembling fingers, pulled on layers of clothing, then grabbed my saddlebags and stuffed them with food I had stored—some dried salted meat, *jerkmeat* they called it here, nuts, bread, and a canteen I rattled angrily, annoyed to find it empty. I could fill it up in the river on the way. I stepped outside into the chill, pink morning—just as Junior's glistening black mount disappeared through the forest.

I sneaked into the cabin to steal her Bavarian cuckoo clock.

I led Reggie out of the stable, fed and saddled. I retrieved my bags from the shed and slung them over the saddle. Then I hesitated, unsure what to do next. It was well past sunup. I tapped lightly at the door of the cabin—heard nothing. I found Abe slumped in a chair, his whittling knife hanging loose in his hand, unfinished letters strewn across the kitchen table. Vera was gone. He looked defeated, muttering gibberish to himself. The sight of his resigned form angered me.

Domingo went with them, I told Abe.—Listen, you'll have to make do on your own for a bit. I lowered myself on one knee at his side. He wasn't seeing.

Abe, it's me. It's Doll. What will you do? I asked urgently.

My mother, he said, used to take a stroll in the garden with the pet peacock on one side of her, her dog on the other. They strolled in the garden like that, every day, before she got sick.

What are you writing? I asked him.

I was writing to my mother.

Abe?

What? he turned, suddenly taking me in. Where do you think you're going?

I won't sit here. I can't do nothing.

You won't find Vera.

I can't sit here!

Well, I can. Years of practicing sitting, Doll.

You didn't sit when your books were being attacked in the old country. You taught us how to fight, didn't you?

To flee. I taught you how to flee.

No.

Self-preservation.

Rubbish.

I've aged a hundred years.

I'm your age, Abe.

I wonder how Vera will get on.

Now you wonder!

My dear mother died in hideous pain.

Abe, I'm going.

They'll find you.

So they can boil me and eat me, too.

I held out my hand to him. He averted his face, so I kissed him on the forehead. His skin possessed the remarkably cool, smooth surface of temple marble. I touched the scrubby red hair at his ears. I hovered over him—how frail my hero looked now, how small. And then I retreated quickly, casting a quick glance at the state of the kitchen—the tea things scattered about where he and Vera had cobbled together a hasty breakfast. A letter lying on top of the table—addressed, I noted with a start, *Dear Doll. . .* and nothing more. Had I really taken her prized possession in my dreams? I knew if the clock was missing from its place she wouldn't be back. But I didn't look, and heard nothing.

There were four of them: I tracked them for three days. Across the valley, then up the north face of the Sacred Mountain. There was nowhere to go but upward. The horses left a trail that even the scouts couldn't obliterate. I followed at a respectful distance, and at night smelled their campfire. They knew I was following. The first morning I spotted the feathers of a wily scout twitching from behind a boulder where I was giving myself a spit bath. I stifled a scream, my heart seizing in fear. Then I recognized the boy by the raccoon circles around his eyes—he couldn't have been older than sixteen. I let him watch, but shook a finger at him to let him know I knew what he was up to. I didn't take off my knife at night when I lay under the stars on my blanket. And the nights were even more astoundingly beautiful up on the mountain. I could see straight to Kansas—or so Abe had once told me. In the morning I was awakened by the solemn circling of eagles. They were fearless—curious at the sight of me. I wondered when the tribesmen would stop me, and why they didn't.

As I rode higher, sometimes guiding Reggie on foot over rocky, uncertain ground, sometimes letting him meander on his own and graze, I recognized I was angry. It was a dangerous emotion to entertain on the mountain where everything seemed to grow more intensely defined, rarefied, and potent—the light, the thinning air, the colors of wildflowers and delineation of leaves and rocks, the depth of perspective arrayed on all sides of me, and my deepening sense of isolation. I was angry and grew angrier, and as I climbed I turned my anger every which way, examining it like the unfamiliar terrain I was determined to know. And every way I examined my anger I grew more unhappy with myself, more dissatisfied, and thus more angry. I began to assign causes and effects to it. First, I thought of my father. Reggie, who had withdrawn his love once I gained an awkward age and no longer was the comely child. I blamed him. How could a father's love be so fickle, so easily swayed? He stopped loving me when I grew plump and adolescent. My mother had supported her daughters and encouraged us to be self-sufficient despite the pressures of marrying into our station, and yet she, too, had abandoned me once I proved insufficient within the social sphere—inadequate, unmarriageable. My becoming an artist couldn't earn her love for me. I blamed both of my parents for failing to protect me from the scoundrel who stole my innocence, Sir Jeremy. I blamed Sir Jeremy, it went without saying—had I a knife strapped to my thigh back then I would have sliced him to ribbons. And Marcus, my first love, who took advantage of my adoring gazes, my admiration for him as a mentor. I blamed these men for not loving me—but I blamed myself the most for being unlovable! Surely it would have been different had I been born with a stronger chin. There was Lorelei, who had died, taking her love (for I knew she had cared for me, even if her love was full of pity), and my Slade mates, who proved too absorbed in other concerns to join me here on a lifetime adventure. I blamed them for their short-sightedness. And I was angry at Junior for his arrogance—for marrying a white woman and imagining he could straddle two worlds effortlessly. I blamed Janie, but somehow she was less blameworthy than Junior, since he knew better, being of a wiser tribe, steeped in ancient wisdom. Janie was powerless, really, despite her wealth, or because of it.

And when I thought of Abe and Vera, my anger boiled over. Ceaselessly I thought of them, and again I felt abandoned. We had come to this land together and been forced apart. Vera had helped the tribeswomen, and gained a personal power. She possessed a charisma that rivaled Abe's. She had felt a calling to aid the women, gathering them to her like her brood, dispensing her old-country wisdom. While she had helped them, cured evils of the head and womanly sicknesses, she had also caused a schism among the tribe, and we had all had to pay for it. Again we were cast out, scattered to the winds. Abe would be uprooted again, goaded out of his community—a pariah. Though he was ill now and limping, he was a phoenix, and he would rise from the ashes: someone would come, a disciple from the old country, and claim him, and he'd find a new place, a warm, dry place, and he would manage to start again. For Abe had proved he could do this, again and again.

And what about me? Who would come and claim me and find me a warm, dry place to live?

I plied my way up the mountain, dragging the reluctant horse, my anger exhausting itself. Occasionally we came upon a gurgling brook, leaking the pure snow from the ice caps, and I let Reggie go to drink thirstily. I caught rabbits in the dead-fall traps Domingo had taught me how to make; I skinned the creatures and roasted them over my fire. I sucked on yucca, and bathed in a waterfall. I waited for a sign of movement from the tribe before setting out in the morning to follow. There was little distance to cover. Snow clung to these nether regions, and the sun was high, stark at this altitude, warm at midday when I covered my face with my hat and lay for a rest on a rock. I lost track of hours. The Sacred Mountain was playing its mischief. I was feeling dizzy and disoriented.

On the third day the scout reappeared, feathers dancing over the boulder where I rested, giving me the fright of my life. In plain gestures he indicated that I was to come with him. So I packed my camp up, gathered Reggie's halter, and followed the boy. I stumbled over the rocks. I smelled the strangely alluring, holy odor of incense as we reached what must have been the summit. The smell unhinged my already loosely bolted head. It was an astonishing sight, standing on top of the Sacred Mountain that just grazed the sky, and beneath us in all directions extended the brown, flattened Southwestern desert. I felt an attack of vertigo and sank to the snowy ground. The tribesmen had erected slender, white wigwams around a cave dug through the mouth of a boulder, and from this orifice the incense was wafting. I knew that Vera was there, inside the cave. But I couldn't move, my limbs trembling from lack of nutrition, my mouth parched from thirst, and my head reeling from the height and inebriating smells. Someone handed me a warm baked yam, wrapped in a yucca leaf. I ate hungrily.

I awoke in the cave. Candles flickered; it was night. Junior sat cross-legged at my side. He smoked from his pipe, his eyes watching me in his imperturbable fashion. I smiled to see him. I tried to lift my head, and was greeted by needling pains through my skull. I grimaced and Junior put the pipe aside.

You should not have come, he indicated in our sign language.

My head, I signed.

He motioned the great height of the mountain.—Go back. Go home.

I have no home.

Abe, he indicated, sketching a red beard.

Vera, I delineated the Yellow Woman.

Not the time to be stubborn, he told me. *Danger*.

What danger? I wanted to know.

This is not a place for you.

You mean women. Then let me take Vera home, I indicated.

No. Go. He was being stern with me.

I want to see her.

Mule-headed, he signed, indicating the ears. I had to smile. I could match him in stubbornness. After a while he got up, adjusting his blanket around his shoulders, and went out. When he returned he held an earthenware bowl steaming with a fragrant mash. I eyed it suspiciously, and sniffed at it, but was too hungry to refuse. I sat up with difficulty and took the bowl from him and put it eagerly to my lips. He offered me a pot of water, which I smelled first, too, but that was a show, because I would have drunk anything he offered. I gulped down the water in a hurry.

When I woke again I saw Vera like a vision, embroidering by firelight—a dozen small torches set up around her, on rocks, ledges, even in the dust where she sat. It was night. She wore her glasses perched at the end of her nose, while a cigarette burned in a clay pot beside her. I imagined they kept her handily supplied with tobacco—the good, strong black kind she liked. She didn't seem surprised to see me, gazing over her nose to squint at me on the ground. I looked quickly around to see that we were alone.

She put down her embroidery and lowered her brows at me.

I'm here to bust you out, I whispered.

She considered me and laughed. Ha! Dolly the gangbuster. Oh, go back.

What are you doing, Vera? Come back to the cabin, to Abe.

Ach. We've already said goodbye.

She was handsome and full of secrets, and then I detected a slight incongruity about her—her smile. She began to perform her toilette. She combed and smoothed her hair, using a shard of mirror she had packed in her bag, and pulled up the pale wisps. Then she stripped to her knickers and washed her limbs, dousing herself briefly from a jug of water. I watched her out of the corner of my eye. When had she ever been so fastidious, so wasteful of time? She dressed now with more care than I had ever noticed her taking about her rather slovenly person; she straightened her clothes, brushing her buckskin riding gear. At last she tied the strings to her cotton shift, tugged on her suede vest. She sat on the ground and smoked silently. I noticed the embroidery she had been working at the night before and asked her about it.

A cap, she said with a perfunctory air.—I'm making a burial cap.

Junior's drum sounded the signal, and the mountain reverberated in assent. Vera fitted the embroidered cap on her head, a small, white skull cap she set delicately with pins to the crown of her thick, blond hair. Then she stood up purposefully.

Don't wear that!

I reached for her. But she was stronger, and pulled me to my feet. She pushed me toward the mouth of the cave. I tried to grab her, to bring her out with me, but she rebuffed me.—Go! she cried, and shoved me harder outside so that I fell on my side. The earth shook with the hard stamping of feet, and I scrambled around the boulder and hid from view. Framed by the night sky, the ancestral crowd of constellations, Junior led the men, dressed in resplendent headdress and war paint; he alone entered the cave while the tribesmen waited. From their slender hips hung tomahawks and knives and other hunting weapons, their faces and hands smeared with colors vivified by the torches—red, mostly red. Soon Junior emerged, and Vera with him; he led her by the hand, rather tenderly, it struck me. He led her by the whisper of fingers. Guided by the torches, they headed to the top of the mount, where there was a clearing, and a large flat rock. Here the sacrifices were performed—I knew because Domingo had told me. Junior's knife was held at the ready, like Abraham ready to sacrifice his son Issac. There was the insistent pounding of the drums, the pungent odor of incense from the cave. I watched in horror from my hiding place, frozen as one feels in a dream when pursued by a beast and one's feet turn to clay. Would he kill her? Then, incredibly, a motorcar appeared at the summit, picking its way over the rough terrain like a sand spider. It approached gradually, and halted before the awaiting tribesmen. I saw that it was Janie's car. The brand-new black Chrysler appeared like a mirage over the crest. The side door opened and Junior guided Vera inside, holding out her arms like a dancer. She seated herself, and he climbed in after her. The door closed, the car quivered, reversing elegantly in the narrow space under the moon, then headed back down the route to town.

This I swear I saw.

I woke with a snort from Reggie—there was no camp, not even a scout to direct me homeward. The Indians are stealthful that way. Only Reggie stood warily, saddled and hobbled. I gazed at him in astonishment. In the morning light I recognized with a wild glee that I had reached the summit of the Sacred Mountain—I was there.

At a certain point a person has to face up to the fact of her death. Either she accepts that her *leaf has fallen* or she defies the Great

Spirit at her own risk. Being with a younger man has this curious effect on me: in my lover's eyes I face my death. I haven't dwelled on death before meeting Akbar—I am healthy enough, healthy as a horse, they say about me, slogging through my days as a painter living out by herself on Avenida Mañana. No one bothers me or takes much notice of me except tax collectors, and from time to time an errant biographer of Abe Bronstone or some bored gallery owner picking through an art history. Death doesn't pester me—I'm not important enough. I can't think about dropping dead and no one finding me. Who cares? In fact, nothing can *kill* me. Sometimes I wonder if my sojourn atop the Sacred Mountain prolonged my life—I'll never know. I see how death stalks others, Johnny Copper for one, who seems chronically racked by ailments and complains always of escaping the Reaper's clutches. Bowed low, he grapples and rails against whatever pursues him. I haven't been afflicted, never in my life, and here I am an old lady, by most standards, though Akbar doesn't think so. By most standards I am decomposing, my flesh gradually giving way to the supremacy of the earth's gravity and sinking into the soft, snaggy mudslide of mortality. Sadly, this is the way I must look, and I have stopped looking. Certainly my breasts in the bathroom mirror have the sad, flattened sinkage of a very aged Venus of Wollendorf. But Akbar delights in my toppling cleavage. My drooping decurrence. And, curiously, it isn't until he takes notice of me in that particular sexual way which men have rarely afforded me—not even in my youthful buoyancy, let's face it, and seldom in the past thirty years—that I begin to regard myself as mortal, and thus fragile, and evanescent. Akbar's vim does not make me feel regenerated, indeed. My initial explosion of orgasm subsides into a gnawing anxiety about dying *in flagrante delicto* in my lover's arms. My strength will desert me, my heart will give out at the moment of climax. And my poor darling will be left with his bloated grandma's corpse.

I don't have to bring up my fears to Akbar. He brings up the subject himself—the subject of mortality, that is. His own. Since our encampment in this Mexican town he has dedicated himself to a serious regime of introspection. He watches the sea most of the day. He grows gloomier—I watch him uneasily. Clad in a floppy hat and gauzy shirt to protect his fair, freckly skin from being scorched, he drags a low beach chair down to the surf most mornings and sits with his legs stretched out so he can catch with his toes the advance and ebb of the waves. Sometimes the tide rushes in precipitously and he is overrun in his chair, but the water tickles him, even if the merciless sun does not, and he throws back his scraggly beard and laughs at the sudden refreshment of water over his knees and into his lap. He has been dozing and the coldness of the water startles him. He isn't a reader—his cross eyes have gone untreated for the most part since he was a child. The words swim on the page before his eyes and tire him easily. He prefers to sit and watch the rise and fall of the surf and train his gaze to the farthest point on the horizon. From time to time a boat will pass, a freighter on its way south to Guaymas, or a gringo's sailboat. The gulls are noisy companions and greedy scavengers along the beach. Akbar is so still that they don't bother about him, and when they swoop and dive they sometimes graze his sleeve with their wings. Occasionally, a family of rotund, brown bathers—mother, father, and several niños, *saltimbanques* from a Picasso painting—set up camp on one side of him, and he has a spectacle to observe. Sometimes he even gets out of his chair and kneels in the sand, ghostly white limbs jutting at odd angles, and I watch him surrounded by children digging in a mud pit with colored shovels. My darling boy loves playing with the kids. I stay near the hotel and set up my easel on the boardwalk and execute a few seascapes. When the sun nears its zenith he turns back, and together we pack my things, then crawl into the shelter of our hotel room. We eat tomato sandwiches and drink warm orange fizz. With the fan rotating squeakily overhead we sink into the bed and roll about until we pass out from the electrical outtage of skin overheated. After a while Akbar climbs out of the bed and sits naked at the desk, hunched over, sweating, his spindly knees drawn up. He rolls a fragrant cigarette.

He has made some friends during his meditations on the beach and they keep him supplied with the good stuff. He drinks deeply from his cooler of electrolyte water. Sometimes he speaks over the whir of the fan and I watch his lips:

I've got nothing to go back for, he says.

I don't answer right away—I know his mood is growing darker and he isn't asking me for anything. I don't answer in jest, Bunkum! My first quip is that he has his mother to go back to, but I don't let that slip. I turn over languorously and harumph a bit and wonder if we're headed for another discussion about having a child. Is he considering adoption? Actually, it isn't a discussion, technically, since I have nothing to say on the subject. I am mum, closed up tight. It is more like Akbar's Complaint.

The fan whirs and squeaks and might even take off flying on its own. Instead, I call his bluff.—Then, darling boy, let's stay.

He smiles, looks over at me, distinguishes me through the fragrant smoke.—That's my Doll, ain't you a sport.

I can paint here, as well as anywhere, and I'm getting kind of used to seeing water instead of sand. Is that what you were thinking? I ask gingerly, the old fears of rejection resurfacing, afraid that what he *means* is he wants to stay here alone.

Nah, that ain't what I mean.

No, I didn't think so.

Akbar has a bad bite from the black dog.

We take a walk and have a coffee at the Café Havana on the strand. We usually end up there in the late afternoons to welcome in the first breath of the evening and watch the visitors gawk at the sunset. And don't we know sunsets? There isn't another café around, so all the inhabitants of the town and the rest of us passing through end up at the Havana. The Picasso family is there, slurping at sodas; the kids hop up and down to see Akbar, who peeks out of his hair coils fanned out around his shoulders. They shriek with laughter. He orders the orange-fizz belly wash they all drink here and I order a glass of gin—neat. This is my favorite time of day, when the sun finally blinks and the salt breeze fans our sun-sore skin, and I'm holding a glass of gin in my hands which are stained with paint and stinking of thinner. I know that Akbar's skin smells the same. I am content, I have accomplished something this day, and am not expected to be entertaining. Usually we don't talk—it is too trying to hear over the din—and that suits me fine. But something is nagging at Akbar. He's mired in his torpor, and he leans heavily toward my ear and says again:

I ain't got nothing to go back to.

I look at him helplessly. He *is* blue; he can't shake it this time. The smoking of his fragrant cigs isn't helping. Behind his mirrored shades pulled down to the base of his nose I can see his translucent grey eyes, bloodshot and terribly hang-dog. I detect a resignation and it frightens me. What is happening? Haven't we made love with some spirit only an hour before? And yet the light is dimmer today, his effort listless and perfunctory. He hasn't wanted to ejaculate. And I haven't wanted to notice for days that he isn't *all there*, that he hasn't released himself, that there isn't much of him left. His weightlessness worries me.

Where are you going? I ask.

I'm nowhere, he says, and laughs.

But. . . darling boy?

I want to be dead.

You're frightening me.

Death is frightening.

What are you saying?

He mouths the words that are too low for me to hear: *You know what I'm saying.*

No.

I ain't for this life, he says.

Come on! We've gotten this far—look at me! I'm what the cat dragged in.

You're a survivor. I ain't.

Let's make a go of it together, I tell him hopefully. I take his hand. I shake a lock of his hair to make him smile. I try to humor my man. I want more than anything for him to believe me. But he simply gazes at me with his forlorn eyes and I know what he's saying. He's leaving me. He is telling me he has given up. Maybe he has been summoned—his leaf fallen. But he's made up his mind, he says. He's a man, ain't he, and he's made up his mind and something in the way he says this stops me cold.

Can I go with you?

You can't, says he.

Don't say it.

Doll, baby, he says, you ain't like me. You're a fighter. I ain't for this life.

But it's good here, isn't it?

Yah, it's good, he sighs.

We don't mention it again. He gets so blue he can't speak. I know he has his connections on the beach and he makes a trade— the cloth wallet is missing. I don't know what he takes. There is a plastic bag he leaves out on the bedside table, emptied, and he leaves it for me to find, as if not to worry me. But he doesn't share with me in the end, and not out of meanness. My darling boy cannot be mean. He goes his way by himself and he knows I won't follow, for how can I? How can I come all this way, from my little island across the ocean, two world wars ago, and all the strife I've known between, to take my own life? He inserts his earplugs, dons his eye patch. He kisses me goodnight and wraps his long, sinewy limbs around me. We sink deeply into the doughy mattress. I listen to the decrescendo of his heartbeat. I hear the ebbing of his life. And in the morning he is so still, his freckled skin grey and cold. He holds me in his umbilical grip, and calmly I carry him, until I know it's time to climb out.

And I go back. Someone has to keep going, and that's always been me. Also I have to inform his aged, lonely mother. In a week I return home in the woodie. The body has gone its own way, arrived separately. The body has been burned, an urn of ashes rests at the adobe hearth. She is not angry, not surprised. The two of us sit on her patio together, overlooking the Sangre de Cristo. We watch the sun go to sleep in splendor. We are not sad. This is not the country for sadness, and we are hardened like criminals. Baked like the dust. We drink a gin-and-Dubonnet together—in equal measures, with two lumps of ice and a slice of lemon. The favorite cocktail, I tell her, of the Queen. She is delighted to hear it.

Acknowledgments

A novelist is by nature a thief, and I have freely lifted from the life and writing of the following people in order to create my own work: Leon Trotsky, G. I. Gurdjieff, William Bradford, Ann Hutchinson, D.H. Lawrence, Frieda Lawrence, Dorothy Brett, Mabel Dodge Luhan, and Vera Brittain. I am grateful to the librarians at the University of New Mexico's Southwestern Collection, Albuquerque. I referred to Sean Hignett's *Brett: From Bloomsbury to New Mexico, A Biography*, Willa Cather's *Death Comes to the Archbishop*, and Frank Waters's *Of Time and Change*. I acknowledge the authors of the innumerable books I have reviewed over the years from which I no doubt extracted ideas or phrases—and whose names I don't remember. I extend many thanks to Margaret Bullock of the Harwood Gallery, Taos; Steve Slick of the Hotel La Fonda, Taos; the Daitz family of Corrales, NM; Judith and Martin Shepard; and Thomas, Charlotte, and Terence Nugent. And to Michael Scharf, who dragged Höhlenfrau into the light.